And Justice for Some

Deputy Ricos Tale 7

By

Elizabeth A. Garcia

Siete Leguas
Press

Cover and interior designed by Antonio S. Franco
Cover photographs by Tim McKenna

ISBN-10: 1987480139
ISBN-13: 978-1987480139

This novel is dedicated to Tony, Lynda, and Elvira, my invaluable first readers; and to Julie and Tim, and Margarita and Amber, who help me in countless ways. With much love and appreciation to all of you

Dear Readers,

Please put away your maps. You won't find Carterton or Simpson, Texas because I made them up for use in this story. It is a work of fiction, after all. The names don't matter, anyway. It's what happens in the towns that matters.

Thank you, Tim McKenna, for allowing me to use your stunning photograph. It could not be more perfect for the cover of *And Justice for Some*. It's as if you read the novel and then shot the cover photo. Thank you to Tony Franco for taking Tim's work and turning it into a cover.

Tony's talents go far beyond covers; he also formatted the interior. In other words, he took my manuscript and turned it into a book.

Lee Porche edits my work and puts up with me and my (at times) computer illiteracy. For that, she deserves big kudos. Thank you, Lee.

It's difficult for me to believe that this is the seventh Deputy Ricos tale! Where will Margarita go next? Who's in trouble now? Is she the one in trouble? I guess I should check in with her—but not yet. I need a few weeks of rest.

Peace and love, my readers,
Elizabeth A. (Beth) Garcia

CHAPTER 1

Moon-drenched fog swirled across the pavement, reducing visibility, and forcing me to slow down. Rounding a curve, I spotted something pale and gauzy gliding along the shoulder of the highway. The hair at the base of my neck stood up; it's a wonder all the hair on my head didn't stick straight out. I slowed my official Brewster County Sheriff's Office truck to a crawl and peered at the—what in the world? I clicked off the radio because The Thing was creepy enough without background noise.

The unknown subject looked like a ghost or what you'd expect a ghost to be: filmy, there-but-not, drifting along without feet. I pulled my Beretta out of its holster in case it wasn't an apparition, or even if it was.

Edging closer, I saw that the "phantom" was a small person wearing a long white veil. It covered her and, because she was short, it had bunched up at her feet, hiding them. It was still eerie, but at least she had feet. I assumed. Walking the road on a foggy night while wearing a bridal veil is not illegal, but it *is* weird.

It appeared I'd found the missing girl. I pulled up beside her and put the passenger-side window down. "Hi! Aren't you Cecelia Florence?"

The child looked spectral as she turned to face me, the veil shifting in the slight breeze. She stared at me with owl eyes, a small female with blonde hair. She didn't appear to be in distress, but the veil made me wonder.

"Cecelia? Is everything all right?"

"Who wants to know?"

"Don't give me that; you know who I am."

"Yeah, you're Deputy Ricos."

"Please get in the truck. My partners and I have been trying to find you for two days."

She shrugged.

"Where have you been? Your parents are worried sick about you."

"Where are *they* is the question."

Her tangled blonde hair hung down to her shoulders. Dirty white jeans and a stained tan jacket contrasted sharply with the stark white veil.

"Why are you walking alone on the highway in the dark?"

She rolled her eyes. "It's no big deal."

"It's dangerous, so it is a big deal. Please get in."

"Why?"

"Stop giving me a hard time and get in."

"I don't want to go home."

"Get in and we'll talk about that."

She took a tentative step in my direction. I leaned across the seat and opened the door for her. After another step, she informed me that she was no longer called Cecelia.

"What should I call you?"

"Cissy, with a 'C.'" She gathered the veil and tried to step up into the truck, but got entangled, stumbled backward, and almost fell.

I got out to help. "Could we set this veil in the back seat for now?"

She kept a tight grip on her prize. "I want to wear it."

I lifted her, veil and all, and set her in the seat.

She huffed. "This is practically kidnapping."

"It's not anything like kidnapping. Your parents said they didn't know where you were and asked the sheriff to find you."

"How come he's not looking for me instead of you?"

"He asked me to do it. I work for him."

"He's lazy, in other words."

"He's not lazy. His office is in Alpine, and he has responsibility for a lot of different things. That's why he needs deputies."

"Will you give me a ride to the Ghost Town?"

"Why go there? The businesses are shut down for the night, except for the bar, and I know you aren't drinking age—"

"I'm looking for my friends. They're having a party."

"It's a school night."

She shrugged. "I don't go to school anymore."

"Yes, you do. By law, you're required to be in school. And what about your friends? Are they dropping out, too?"

"You're nosy, aren't you?"

"Maybe so, but I have your best interests at heart. You need to be in school because there's a lot to learn, and it's hard to get a job without a high school diploma."

"That's just your opinion."

"It's a fact."

She straightened the veil and made sure it was uniformly spread out around her on the seat. Once she had it just right, her attention turned to me, and she looked me over. "How old are you, anyway? You seem awfully young to work in law enforcement. Do you even know what you're doing?"

Everybody is a critic.

"Yes. I do know what I'm doing." *Though lately, I wonder.*

"Do you know Deputy George?" She referred to one of my partners, Deputy Barney George.

"Yes. I work with him. How do you know him?" I knew how, but I wanted to hear what she'd say.

"He came to my house when my dad started beating up my mom. They'd been drinking and got into it, so I called 911 on them. Deputy Barney came and got them calmed down. I like him."

"Please put your seatbelt on."

I backed the truck, turned it around, and pulled onto the highway.

"Do you have a lot of boyfriends?" she asked.

"Let's talk about you."

She shrugged her thin shoulders. "I'm just a dull kid."

"I'm sure you're not dull."

"Do you a boyfriend or not?"

"No."

"How come?"

"You were going to tell me about you."

"I have a boyfriend," she said.

"Tell me about him."

"If you don't want to talk about your boyfriend, then I shouldn't have to tell you about mine." She threw herself back against the seat in a show of teenage attitude.

"I think I should call you Opinionated Little Girl."

She laughed at that. After a moment, she said, "My name is 'Sissy' for being a sister, not for being a sissy. I changed the spelling to a 'C' because

I don't like it the other way."

"I understand. Why don't you want to go home?"

"It's boring and there's nothing to eat."

"Is that true, or is it things you don't like?"

"It's junk I have to fix."

"Yeah, I get like that, too."

"Lazy, you mean?"

I laughed. "Yep. Lazy."

"We could go out to eat."

"The restaurants are closed. Let's go to your house and wait for your folks. I'll help you fix something."

"Did you talk to my parents?"

"No, but the sheriff did."

"Are they freaked out?"

"They're concerned since you haven't been home in two days or been in school. Why weren't you in school?"

She gave me a stern look. "That's my personal business."

"I serve as a truant officer, so it's my business also."

"Am I in trouble with you?"

"You need to be in school. Is there someone you can stay with until your parents return?"

"No. I can stay by myself. I do it all the time."

"You're not afraid?"

"Why do you think I would be afraid?"

"Some youngsters are afraid to be alone at night."

"I'm not that young."

"You aren't that old, either."

"I can't win with you," she grumbled, but then she laughed.

"I'm trying to get information about you, Cissy."

"I want to know why you don't have a boyfriend."

"That's my personal business and has nothing to do with this."

She shrugged. "What's the big deal about your boyfriend?"

"It's not relevant to this conversation. I try to keep my personal life separate from my job."

"Which is hard in Terlingua."

"Yes. It sure is."

A few miles passed in silence. The full moon shining on the fog made it look like swirling silver. If this show was a contest of wills, the moon was winning.

Cissy said, "I don't think you'd like my parents."

"Why do you say that?"

She turned her gaze away. "They don't like Mexicans or black people or homosexuals or fornicators."

I wondered if she even knew what *fornicators* meant but didn't want to argue. I wanted to go home and sleep.

"They barely like any kind of people."

"That's a shame."

"But you don't care."

I thought I should call her "Perceptive Little Girl" instead of "Opinionated Little Girl."

"Tell me about the veil," I said.

"I bought it for fifty cents at the resale shop. I think it's beautiful."

"It is, I agree. But why are you wearing it?"

"Well, duh, because it's beautiful." She sighed. "I've never had anything this beautiful in my whole life."

"I see."

"What if a boy wants to do sex," Cissy blurted, "and you don't want to?"

"If you don't want to, you should only have to say so. It's personal, and the choice is up to you, not the boy. Any boy who respects and cares about you will understand this."

"Are you a radical woman?"

"That's not radical, Cissy. That's the way it is."

"You're okay," she said, "but I still think you're kinda radical."

"It's not radical to stand up for yourself. Are you having boyfriend trouble?"

"Isn't that a personal thing?"

"It's personal, yes. Whether you want to talk to me about it or not is up to you."

"Hey, my house is coming up on the left." She pointed at a dirt driveway. "Turn there."

I pulled in. My heart sank when I saw where she lived. It looked like a run-down shack, and I wondered if it even kept out the weather. At least someone was working on it. Building materials lay strewn around the yard.

"My dad and Tom McAfee were drinking beer at my house before my dad left for San Antonio."

I almost groaned aloud.

"Do you want to know what they said about you?"

"No."

"They think you're hot."

"They don't know me, Cissy, and they shouldn't talk about me."

"My father was in prison and he's kinda messed up from it. I don't know about Tom." She paused a second. "If I got in trouble, could I call you or Deputy George?"

"Sure. Call either one of us. We have a new partner, too. His name is Deputy Mayhew."

"Yeah, I've seen him before. He's called Buster, and he's cute."

"Shouldn't we go in your house?"

"I guess so, but it's so dark."

"I'll shine the headlights until you get inside and turn on the lights. Why don't you let me carry the veil for you, so you don't trip yourself up?"

She grinned. "Good idea."

Cissy shed the veil, hopped out, and ran towards her house. I called the Sheriff's Office in Alpine to say I had located Cecilia Florence and that she appeared to be unharmed. The dispatcher said he would notify her parents, who were on the way home. He also said he'd call my partners and leave a note for the sheriff.

I turned off the headlights and got out. The place gave me the creeps, and the come-and-go fog creeping around didn't help.

The house proved to be less decrepit-looking inside. The living room was cheerful, with colorful wall hangings and a few photographs. Cissy led me to the small, clean kitchen. We decided to make boxed macaroni and cheese and apple slices spread with peanut butter. There wasn't much else besides canned soup. Not only had they left their young daughter alone, but they'd also left her without adequate food.

"Where've you been for two days?" I asked while we waited for the water to boil.

"Here, there, around, I got tired of being by myself at the house."

"The people who came to give you a ride to school said you weren't home. We checked around, and your friends told us they hadn't seen you."

"They didn't want to get me in trouble."

"Your friends were covering for you?"

"Yeah, you got a problem with it?"

"Yes, I do. We were worried about you. Your parents reported you missing and asked us to find you. It isn't right to have your friends lie to someone who cares about your welfare."

"Okay, okay, I get it. Can you at least let me eat in peace?"

"You're not eating yet."

She sighed mightily. "You're so annoying."

I was starting to like this kid.

***

"Sometimes I skip school," Cissy admitted with her mouth full of macaroni and cheese.

"You should go to school. It's important for your future."

"I knew you would say that."

"I'm serious. Going to school is important for a lot of reasons."

"Yeah, I heard you the first time."

"You must have brothers or sisters if you're called 'Sissy,' right?"

Sadness clouded her face. "I have a sister. We haven't got her back yet."

"Where is your sister?"

She sighed. "Child Protective Services took her away from my mom."

"Why didn't they take you?"

"I was living with my grandma. My dad went to prison because he killed a man in a bar fight, but he didn't mean to. My mom was drinking too much, and she wasn't taking good care of Lesley. My sister's name is Lesley. She's three years younger than me. My parents are trying to get her back." She took a deep breath that became a sob. "I hope they can. I love her more than anyone."

When you ask a child a question, sometimes the answer will break your heart.

* * *

"Seriously," Cissy said with her mouth full, "What about law guys? Do you date law guys?"

"Stop it with the questions. Why are you so concerned that I have a boyfriend?"

She shrugged. "I have to figure out how these things work."

"You have plenty of time for that."

As we finished kitchen cleanup, Cissy's parents arrived. The front door slammed open, and a large man stepped inside. His shirt had been dribbled with something and not changed in a while. His pants were dark, so it was hard to tell, but he had slept in his clothes. His hair hadn't known a brush for at least a couple of days; nor had he shaved. He looked like a crazy person and glowered at me.

"Daddy," blurted a surprised Cissy, "why were you gone so long?"

He glared at me. "What are you doing with my daughter?"

"I'm Deputy Ricos. You reported Cissy missing. I found her and brought her home."

"I better never catch you here again."

"Hold on. I'm only here waiting for you."

"Please, Daddy," Cissy pleaded. "She's nice."

"Shut up, Cissy."

"Mr. Florence, you asked us to find your missing daughter and—"

"What are you doing with my daughter in the first place?" interrupted a mousy woman who squeezed into the room past her husband. She wobbled and smelled drunk and didn't seem to notice when I failed to answer her question. The father appeared to be sober at least, but he was no prize.

"Mom," Cissy said, "she gave me a ride home from Terlingua. She's nice."

"What the hell were you doing over there?" bellowed her father, addressing Cissy but staring at me.

"I was trying to find you." She looked to me to see if I would back up her lie.

"Cissy, we told you we were going to San Antonio. Why weren't you in school?"

Cissy shrugged and studied her feet. I headed for the door.

"I'm Rod Florence." Cissy's father stepped into my path and took a stab at civility. "So, you're Deputy Ricos?"

"Yes. It's late. I'd better get going. See you later, Cissy."

"Go to bed," Rod barked at his daughter. "I mean right now."

"Bye, Margarita. Thank you for the ride."

"You're welcome, Cissy."

Mr. Florence followed me out. "If you pick up my daughter again or come anywhere near her, I will report you to the sheriff." Great. Another critic, and this one smelled like a week's worth of stale cigarettes and dirty laundry seasoned with pot.

"Sir, I was doing my job."

He looked me up and down. "I don't want Cissy around you. Are we clear, or do I need to call Sheriff Duncan?"

"Please call the sheriff if it'll make you feel better."

I got into the vehicle, started it, and put it into reverse. Rod Florence continued to rant at me. As I pulled away, he yelled, "I don't approve of your lifestyle."

What lifestyle? I work. I go home. I run and work out. I rarely date. I live alone except for a puppy. I didn't think that even qualified as a lifestyle.

***

As I pulled into my driveway, Sheriff Duncan called on my cell phone. It was unlike him to call so late.

"I've just been chewed up and spit out by Rod Florence," he said when I answered. "I want to know how he got my home number."

"I didn't give it to him if that's what you're thinking. Isn't it in the Alpine phone book?"

I watched my puppy press her nose against the living room window, her paws on the sill. "Just a minute, Missy," I mouthed, as if that would do any good.

"He's spittin' mad," the sheriff continued. "Never mind the fact that you found his missing child and brought her home safely. He thinks I should dismiss you because of moral turpitude, which boils down to a lot of wild imaginings. That man is dumb as a stump."

"You must have confused him with facts."

He laughed and changed the subject. "Earlier today, I had a call from your fervent admirer, Tom McAfee."

I groaned, got out of the truck, and headed to my house.

"Tom is concerned that you're wrong for the job of deputy. He thinks he's better suited since he's a man, and you're a lovely female."

"I'm familiar with that argument."

"He believes his Army experience should have been training enough to qualify him, and he could be a deputy with his eyes closed."

"There's a scary thought, Sheriff."

"You're not kidding. Hell, there are so many reasons Tom can't have your job, I don't know where to start."

I took a deep breath and opened the front door of my house. Missy shot out and into me and almost knocked me off my feet. It's a wonder I didn't drop the phone. Missy understood a lot of words and commands, but calm and cool weren't in her vocabulary. Although growing fast, she was still a puppy in most ways.

"You can't win an argument with Tom," I said above the whirlwind. I plopped into a rocking chair before Missy could knock me down. She continued to happy dance, not yet ready to settle down and let me pet her.

My boss said, "I told Rod Florence that the next time you pick up his daughter, she'll be brought to Alpine, and the Child Protective Services will be contacted. That took a little of the hard out of his blow."

I laughed at that. Our sheriff is tough when he has to be, and unlike some lawmen, he knows when that is.

CHAPTER 2

I was well over the 75 MPH speed limit on the flats of Highway 118 near Santiago Peak between Alpine and Terlingua, when flashing lights appeared. It was tempting not to stop, but my fellow law enforcement officers knew my blue Mustang. It was not a good idea to show disrespect for them, even if they were as aggravating as a swarm of gnats.

I pulled over as a siren bleep-bleeped a greeting. Thanks to my wide side-view mirror, I watched Trooper Roberts exit his patrol car, adjust his hat, hitch up his leather gun belt, and smooth his tight pants.

I rolled down my window as he stepped up to it. "Hey, Clancy."

He squatted so his face was in the window with his head resting on his arms. "Hi, Margarita. Aren't you going a bit fast today, even for you?"

"I'm working."

His brow furrowed. "You don't look like you're working."

"You wouldn't give me a citation, would you?"

"Speeding is not why I'm stopping you."

"Why are you stopping me?"

"I want to talk."

"I know you have my phone number."

"Face-to-face works better. Besides, you don't always answer your phone." He stood, sauntered to the passenger side, and tapped on the glass. "Open up."

I didn't want to.

"Open up, Margarita, please."

I put the window down far enough to talk to him. "I'm in a hurry Clancy; that's why I was speeding."

He groaned. "Oh, please. Spare me the lies. I hear them all day long. And I happen to know you speed whether you're in a hurry or not."

I unlocked the door. "Okay, get in, but make this fast."

"Listen, I don't think I can say this fast. There's something you need to know, and it's serious."

"What is it?"

"Margarita, it's about Jupiter." He referred to his fellow State

Trooper, Jasper Pierson. I never asked Jupiter how he got his nickname because it didn't matter; maybe Jupiter was his home planet.

Clancy sucked in a deep breath. "You've always been straight up with me, so I just thought..."

"What is it, Clance? Out with it."

"Pierson is talking about you, Margarita."

"What does he say?"

Clancy looked away from me and took a deep breath. "There's no good way to say this."

"Just say it, please."

"He's um, he's bragging to everybody that he's sleeping with you."

I wanted to cry, scream, or laugh hysterically. Or disappear. Poof!

"I thought you should know," Clancy said.

Jupiter had been a bad decision; I knew that, but I hadn't realized the grand scale of it. A private screw-up would've felt better, but it never works like that.

"Please say something, Margarita."

"I feel betrayed—and angry."

"I'm sorry. Pierson is a dumbass who doesn't know when to keep his big mouth shut."

"Thank you for telling me, Clancy, but now I need to go."

"Please don't hold this against me."

"I won't."

"I'm afraid you will."

"I won't, Clancy. I promise you I won't. It's not your fault Jupiter has the maturity of a fourteen-year-old boy."

"Margarita, if I called you sometime, would you consider—"

I held up my hand. "I'm going to stop you right there."

"You're right. Bad timing. I'm going now."

"Bye, Clancy."

He walked around to the driver's side of my car, stooped down low, and said, "Slow it down, Ms. Ricos. Please don't make me stop you again." He winked and walked back to his cruiser.

***

At home, I made hot tea because I find it comforting, and it's easier to make than mashed potatoes. Then I took a steaming mug and my steaming self to sit on the porch with Missy. My baby guard dog surveyed the area for possible threats. Too bad she hadn't been with me when I made the Bad Decision.

When I felt calmer, I called the Bad Decision to tell him adios. Oh, the whining and excuses that ensued. I finally just hung up. Being an adolescent boy, Jupiter would never understand "why" unless he grew up.

A cactus wren landed on the porch railing not far from where my feet rested. I thought she was one of a nesting pair that lived in a cholla cactus in my backyard. Ms. Wren scrutinized the scene and then scolded us with her heart in it.

Cactus wrens make a raw, scratchy sound, like somebody trying to start a car. They're entertaining and gregarious, but this little gal had had enough. Maybe a sweet-talking, good-looking, male cactus wren had kissed her and told everybody.

"Hey," I said, "I know a state trooper who should hear that rant." A cactus wren scolding was just what he needed.

The bird flew off as suddenly as she'd arrived. Missy turned to me, confused, as if to say, "What was that about?"

"It beats me, girl."

She sighed and rested her head on her paws.

"People can be so disappointing, Missy."

She looked up at me with sad eyes. That was old news to my pup. She'd learned about disappointing people from her former human.

As I finished the tea, I realized I needed perspective, a change of view, and a change of attitude. In other words, I needed a long run.

Before I went inside to change clothes, Barney pulled up in his Brewster Country Sheriff's Office truck. Missy ran to greet him and make him feel welcome. Of course, Missy thought he'd come to see her.

"Hey, Barney."

He plopped into the chair next to mine. "Hey yourself, Ricos. I just came from town." By "town" he meant Alpine.

"I guess that explains why you're still wearing your uniform."

"How come you didn't tell me that you and Jupiter Pierson were such a hot item?"

"Jupiter is a mistake I made, Barney."

"He doesn't think so. I'm going by what he says, since you don't tell me anything."

"Would you like to tell me about all of your mistakes?"

"Nah, I'd rather not."

"Did you speak with Jupiter or did someone else tell you?"

"I stopped to get gas, and the trooper himself was at the pump next to me. I gave him the howdy nod because I don't really know the guy."

"What did he say?"

Barney mulled my question, as if it was a hard one. "What he said, translated, is that you two are dating."

"What do you mean by 'translated?'"

"He asked if I'd heard that you and he are together, and he made it sound serious. I didn't know what to say because I hadn't heard a word about it. I felt bad that you hadn't told me anything. I said something stupid, like 'it takes dedication to date a woman in Terlingua when you live in Alpine.' He said you were worth it, and anyway, you go to his place because of all the Terlingua gossip and such."

"You didn't answer my question about 'translated.'"

"Jeez, Ricos. All right, well, the truth is that he went locker room on me. Way too much information, if you know what I mean. I work with you, and you're my friend, and I don't want to hear that kind of talk." Barney glanced at me and took a breath. "I got the hell out of there before I decked him. He's an officer of the law, and he should have more respect. I'm an officer of the law also, and I know my boss would not care to hear that I laid a state trooper out flat at the gas station."

"That's true, but I would've liked to see that."

"Want to take a quick run to town?"

"Yes and no," I said. After a short pause, I added, "I heard about Jupiter's bad behavior from Clancy Roberts."

"The state trooper Roberts?"

"Is there another Clancy Roberts? He stopped me for speeding earlier today and told me about Jupiter's flappy mouth."

"Did he give you a ticket?"

"No. He never gives me a ticket."

"He stops you because he likes you."

"I like him too, but right now all State Troopers are under suspicion."

"I can understand that. Have you spoken with Jupiter?"

"I called him when I got home and told him I'd made my last trip to Alpine that would include him."

"How'd he take it?"

"Not well. He doesn't understand why I won't give him a second chance. He thought we hit it off, and everything was great, and whiny, whine, whine. He made it all about him, which just made the whole thing worse."

"Wow."

"I feel so disappointed in him, Barney."

"You know that some men never grow up, right?"

"Yeah, but I thought Jupiter was a grown-up."

"Just because a man is large doesn't mean he's mature."

"Okay, I get it."

"How long have you been dating him?"

"To be truthful—and I don't want to hear any crap from you about it—I wouldn't have called it dating."

"So, what was it, a sordid affair?" Barney feigned shock.

"Enough about me. Can I interest you in some tea?"

CHAPTER 3

The morning started out fine, with no hint of disaster to come. It was wickedly beautiful at my end of the county. As I left my house, the rising sun painted the sky a pinkish-gold color, even though it was still behind the mountains of Big Bend National Park.

I left Missy with my mom and headed to meet with the sheriff at his office in Alpine, eighty miles away. Sheriff Duncan and his deputies cover Brewster County, the largest and most scenic county in Texas. There are over six thousand square miles and more mountains than a person can count, although I could spend the rest of my life trying.

When I arrived in town, I pulled into a gas station. A State Trooper pulled in behind me and right into the back bumper of my Sheriff's Office Ford truck. Tapping the rear end of my vehicle was one of the multiple ways the bad boys of Brewster County law enforcement entertained themselves. Usually, I remained calm and above it all.

Sometimes, enough is enough and then some.

It took one second to jump out of the truck and begin to rant. "Jupiter!" I yelled. *"Cabrón!* What do you think you're doing?" I stomped and flailed my arms. "What are you trying to prove?"

The big idiot leaped out of his cruiser and stood next to it looking sheepish. "You in a bad mood, Margarita?"

Bad mood? A bad mood would've been a relief.

"Listen, you pathetic little boy, haven't you ever had sex with a woman before?"

"Well, of course, I—"

"Don't you dare speak to me!"

"But you asked me a—"

"I said not to speak to me!" I continued to rant at him in English and then in Spanish, even though I knew he spoke no Spanish. I accused him of acting like a 14-year-old and told him he was a pathetic example of a man and on and on. When I ran out of steam, I did not feel better and instead, felt ashamed of myself and even more stressed out.

I hopped back into my vehicle and chewed my lip all the way to the Sheriff's Office. When I parked next to the sheriff's truck, I took a deep breath and tried to calm myself before going in.

I stopped at the secretary's desk to say hello, and then strolled into my boss's office as if everything was as peachy as a Terlingua sunrise.

In place of the usual hello conversation, he said, "Margarita, is Jasper Pierson stalking you?"

"Why do ask that, Sheriff?"

"Please answer my question."

"No; I don't think so. Please tell me why you're asking me about him."

"Cliff heard some talk he didn't like." He referred to Cliff Selby, our lead deputy. "He told me about it, and I don't like it either. It's not my business or Cliff's, but Pierson put us into it by talking out of school."

Oh man, I only thought I wanted to disappear before.

"Sheriff, I only went out with him a few times, and I already told him I didn't ever want to see him again. He and I didn't click."

I couldn't tell the sheriff I'd slept with Trooper Pierson in a futile effort to ease the pain in my heart, to feel alive, to be held by a man. I didn't even understand all the reasons. And it hadn't worked anyway, except for a few hours. I'd been drinking at the time, and I couldn't tell the sheriff that, either.

"Regardless of Jasper Pierson, I believe there's something going on with you."

"Sheriff, you know the time off you offered me a while back?"

"Yes. You refused to take it, as I recall."

"I need it now. I feel like I'm about to unravel. When Rod Florence ranted at me, it felt like the last straw. He doesn't want me to come near his daughter, and I'm a bad example, and he doesn't like my lifestyle. Usually, I let things like this roll off my back. It took all my restraint not to kick him in the teeth. I almost drew my weapon, Sheriff. Who knows what would've happened then?" I paused for a breath. "I don't even know if I want to stay in law enforcement."

"I feared this would happen, Margarita. I'm sorry I didn't force you to rest when you were injured. So much has happened to you in such a short time."

"Please don't blame yourself. It'll just make me feel worse."

The sheriff's secretary knocked and then popped her head in. "Excuse me, but Trooper Pierson is here, Sheriff. He says he needs to see Margarita."

The sheriff's eyes narrowed. "Please tell him that Margarita and I are working on something important. He should go on about his day."

"I told him that, sir, but he won't leave."

Sheriff Ben stood, and to me he said, "I'll be right back."

I considered climbing out the window while he was gone.

The sheriff came back carrying a cup of coffee. "Pierson left, but he's going to call you later. If he becomes a problem, please let me know. I'll speak with his boss if I have to."

"You won't need to, Sheriff."

"How much time do you need?"

"Can you spare me for two weeks?"

"Yes, but I think it should be a month. I know how you hate my opinions, but I'm going to give you one anyway. I think you should get away from everything. Go somewhere. Take a vacation. The point is I want you to come back to work at the end of it, Margarita. You're a fine deputy, and I don't want to lose you."

"Thank you, sir. I just need to figure out where to go from here. I feel as though I've lost my way."

"Does Trooper Pierson have anything to do with this?"

"No; he's more of a symptom than a cause. Now he has increased my stress, but I can't blame anyone but myself for him."

"Nobody makes the right decisions all of the time. Please remember that, Margarita."

"I will. Thank you, Sheriff."

When he didn't say anything more, I asked, "Didn't you need me to do something here today?"

"I'll free up someone else. You go home and take care of yourself."

My boss walked me out to my car, talking the whole time. He made it look casual, but I knew he was checking to be sure that Trooper Pierson was not going to accost me in the parking lot.

***

I sat on my porch with Missy, and we contemplated the steep up-

and-down rock faces, sharp spires, and the huge boulders littering Cimarron Mountain. My eyes took in the surrounding mountains and acres of desert and then returned to my mountain. I like to think I'm part it. For certain it's part of me.

Barney drove up in his Sheriff's Office truck.

Missy ran out to greet him and made a big fuss over him. He bent down to show her some love and then plopped his six-and-a-half-foot frame into the chair next to me. The pup lay down between us.

Barney stared at me with an incredulous expression. "I just spoke with the sheriff, and he says you're taking a month off."

"That's true. I asked for two weeks, but he thinks I should take a month."

He heaved a sigh as though the end times were upon us. "A month, Ricos?"

"Yes, a month. Thirty days."

"Why didn't you tell me about it yourself?"

"It just happened, Barney. When I walked into his office, I realized I needed time off."

"Yeah; that happens nearly every time I go in there." He ran his hand over Missy's back and then asked, "What's going on with you, Ricos?"

"I need a break, that's all."

"That doesn't tell me anything. Is this about Jupiter?"

"No, Barn. Jupiter is only a symptom."

"A symptom of—?"

"A symptom of something wrong in my life. I'm not satisfied in this job anymore. I put myself in harm's way for people who call me a slut or a bitch behind my back or even to my face. They accuse me of being a lesbian because I carry a gun. What if I was? How would that affect them? Would that keep me from doing my job? And then there're the ones who dismiss me as 'hot' or 'the girl deputy.' That's even worse."

"Some people call you Batgirl and know damn well how brave and capable you are."

"Thank you, but that's only you."

He shrugged.

"Do you want to hear the rest of my grievances?

"Yes. Go ahead."

"Some idiots send their drones to spy on me."

"Well, you took care of that."

"Sure, but he'll just get another one. Also, people think we have a continuous orgy going on in the office because I'm a woman working with two men."

Barney chuckled. "Yeah, Julia hears that one."

"The last case, or I should say cases, put me over the edge. You were shot, and we didn't know if you were going to live. It hit home the kind of danger we're in sometimes. Also, my precious friend Austin was accused of rape. Then I got beat up by those scumbags. Lying Brenda came on the scene and claimed to have a child by Kevin. Talk about stress?

"Yet again, we had to clean up a bunch of messes we didn't make. And don't forget that innocent young woman whose death went undiscovered for more than twenty years. And the disgusting, unforgivable reason she died. It's not just one thing. It's everything all together."

"I understand."

"Oh—and the people who gossip about me? Who do they call if they're in trouble?"

"I'm surprised we have the strength to answer the phone with all the sex and partying going on at the office."

"Yeah, no kidding."

"Look, Ricos—"

"The truth is, I started drinking."

"Oh, no."

"I don't need a lecture about it. Believe me, I beat myself up worse than you ever could."

"I wasn't going to lecture you or beat you up, Margarita. I'm on your side. If you want to talk, you know how to reach me."

"Thank you, Barney."

"Does the sheriff know you're drinking again?"

"No, and please don't tell him."

"Have a little bit of faith in me. I would never tell the sheriff. I want you to come back to work, not get fired."

"I need to work some things out."

"Do whatever it takes. If you want to sit by the Rio and contemplate the vastness of the universe, you know I'm into that."

"Thank you. I do know that."

"How can we be the most kick-ass deputy duo in the West if you're sitting on your rear all day getting fat?"

CHAPTER 4

Because I was lying on a boulder like a lizard, and because the best dog in the world lay at my side, and because the boulder was halfway up Cimarron Mountain; and because I had an abundance of endorphins on the brain and no cares whatsoever at that moment, I took Jupiter's call.

"Please don't hang up," he said after I said, "Ricos."

"I won't."

"I just want to say that I screwed up big time and I know it. Then I made it worse by having a tantrum. I hope you'll forgive me because I like you a lot. I don't want you to feel that you can never speak to me again or that I'm a creep."

"I wish you well, Jupiter."

"Take good care of yourself, Margarita."

To Missy I said, "And that, my curious little pup, is how a few-night stand is supposed to end."

***

As I wound down from a long run, drank water, and started feeling better about everything, Barney called from the office.

"Are you on leave, or what am I supposed to tell people?"

"Tell them I'm on vacation if you have to tell them something."

"Can we talk about the school?"

"What about it?"

"The secretary called for you because your little friend Cissy Florence slipped away during lunch and nobody knows where she went."

"Cissy is a big fan of yours, Deputy George. Why don't you look for her? Or, you could send Buster and make her day. She thinks he's cute."

"That figures. He's about her age."

"I think you should stop ragging Buster about his age. He can't help being young and looking it."

"Do you think he's cute, Margarita?"

"I refuse to answer any of your trick questions."

"You have a thing about him, don't you?"

"If by 'have a thing' about him, you mean like and respect him, then yes."

"Un-huh."

"Stop trying to make problems."

"If you'll look for Cissy, I'll stop making problems."

"Oh, sure."

"How about if I owe you one?"

"Okay, but after this, I'm on vacation. Do you get it?"

"I can already smell the sunscreen, Batgirl."

***

I checked at the Florence home, then drove up to the Ghost Town, and I asked about her at various stores. No Cissy and no parents of Cissy.

When I dropped by my house for a drink of water, Cissy was waiting on the porch.

"Please don't be mad," she said as I walked towards her.

I sat down next to her. "Tell me why you aren't in school."

"I don't like it."

"I'm sorry, but you need to be there whether you like it or not. Surely there's something about it you like."

Her brow scrunched in thought. "I like P.E. and boys; and I like math."

"Well, there's something."

"I want to live with you," she blurted.

"Cissy, you barely know me."

She shrugged her skinny shoulders. "I know you good enough. You care about kids, and I can talk to you about things, and you're not real old, and you don't smoke pot or drink. You have a nice house and a puppy. Also, you're pretty."

"Thank you, Cissy, but I don't think I'd make a good mother."

"We could just be friends."

"Cissy, if your father finds out you're here, we'll be in trouble."

"How will he find out?"

"People talk. He told me he didn't want me around you, so it'd be wrong for you to be here behind his back."

"My parents are never home. I was thinking you could adopt me and then we could get my sister. They're not going to let my parents have her, but I bet they'd let you 'cause you're a responsible person."

That was debatable.

"Cissy, I don't know anything about raising children. I don't even have a husband...or time for a child."

"You don't need a husband to have a child. And you could make time. I think you could do it fine if you would only try."

"I appreciate your confidence in me, but your parents would have to be told you're here, and your father will be furious. Is there even a way to reach him?"

She grinned. "He bought us cell phones, and I have his number."

"In that case, why don't you call and ask him?"

She didn't want to do that anymore than I did.

"I'm going to take you back to school and after that, we'll figure something out."

"Margarita, I asked my father who would take care of me while they're gone for three days, and he said, 'figure it out.' So, I did. I'll stay with you."

Before I left the school grounds, I called Sheriff Ben and tried to explain what had just happened.

"Well," he said after some thought, "I could call the Florences and tell them she can either stay with you, or I'll call Child Protective Services, their decision."

"But CPS will take her away, and she could be put somewhere worse than where she is. On the other hand, I don't need a child, not even for three days."

"I think it would be good for you."

I groaned in my head. Anything someone else thought was "good for me" would probably be hell.

"Well, you can't have it both ways," the sheriff said. "If you can't keep her, I have no choice but to call CPS. The parents have left that little girl alone and defenseless in a house out there on the highway. She won't stay in school and anything bad could happen to her while they're gone."

"Okay, I'll take her for three days if they agree to it."

I could practically hear him smiling. "I'll call you back in a while."

"All right, Sheriff."

There wasn't anything I needed less than a child, unless it was a man.

***

I went by the office to see what Barney was doing.

"Damn it, Ricos," he said when I walked in, so it was just like I was still working.

"What's going on?"

"I don't even know where to start. Sit down." He leaned back until his chair hit the wall. He jumped, as if surprised the wall still existed.

I sat in the visitor chair opposite him. "Start somewhere."

"This is not for public knowledge yet, but a convicted sex offender is moving to Terlingua."

"You're kidding me."

"I wish."

"That doesn't make sense. This place is too small, and everybody knows everything. Did this come from the sheriff?"

"Of course."

"And he approved it?"

"He doesn't have a choice. The Texas Parole Board approved it."

"But Terlingua isn't convenient. He'll have to drive to Alpine to see a parole officer. I bet he doesn't stay a week."

"I hope he doesn't come."

"When he sees how remote it is, he'll change his mind."

"You and I both know he'll come and bring hell with him," Barney said.

"What did he do?"

"He raped a twelve-year-old girl when he was nineteen."

"What? And they're allowing him to come to Terlingua?"

"He did his time, so..."

"But no amount of time—"

Barney held up his giant hand. "I know what you're about to say, and I agree. We don't have a choice in this. He did his time and now he's free."

I didn't speak. What was there to say?

"He's been in prison seven years, but he was originally sentenced to ten. I guess he got out on good behavior or..." Barney didn't finish the sentence.

"When this guy registers, it'll be non-stop hysterics and pervert sightings," I said. "I can already hear the whining. *He looked at me funny.*"

Barney laughed and then got serious. "I wish you didn't have to be on vacation right now. I need you here."

"You have Buster."

Barney rolled his eyes.

"Sorry, but this vacation is something I need. If I didn't, I'd just come back to work. Buster will help you, Barney. He'll need some direction from you, but he's sharp and he works hard."

"I get it. I just have more faith in you."

"Thank you, but you'll have faith in Buster once you work with him more. There was a time when you had to explain things to me and show me what to do. I wasn't always the stellar officer you see before you now."

"Oh, right. You mean a Batgirl wearing cutoffs?"

"I don't need a uniform to do my job."

"I know that's true. Back to the subject of the ex-con. Sheriff Ben says he refused early release to avoid chemical castration. He could've been free a year ago if he had agreed to it. The sheriff is afraid that not agreeing to the castration means he's planning to continue his dark activities."

"Who the hell would volunteer to be castrated, chemically or otherwise?" I blurted. As my old friend Craig would say, *lordy, lordy, lordy.*

Barney grimaced at the suggestion of it.

"Maybe he refused treatment because of the side effects," I said. "Men don't want to have breasts or lose the ability to—"

"Okay, Ricos; stop. I get it."

I was going to say *lose the ability to have an erection,* but I thought I should leave it alone. The offender had his reasons, so I didn't need to go on about it.

"I'll tell you one thing about this guy," Barney said. "We'll have to protect him from the community as much as the other way around."

* * *

After a while, I went into my small office and sat in the overstuffed chair with my boots on the desk to look out the window at a hill that abuts the back of our parking lot. It can't be called a mountain because it isn't high. Yet the word *hill* makes it sound ordinary and it's not. It's a work of art from the hunk of reddish-brown rock perched on top to the boulder maze strewn at its base. It gives thick stands of prickly pear cacti a place to set down roots, along with yuccas and stabbing shrubs like mesquite and catclaw acacia. A family of desert willows lives out there too, growing steadily upward, egged on by the sky.

"Ricos! Are you listening?"

"What is it, Barney?"

"The sheriff is on the line for you."

"How does he know I'm here?"

"I've told you before, he's like God."

I leaned across my desk and picked up the phone. "Hello, Sheriff."

"The Florences agreed to it," he said, proving wonders never cease. "They'll pick Cissy up from you upon their return."

"Which will be when?"

"He was cloudy on that, but within a week."

"Sheriff, I can't keep her longer than three days."

"You can hope for the best, Margarita."

I went back to studying my short mountain. The Chisos range can be seen from my window if I turn my head in a sharp right. But the Chisos are distant. Cactus Hill is close and personal. I observe it any time I need to think, but I study it intensely when things don't make sense, which is most of the time.

***

"Cissy seems like a great kid," Barney said.

"Maybe you could keep her for a few days."

"Are you kidding? Julia would kill me." Barney referred to his wife.

"Cissy would be a built-in babysitter."

"Nice try Ricos, but this is an enriching experience you should have. I wouldn't want to rob you of it."

Well, crap.

I returned to studying my hill.

CHAPTER 5

My mother was no help. She found my dilemma amusing.

"It'll do you good," she said, which meant it would be misery. "Maybe you'll appreciate what your parents went through."

I already appreciated my parents.

My first disagreement with Cissy occurred soon after I picked her up from school, and it was about homework. She wanted to watch television instead of doing it.

"I never do homework," she proclaimed.

Missy cocked an ear at the tone of her voice.

"That's one of your problems at school. In my house, you're going to do it."

"I'll do it later." She lifted Missy into her lap.

"I want you to do it now. I'm going for a run before it gets dark. When I come back, I'll make dinner. Then we can watch a movie. I have no satellite service, so get used to the idea."

She looked horrified. "But everybody has satellite or else Internet."

"I don't have time for TV, so it wouldn't be worth it." I had Internet, but I had never signed up for any of the movie-streaming channels.

"If you adopt me and Lesley, you're gonna need it."

Instead of trying to explain why adoption wasn't going to happen, I said, "Will you promise me you'll do your homework while I'm gone?"

"How long will you be gone?"

"About an hour. If you finish before I get back, take a bath."

"Do I have to?"

"Are you going to give me a hard time about everything? Yes, you do have to. In my house, we do homework and take baths. You'll find all kinds of shampoos and soaps. If you want to take a bubble bath, there's some nice-smelling stuff for that. Or you can take a shower."

Her eyes darted to my computer, so I nipped that in the bud. "You need a password to get into it, so forget using it until I return. If you cooperate with me, I'll let you use it."

"I didn't know you'd be such a hard-ass."

"We'll have fun, but I have my work and you have yours. Since you're staying with me I expect certain things. You expect me to feed you and give you a safe place to sleep, right?"

She nodded, a small girl with serious eyes.

"I'll do my part, Cissy, but you have to do yours."

"Why do you run, anyway? What are you running from?"

"I run because it makes me feel free. It feels good to my body, and it makes my problems stand back."

"Like what problems?"

"My work and people talking about me, and mouthy little girls who want to stay with me but don't want to do their homework."

"Okay, I get it. Can you at least leave Missy with me?"

"I can do that, but I'm not kidding about a bath and homework."

"I'll do my homework," she groused, "but only 'cause you're forcing me. When do we get to have any fun around here?"

* * *

Another reason for running is drinking; somehow, running keeps me from it—almost always. I didn't want to mention that to Cissy.

I drove to a dirt road near the Terlingua Ghost Town and left my car. I'd picked the wrong day to run that route because Tom McAfee was on the prowl. Tom is a strange man of 40-something who wants to "date" me. I don't like him and therefore have no interest in him. It has nothing to do with his age.

I took off along the edge of Highway 170. Tom passed in his Jeep, but I barely noticed because a man came on foot from the Ghost Town road and began running along the other side of the highway. He was a big man with blond hair pulled into a ponytail and*, ay Dios,* he was built.

Tom turned his Jeep around and came back. He blocked my line of vision, so I lost sight of the runner.

"Hey, Margarita, what are you doing?"

"I'm running."

"Hop in and we'll go do something." Tom was easier to read than *See Spot Run.*

"I need to exercise."

"I don't see how missing one day could hurt."

"Later, Tom." I took off, leaving Tom to pout or whatever.

I headed to Long Draw, an arroyo that crosses the highway in several places. I ducked off the road and into the first part of the dry creek bed, where the hard-packed sand makes running easier. I seldom see a sign of humans there, and I like it that way. Peace washed over me, displacing anger. I kept running until I crossed the road again and into the best part of the arroyo, the canyon.

After a while, I sat on a boulder to rest and drink water. Before long, I heard gravel crunching and heavy breathing. When I looked up, the unknown running man was jogging down the arroyo towards me.

"Hello," he grunted with a nod as he passed.

I returned his greeting and smiled. He looked angry, a typical stone-faced bad boy, but you sure don't see muscular legs like those every day.

To my left loomed a rough wall that forms the highest side of the canyon. In some places prickly pear and strawberry cacti hang from precarious positions and appear to grow right out of solid rock. Waterfalls rage from the top of the mesa during downpours and leave rough-and-tumble pour-offs that are dry most of the time. Despite that, a thick community of desert willow, cat claw acacia, mesquite, and native cottonwoods grow along the bottom of the wall.

I was about to continue my run when I heard footsteps and labored breathing. Tom McAfee headed towards me. I doubted he had taken up running, and he wasn't dressed for it. Most likely he'd driven his Jeep as far into the arroyo as he could get it. He wore a smile plastered in place, but he looked pale and out of breath.

"Why did you follow me, Tom?"

He plopped down next to me, and I jumped off the boulder.

"Don't. Be. So. Jumpy." He fanned himself with a brown cap with a Big Bend National Park logo, and he spoke in gasps. "I hoped. You'd be. Over that. By now."

"Something is wrong with you."

"You're. Obsessed. With running."

"Tom, leave me alone. Can you get it through your head, or do I need to get a restraining order?"

"I have to admit it's a nice afternoon for a run."

"Restraining order, it is." I turned away to continue my run. I realized I didn't have to hurt or threaten him when I could outrun him.

Tom grabbed my arm. "I'll give you a ride, Margarita. Don't go yet."

I jerked away. "Don't grab me!"

"I didn't grab you," he said and grabbed me again. "Why are you so afraid of me? You're the violent one."

"Violent?"

"You shot my drone out of the sky."

"I shot your spying drone at the edge of my porch. You can't say I didn't warn you dozens of times."

"I like you anyway, Margarita," he said and grabbed me again.

"What is wrong with you?" I yanked my arm back and moved out of his reach. "I don't want you to touch me."

"Look." He held up his hands. "I want you to have a beer with me. What is so wrong with that?"

About a hundred things. "I don't want to do that."

"It's only a beer with no strings attached. I can bring a couple of bottles from my Jeep if you want to drink them here."

Nobody could be that dense. Again, I turned to run, and he grabbed me from behind. I tried to throw him, but he was too heavy, and he'd caught me off guard.

"Let me go!"

His arms held me like a band. The sound of gravel crunching from behind alarmed me. I feared that a few of Tom's pals had come to join the fun and games.

"The lady said to back off, mister." Running Man!

He glared at Tom. "Let her go. Now."

Tom jerked me around so that I was between him and my defender.

"Let her go," my muscled champion warned again.

"You stay out of this," Tom snarled.

"Don't put her between us, you coward."

Tom shoved me aside so hard that I stumbled into the boulder and skinned my hands and knees.

The men faced off, assuming fight positions. It was easy to see that Running Man could kill Tom, maybe with one blow.

"Stop it!" I yelled. "There's no reason to fight. Go on, Tom. Get out of here."

Grumbling and cursing, he headed back to his Jeep.

I smiled at my rescuer. "Thank you."

"Don't mention it." He wheeled around to continue his run, and his gold-streaked hair gleamed in the fading light. It was beautiful and didn't go with his tough growling-guy image.

"What's your name?" I called after him.

He turned back, but not enough to face me. "Why?"

"My name is Margarita. Do you live here?"

He shrugged and took off up the arroyo.

That is not how the brave rescuer of a damsel in distress is supposed to act. I dragged my wounded self-esteem home.

CHAPTER 6

"I need advice about my breasts," announced Cissy as I came through the door. I hadn't noticed she had any, and that was the source of her concern.

I scooped my enthusiastic Missy off the floor and sat down with her, so she'd know I was happy to see her, too.

"What would you like to know, Cissy?"

"When did you get them?"

"I was about your age, I think."

"Mine aren't growing."

"They will; give them time."

"But I should at least have bumps by now."

Missy cocked her head at the frustrated tone of our young friend. She didn't care about breast development, but she loved Cissy.

"Cissy, your body is going to grow at its own pace. You can't compare yourself to other girls. The sooner you get over that, the happier you'll be. Celebrate the things about you that are uniquely yours, and don't let anybody put you down."

"Like what is uniquely mine?"

"You have blonde hair that is soft and beautiful when you brush it and keep it clean. You have big blue eyes and a pretty face and a smooth complexion. You're going to be a gorgeous woman one day, but not overnight. Also, it's not only about looks. You're bright and outspoken. You seem to have a kind heart. Those things are most important of all."

"My mother's not gorgeous or bright or kind."

"But you are, Cissy; it doesn't matter about your mother. You can be who you are and make your life different from hers. Your mother doesn't take good care of herself, does she?"

"No, and she drinks too much. My father is mean and not good-looking."

"None of that matters. They have their gifts, I'm sure, but your concern is with your gifts. I tell you to go to school because being educated will be your ticket away from here. You can make your own life exactly as you want it. How great is that?"

"That's pretty great." She glowed with the prospect of it.

"Go to school and pay attention. Do your homework, always. Try to learn things on your own. Read instead of wasting time in front of a TV. Another way to take care of yourself is to eat good food, get plenty of exercise and rest, and don't put yourself in situations where you could get hurt."

"Like walking on the highway at night?"

"That's right."

"And not going to late parties on a school night?"

"That, too. Definitely that."

***

At bedtime, we sat together on my bed, and then she flopped down on it. "Would you read to me?"

"It would be good practice if you read to me."

"But nobody has ever read to me."

"In that case, what should I read?"

"Something you like."

"Have you ever read *To Kill a Mockingbird*?"

"No. Is it good?"

"It's one of my favorites."

She patted my pillow with her small hand and her eyes shone. "Then lie down right here and read."

I lay down right there and read.

***

At breakfast the next morning, Cissy was animated about the book, talking about Scout, Jem, and Atticus Finch as if she knew them personally. She couldn't wait to meet Boo Radley, but the mystery of it frightened her a little. She loved being read to and cuddling next to me, feeling safe. I had liked that too.

When I mentioned oatmeal for breakfast, she stated with haughty certainty, "I'd rather starve than eat that." But when I set it in front of her with sliced banana and strawberries on top, she devoured it, talking all the while. I didn't know if she liked it or ate it without a fight so that I would keep reading to her.

***

After I dropped Cissy at school, I went by the grocery store. Don't picture an H-E-B or Albertson's; the place is small compared to them, but it's still a great store. My point is that I ran into Running Man again, except I now thought of him as That Rude Runner.

I stood behind him in line at the check-out counter, and when he turned to leave he almost ran into me. "Oh. It's you."

"Yes. Try not to sound so enthusiastic about it."

He mumbled and hurried out.

That Rude Runner waited outside the door holding two grocery bags. "You're Margarita, right?" He took a baby step towards me.

"Yes."

"May I speak with you?"

"Okay."

"I—uh—want to—uh—apologize for being rude yesterday. I'm not good with women. I mean people. I mean regular people, especially women." I hadn't seen a male fidget like that since junior high dances.

"It's all right," I said. "I'm not going to bite you."

He laughed uneasily, and then an awkward silence ensued.

"My name is Randy." It took him so long to tell me his name that I wondered if he'd made it up. "You asked if I live here and I do."

"Maybe I'll see you around."

"Do you run a lot?"

"Yes. I guess you could call it a lot."

"I never saw you in that little canyon before," he said.

"That's because I don't run there often."

"Where do you run?"

"All over, but I like the dirt roads near my house."

"Okay. Well, so long." He took off as if being chased. Jeez.

Randy had made it at least a mile from the store by the time I passed him in my Mustang. I stopped, backed it up, and put the passenger window down.

"Would you like a ride?"

"I live in the Ghost Town."

"That's okay. I know where the Ghost Town is."

He got in as if it would be his last ride and set the bags on the floor.

"Nice car," he said after a while. "Do you ever open 'er up?" He grinned for the first time and it changed his face from hard to handsome.

"Oh, yeah, I love to speed."

"I do, too, but you wouldn't know it. I drive an old Chevy truck that barely makes it to sixty."

"Sometimes I go out to the flats on Highway 118 and fly back and forth. It helps me think, or not think if thinking too much is my problem."

"It's good for what ails you, in other words."

"Yes, and if nothing is ailing me, it's still great."

"I know what you mean."

"The Ghost Town is a long way from the store. Did you walk?"

"I was walking, but a woman stopped and gave me a ride."

Of course; who wouldn't?

"Have you lived here long?" he asked.

"Yep. I was born here."

"This seems like a great place to grow up."

"You can say that because you didn't grow up here."

"So, it wasn't great?"

"It was in some ways, but it was also boring at times. There was no radio station or movie theatre or skating rink—nothing like that. I got to go on the river a lot and through all the canyons, so I shouldn't complain. I know the backcountry well, and the national park."

He didn't say anything, so I thought I had said too much. "Where are you from?" I asked to give him a chance to speak.

"I'd rather not talk about it." He returned to his glum face.

I thought he was like a mountain lion: awesome to look at, but you wouldn't want one in your house.

When we reached the Ghost Town, Randy guided me in monosyllables to his home, which was one of the rock houses built by the miners when the cinnabar mine operated there. It looked broken-down. A broken, duct-taped window caught my attention in the front. Some of the rocks had fallen from the structure and lay in short piles along the sides. It looked like it had been abandoned since the days of the mine. Weeds and wildflowers stood together in the yard in lonely clumps.

"I'm working on it," he said when he saw me looking at it, as if daring me to suggest something different. Then he got out of my car and murmured, "Thank you." He didn't smile or even look at me.

"You're welcome, Randy. I hope you enjoy living here."

He gave me a hostile look, turned, and disappeared into his house.

"You don't need that kind of aggravation in your life," I told myself as I backed out of That Rude Runner's driveway and his life. I thought.

CHAPTER 7

When I returned home that morning, Veronica Frances was sitting on my porch with a file on her lap. Ms. Frances teaches math, and I had met her through my husband, Kevin. Our paths seldom crossed since he died. Maybe she avoided me because of the pain of that loss, but I thought it had more to do with our jobs keeping us busy. I can't imagine harder work than being a good teacher.

After we greeted each other and got past all the well-meaning questions that made us both feel sad, she said, "I guess you wonder why I'm here."

I sat down next to her. "That question crossed my mind."

"This is my planning period, so I don't have long. I want to talk to you about Cissy Florence. I heard you were trying to adopt her."

"You must have gotten that from Cissy."

"It's not true?"

"No; I'm only taking care of her for a few days. She thinks she wants me as her mother, but the reality of that would be—"

"Hard on you," she finished my sentence, but that wasn't what I was going to say.

I laughed. "True, but I don't think having me as a mother would be the carnival ride she envisions."

"Margarita, that child needs somebody to parent her, or at least love her and take care of her. I assume you know her parents."

"I know them well enough to understand what you're saying."

"They don't know where she is most of the time, and anything could happen to her when they leave for days on end. Also, she misses too much school."

"That's why I'm keeping her. Sheriff Duncan gave her parents a choice of Child Protective Services or me."

"If CPS ever gets hold of her, those so-called parents will never get her back."

"I know. What do you need from me, Veronica?"

"I want to tell you that Cissy has a mind for math. She said you made her do her homework, and I want to encourage you to continue doing that."

"Don't worry. If she's staying in my house, Cissy will bathe and do homework and go to school."

"I wish you could keep her all year."

I couldn't even imagine how that would go.

"Also," Veronica continued, "I think it'd be awesome if you adopted her."

"Why don't you adopt her?"

"Are you kidding? I deal with kids all day long."

"It'd be different if she was yours."

"Stop it, Margarita. I don't even have a husband."

"That was my argument too, but Cissy doesn't care about that."

She sighed. "Poor child, she has so little chance and yet so much potential. Cissy is one of my brightest students."

I agreed on Cissy's intelligence but had no clue what to do about it.

When the math teacher left, I changed into shorts, fixed a glass of iced tea, and sat on my porch with my bare feet propped on the railing and Missy at my side. As I studied Cimarron, I decided that being on vacation was great and, taking that a step farther, maybe I should quit altogether and stay on vacation. That happy thought lasted seconds before reality set in. I have bills. I need to work. I need a focus. I need to get a grip. I need... *Enough of this!*

I needed to run. Running doesn't pay bills, but it's positive and keeps me from gnawing my fingernails. It keeps me from drinking and going to bed with men I should leave alone. It keeps me, no matter how temporary it is, from beating up on myself for drinking and going to bed with men I should leave alone.

***

I have a friend named Billy Warren. For a short time, he'd lived in Lajitas, a golf resort on the nearby Rio Grande. He'd worked as a waiter in their restaurant. Through his job he met a hotel guest. They fell in love, and Billy moved away. When I returned home that morning, he was sitting on my porch with two suitcases.

"Billy!"

With typical Billy enthusiasm, he ran to me, hugged me tightly, then lifted me and spun me around. "Oh God, I missed you!"

"I missed you too, but you're making me dizzy."

He set me down and kissed me on the cheek. "You look great, Margarita."

"Thank you. I'm glad you think so."

"Do you know there's a dog in your house?"

I laughed. "That's Missy."

We walked over to the porch, and I said, "I'm going to let her out, so you'd better sit down. She's super-enthusiastic—like you."

He laughed and sat in one of the rocking chairs. I managed to grab Missy by the collar as she bolted out the door, so I saved Billy from her frenzied greeting and introduced them in a more toned-down way.

"Are you back or just visiting?" I asked after Missy got over the excitement of a newcomer.

"I'm back."

"What happened?"

"I was like a new toy. He got tired of playing with me and moved on to a new one." He sniffed with indignation. "I decided to come back to the place where I was the happiest I've ever been."

"Oh, Billy, I'm so sorry it didn't work out."

"I'm doing all right."

"You look wonderful. You two must have gotten along well for a while, no?"

"We did." There was a two-second pause and then, "Barney told me you're on vacation but that you might quit for good. Why would you do that?"

"I've let this job get to me, Billy. I think I need to do something else, something that doesn't entail dead bodies or shooting people or getting shot or being beaten up."

"I thought you loved your job."

"I do—did. I'm disheartened by the horrible things people do to each other, and I'm sick of cleaning up other people's messes. I can make my own messes, thank you."

"Yes; we all know you can."

"I'm taking time off so that I can figure out what's what."

"If you do, please let the rest of us know, because we're all floundering around with that question." Billy laughed and then said, "Barney commanded me to convince you to stay on as a deputy."

"He shouldn't have done that. I need to decide this for myself."

"I agree. Who is this Jupiter fellow your partner mentioned? You never told me about him in our talks."

"Barney shouldn't talk about him, either."

"He knows I love you, and he believes this character hurt you, but that you won't admit it. So, he expects me to find out the truth."

"Jupiter was a two-night stand."

"For real?"

"All right, maybe four."

"You say you don't like those kinds of relationships."

"I don't."

"You'd been drinking, hadn't you, when you got involved with him?" His statement wasn't accusatory or judgmental, but it was full of the tender understanding of a friend.

"Yes. I was drinking."

"Did you stop?"

"Yes."

"What's your plan now?"

"I have a month of vacation, so I'm going to have fun and do some things I want to do. Hey—do you want to go camping with me?"

"I'm too broke. Also, a job is waiting for me in Lajitas."

"Maybe we could go on your first days off—just a quick trip into the Chisos. I'll pay for everything, not that it'll cost much."

"I'd love that."

***

"About tis girl child," Billy said.

I'd had to explain about Cissy when we entered the house since her things were all over it. Billy and I were back on the porch, having made and eaten lunch.

"Her name is Cissy. What about her?"

"I don't guess you'd let me stay here a couple of nights until I get my old job back? They agreed to hire me, and they'll give me an apartment."

"Then I'll have two children underfoot."

"Well, Mommy Dearest, I know you can handle it."

"Her father is rabidly anti-anybody who isn't white, straight, and boring."

"I'm white."

"True, but you aren't straight or boring."

"Well you're Latina and not boring, either."

"I'm straight."

"Frankly, one out of three is not much to brag about."

"Look who's talking."

"Her father's not staying here, so what's the problem?"

"No problem. Of course, you can stay. Cissy can sleep with me, and you can have the couch."

"You have that backward, Babycakes," he said in a thick New Jersey accent. "Let the kid have the couch."

* * *

Cissy fell for Billy the minute she saw him. He was sitting on the porch with Missy in his lap when we pulled up after school.

"Oh my God," she gasped, "You didn't tell me he was so dreamy. Who cares if he's gay? I mean, that isn't set in stone, is it?"

"I believe it is, but the biggest problem with what you're thinking is that he's twenty-eight, and you're thirteen."

"He's just so *handsome*."

"Yes, he is."

Billy is tall and slender with white-blond hair cut in a spiky style, and he has sparkling blue eyes with dark lashes. The first time I saw him I fell for him, too. He has a personality that never quits and a sensitive heart, but Cissy didn't even know about that yet.

"A girl can dream," she said as she got out of my car.

No doubt.

Billy stood and introduced himself in a gentlemanly way, then bent down and hugged her. Cissy gave me a smug look over his shoulder.

* * *

The following day, Billy shocked me speechless by bringing That Rude Runner to my house. He (Rude Runner) was wearing a green Texas

Rangers cap—the baseball team, not the law enforcement team—which at first distracted from the fact that his hair was gone. Also, he wore jeans and a green shirt that had been ironed. Ironed, no less. He looked nice, and different somehow, and I thought it must be Billy's influence.

After the most awkward introduction of all time, Billy went into the house to get three glasses of iced tea.

I invited Rude Runner to sit and he did.

"You must think I'm an asshole," he said.

"Well..."

"I'm sorry. I don't relate to people well."

"Then what are you doing with Billy?"

He got redder than a Big Bend sunset and began to stammer.

I held up my hand. "I'm sorry. Please let me rephrase that."

"I just met him. What I'm doing is getting to know him. He wanted me to meet his best friend, and here we are."

"Yes. Here we are."

"I guess this was a bad idea."

Billy returned using a cookie sheet as an impromptu tray. He brought three glasses of tea and his happy attitude. "You lack supplies," he said when he saw me staring at the "tray."

"Really?"

"You're hopeless." He looked at Randy. "She's hopeless."

Billy's presence changed our snipe fest into more pleasant conversation, and I discovered that Randy was not as rude as he appeared on the surface. He was from Carterton, a small town in Texas "not nearly as beautiful as here. In fact, it's nothing like here." He worked as an auto mechanic but stayed evasive about why he left his hometown and his job.

"Will you open a business here?" I asked.

"I don't have the money to set myself up, but I planned to talk to that mechanic shop and try to get hired there."

"I bet you will. They need a good mechanic."

"What do you do for a living?"

Randy looked at me, so I said, "I'm a deputy sheriff."

His mouth opened in surprise. I hate when men do that.

"What is so shocking?"

"Well, nothing. In truth, I heard about you already.'"

"Oh?"

"A bunch of gossipy guys at the café were yammering about you. I overheard them while I ate breakfast."

"How did you know they were talking about me?"

"Um, they described you."

"I see. What did they say?"

"It was man talk. It'd just make you angry."

"Don't make her angry," Billy said.

Randy smiled at him and continued, "Your friend from the arroyo was there. What is his problem? It's not any of my business, but you should keep away from him. I think he could be dangerous."

"If he touches me again, I'll get a restraining order."

"Don't give him a chance to touch you. Stay away from him. I'm not a violent man, but I'd like to give him a merciless ass-whooping."

"Yeah, me too, and I'm not a violent man, either."

Billy laughed, and Randy almost did.

For a while, we stayed quiet. The red-tailed hawk I'd been watching earlier took a plunge but came up empty-handed. She screeched in outrage and returned to the sky.

"I never would've guessed you were in law enforcement," Randy said. "I figured you for a teacher or a park ranger, something along those lines."

"Do you have something against deputies?"

"Yes, plenty, but that has nothing to do with you." He glanced over at me. "I'm sure you're a good one."

"Yeah, well..."

"Are you a hard-ass?"

"About?"

"In general, I mean."

"No, I'm not unless I'm forced to be. Anyhow, I'm on vacation, so I'm taking a break from that for a while."

After a short silence, I blurted, "What happened to your hair?"

"I shaved it off."

"But why?"

"It reminded me of things I don't want to think about."

"But it was so beautiful."

"It'll grow back," he said as if it were no big deal.

But it'll take so long!

Billy gave me a look I couldn't read, so I shut up about Randy's hair.

* * *

"It's time to get Cissy from school," I said.

I left Billy to explain about her.

On the way home, I explained to Cissy that a friend of Billy's was at my house.

"Ooh-la-la," was her single comment.

Then she met him and stared with her mouth open. Cissy followed me into the house. "You didn't say he was so *gorgeous*. You sure do know a lot of hunks. I thought you said you didn't have a boyfriend."

"I barely know him, Cissy, so calm down. He's not a boyfriend."

"Well, he should be. I hope you're not going to let him go to waste."

* * *

"You have a great view here," Randy said.

"Yes, and this is a pretty time of day. This country really shines in the early mornings and late afternoons. Every time I sit here, things look different, depending on the location of the sun."

"Yeah, I've noticed how the sun has its way with everything," he said. "The scenery changes from moment to moment."

"Now you see it, now you don't," Billy added.

"Is it just me or do mountains pop up and disappear?"

"It's a trick of the sun's position, the distances, and the clouds," I said.

"Terlingua is a beautiful place," Randy said. "I want to stay."

"I hope you can," I said.

Billy didn't need to say anything; his expression told what he thought.

* * *

Randy stayed for dinner, during which someone brought up the subject of salsa, both the music and the dancing. Randy and I discovered that we both love to dance. After eating, we moved the furniture out of the living room and demonstrated the tango, the mambo, the cha-cha, and the samba. Billy and Cissy were entranced, but that was probably about Randy. He was a confident, smooth dancer, and dancing with him was fun.

Missy thought it was the most entertaining thing she'd ever seen humans do, but she soon got over it and passed out in a corner.

When we began teaching our protégés to dance, they became frustrated and swore they'd never catch on. We took turns partnering with them until they began to understand the relationship between the beat of the music and the movements. It's not as baffling once you get that.

First, I danced with Billy and Randy with Cissy. When we switched, I thought Billy was going to pass out. He paid close attention as Randy counted the steps out loud for him and gave him pointers.

I had fun with Cissy, even though she was uncoordinated and had trouble with the order of the steps. When Randy and I would demonstrate, she laughed and said it was "old people dancing." He pointed out to her that none of us were old, except compared to her. She gave it an honest try and especially liked the cha-cha and dancing with Randy. Both of my friends dropped me enthusiastically every time he said we should switch partners. I tried not to take it personally.

Cissy got angry when I said it was time for her to go to bed but got over it when Randy promised to come back soon for more lessons.

"Dancing takes practice," he said. "One lesson is never enough."

"You can come back every night," Cissy suggested brightly, and gave him a big hug, which he returned.

"Cha-cha-cha, Cissy," he said and sent her into gales of laughter.

I tucked her into my bed and promised I'd read double tomorrow if she let me off the hook tonight.

"Ooh-la-la," she whispered and then winked.

***

After Billy took Randy home, we sat on the porch.

"Are you okay, Billy?" He seemed too quiet.

"Beautiful stars tonight."

"Yes, just like last night and the night before that."

"It was just an observation. No reason to mock me."

"What's with you? You're not acting like yourself."

"It made my heart pound to dance with him."

"I know what you mean."

He became too-quiet again.

"Spill it, Billy Bob."

"Randy is gay."

I laughed. "I'm slow, but I figured that out when you walked onto the porch with him."

"I can tell you like him, and I don't want you to hate me. And we promised never to fight over men."

"Damn it, Billy."

"I didn't make him gay."

"I know that. I ran into him everywhere I went, and I just thought... Never mind. You obviously bring out the best in him."

"He acts like a tough guy, but he's not really."

"Why do I fall for gay men? I must have a programming error in my brain."

"There's nothing wrong with you. You're attracted to good-looking men your age, and the law of averages says some of them will be gay."

I felt around on my head. "Maybe I have a chip missing."

"Jupiter Pierson wasn't gay."

"Oh, shut up, Billy. Jupiter means I have a different kind of chip missing."

He laughed. "You're not missing any chips."

"Don't be too sure."

Billy got serious. "Please don't let this come between us. If it's going to, I won't go out with him."

"And let a man like that go to waste?"

He chewed on his bottom lip. "Well, that would be criminal."

"Have fun with him, Billy. I'm angry, but not at you. A state trooper has made me into the latest joke among Brewster County lawmen. Also, I don't know if I want to keep my job. I'm confused about a lot of things, but what I do know is that I want to drink. I'm a mess in general. What man would want any part of that?"

"Well, nearly every man in Brewster County, I hear."

CHAPTER 8

When I returned from taking Cissy to school, Billy had left a note. "Sweetness, I'm off to spend the day with Randy. Love you, Billy."

Then Cissy's parents beat on my door.

"We're here to get Cissy's things," said her mother. "We'll pick her up from school today."

"I'd like to tell her good-bye. Could I pick her up and bring her to your house?"

They looked at each other. "No," they said in unison.

"Did she behave?" her sad excuse for a father asked.

"She's a great kid. She gave me no trouble."

"Would you keep her the next time we have to go away?" asked the mother.

"Okay, sure."

"We'll call you," Rod Florence said.

"Wait, please. I have a novel for Cissy. Tell her she should finish it and the next time I see her, we'll talk about it." I got *To Kill a Mockingbird* and handed it to him.

He took the book from me and looked at it as if it were a piece of unidentifiable jetsam from an alien spaceship. Then he picked up his daughter's things, took his wife by the arm, and they walked off my porch towards their car.

"You're welcome," I called after them. "I'm glad to help."

They stared at me blankly and got in the car.

***

After I cleaned my house and read a while, I went by the office to see how Barney was doing. I didn't have to ask when I walked in on him and Buster having a disagreement.

"You can't make me do everything you don't want to do just because you have seniority," Buster said.

"You want to bet on that?"

"I hope you two aren't fighting," I chirped.

"No way," snapped Buster, and he slammed out the door.

Barney's answer was to glare at me.

"Hey—it isn't my fault if you and Buster fight like little boys."

"I don't like Buster, and he can't stand me, so don't worry about a thing, Batgirl. All is well in the Terlingua office of the Brewster County sheriff."

"That's ridiculous, Barney. You two have no reason to dislike each other. You're too demanding and impatient with him."

"I don't think I need any advice about getting along with others from you, Ricos."

I threw up my hands. "Fine."

"Did you plan your vacation yet?"

"Not yet. Why?"

"Why don't you take Buster with you?"

"Take him to...?"

"Just take him away."

"You can train him right, Barney, if you just have a tiny bit of patience. Look how great I turned out."

"Yeah, look how great. Why are you here?"

"I came to see you because you're my friend."

"You want to aggravate me to death?"

"Well, not to death. What's going on?"

"Nothing you can do anything about. The ex-con moved here, as the sheriff said he would. I'm the only one who knows, but tomorrow all hell will break loose. I need to notify the school and other places where children hang out. I could sure use your help."

"Did you meet him?"

"He had to come in to register, so yeah, I met him this morning."

"Is he nasty looking?"

"No. He seems normal. I think you would say he's good-looking."

"That's not fair. Handsome bad men should have to wear a warning sign."

"You know damn well his life will be hard enough without a sign."

"I suppose."

"I put a copy of his file and a picture of him on your desk, so you'd know not to fall for him."

"That's not funny, Barney."

"I'm only messing with you. You know I'm on your side, even if it's wrong."

"Buster hasn't taken over my office?"

"No way. That office is yours."

"Thank you, Barney. I'm touched."

"Don't let it go to your head."

I went in my office to peruse my hill and to have a look at a for-real child rapist. On one hand, I didn't want to see him. On the other, I had Cissy and a lot of other kids to worry about.

I stood at the window a while and admired the work of perfection that is Cactus Hill. All was as it should be, so I took a seat at my desk.

My eyes landed on a file with a tab that read "Randall M. Green." When I opened it, a mug shot of Randy looked back at me. My gut response was that Barney was playing a not-funny joke. But how would he fake a mug shot? And he had no way to know I even knew Randall Green.

I thumbed through the file, barely seeing anything. The mention of an Ellen Miller caught my attention. She had sent Randy love letters and money. That made me wonder if he was gay or only said he was. But why? Who says they're gay if they're not?

Included in the file was a photo taken that morning by Barney, in which Randy wore the same green shirt he'd worn last night at my house. A child rapist had been in my house. With 13-year-old Cissy. He'd danced with her and hugged her more than once.

Oh, God.

And he was putting moves on Billy. Billy's heart would be broken. Would he hurt Billy? If he had raped a girl, he probably wasn't gay after all. Besides that, most pedophiles are heterosexual. Why would a pedophile have any interest in Billy? Did he think he could use him to get to Cissy? But he hadn't known about Cissy until he came to my house! Did he plan to abuse Billy in a freaky way? My mind twisted itself into a pretzel.

Ellen Miller meant that Billy was wrong about Randy being gay. He wasn't gay, and Billy was in grave danger.

I didn't know what to do first. After a few minutes of gut-wrenching indecision, I hurried out of my office and into the front where Barney sat. A phone call occupied him, so I waved good-bye and slammed through the door into the parking lot and threw up.

CHAPTER 9

After I established that Billy was still not at my house, I changed into a long-sleeved shirt and denim vest. I got my personal Beretta out of the glove compartment of the Mustang and checked it. It had been cleaned recently, and I determined that it was loaded and ready to fire if necessary. I stuck it into the waistband of my jeans where it would be hidden by the vest. After that, I drove to Randy's house like an avenger.

On the way, my head filled with tiny voices, all with different opinions. One said maybe Randy was innocent, falsely accused and wrongly convicted. Another accused me of being my typical naïve self, living in a dream world where everybody is good and just needs a break.

Sheriff Ben's voice sounded a lot less tiny than the others. "Our prisons are full of guilty men who claim to be innocent." It also said, "don't be fooled by a man's looks. The best-looking Prince Charming can be the worst of the bad guys."

Why were *my* Prince Charmings always turning into frogs? Another voice, that of the sane woman who tries her best to live in my head, whispered that I should wait and see, and not shoot anybody just because I'd had such a shock.

Randy's house appeared unoccupied and his truck was gone. The place was locked by a flimsy lock. I broke in and looked around without seeing anything. I'd broken the law, but I soothed my guilty conscience with the thought that I was on vacation. Oh, sure. That didn't wash, but I still looked everywhere Randy could have stashed Billy. There were few places and all of them empty. I called his name, with the only answer coming from my wounded conscience.

I stared at the bed a long time. It consisted of a mattress on the floor, but it was neatly made, and I didn't have the heart to unmake it and really check it out—and besides, how would that tell me if Billy had been there? Without forensic equipment, I couldn't tell one hair or semen sample from another and "anyway," the one sane voice pointed out, "you don't want to look at semen samples, for crying out loud."

I checked the flagstone around the bed for anything, but the room was neat with nothing on the floor but the mattress. The medicine cabinet in the bathroom held a few packages of condoms, but I couldn't fault him for that. I was desperate to see something perverted or grossly out of place but there was nothing, to my great relief and equally great disappointment.

I left Randy's house, relocked the door, and I sat in my car. I'd found nothing. Even ex-cons have rights, and I had disrespected his. He had paid his debt to society according to our legal system. Personally, I don't think the rape of a child can ever be repaid, but the man had served his time and had played by the rules dictated to him by the court.

If the sheriff got wind of this, I would be dismissed, no doubt. I needed Barney's level head and steadying presence, but I couldn't tell him I'd brought the child molester into my life when so recently I had brought in another wrong man, a man who turned out to be a drug lord. There had to be more missing from my brain than just a few chips.

"Get a grip," insisted the sane voice that hangs on against all odds.

I took a few deep breaths and switched the gun to the other side of my pants, but it was uncomfortable wherever I put it. I went over every time I had seen Randy, every bit of conversation I'd ever had with him.

He had come into my house!

I decided to confide in my friend Craig. He lives in a home that's under construction on a 1,000-acre mesa I was gifted in a cold case I solved a while back. Going to Craig's meant I had to exchange the Mustang for my ATV, since the road that climbs the bluff is impassable by anything else. I had the patience and presence of mind to make that exchange, so just the thought of my wise friend had calmed me.

***

Craig heard me coming and stood outside his house holding his cat, Marine. Sawdust covered them. The kitty had grown from a starving stray Craig rescued into a soft, gray and white, long-haired cat. When I saw them, my heart filled with love and my eyes with tears.

Craig Summers is 60-something in age, an ex-marine who was once a prisoner of war in Viet Nam. He's reclusive and shy but not crazy, which is how he's seen by much of my community. I know him as level-headed, brave, and loving.

Craig is intelligent and was trained in combat and covert missions. He hasn't lost his toughness or his skills. He's been my friend since I was a kid. I needed his calm assessment of my situation about as much as I'd ever needed anything.

After I hugged him, and we established that we were all right, and I even held and loved on Marine, we sat on his porch. It faced Big Bend National Park and mountain after mountain as far as the eye could see. Craig's house wasn't finished, but his porch was. He's a lover of the outdoors, so it was likely that only one or two rooms of his home would ever have a roof. At that point only his bedroom had one, and he liked it like that.

It's hard to stay upset about anything when I'm on my mesa. I needed a house there but hadn't gotten around to building one. The 360-degree panorama will take your breath. On that early fall day, yellow and white wildflowers carpeted my land. A few red blooms popped up here and there, standing above the carpet to show off.

"Tell me what's bothering you," my astute friend said.

"What makes you think something is bothering me?"

"You're carrying a firearm in your pants, and the sadness on you is so heavy it's making me want to cry." He shifted Marine around on his lap. "And you're here at an odd time of day."

I spilled everything, beginning with Jupiter's betrayal and moving on to the fact that I'd asked for leave and didn't know if I wanted to stay in law enforcement. I didn't try to make myself sound sane or in control of anything because I knew he was not just listening with his ears, but was listening with his heart as well. I even admitted that I'd slept with Jupiter and why and that I'd been drinking at the time.

Craig knew all the reasons why taking a drink was bad for me, but he didn't chastise me or even comment until I stopped talking. One reason I could tell Craig anything was that he never judged or tried to give advice unless I asked for it. He allowed me to have faults and human failings. Craig took everything in stride. He'd never even had a child, and he made the best grandpa in the world.

Craig saw the tears coming before I knew I was going to cry. He set Marine down and motioned to me. I laid my head against his strong chest and cried until I had no more tears. After a while, I sat up and dried my eyes on the hem of my shirt.

"As for the way that man acted, shame on him, but this isn't about him," Craig said.

While still after-sobbing, I gave him the news about Randy from beginning to end, including the fact that my friend Billy was with him, and that I had danced with the man and enabled him to be around a young girl who was in my care.

Craig thought about it and then said, "Anybody could've made the mistakes you did, but I think the important thing is to find Billy. Something is off about this. I need to think on it but meanwhile, let's get moving."

"Oh, Craig, you don't have to come with me."

"I know you didn't come to me just for a good cry."

I felt real pity for the people who thought Craig was crazy and, based on that, refused to know him.

***

On the way down from the mesa, I stopped the ATV and admitted to Craig that I had broken into Randy's home and found nothing incriminating. He gave me a stern look, but we both knew it was the kind of thing he would do. Except he hadn't had "the law" instilled in him the way I had. I had taken a serious oath.

It made me feel better when he said, "At least we got that out of the way." In fact, it made me laugh.

We went to my house to exchange the ATV for the Mustang. Billy was not there, nor did he answer his phone; nor was there anyone at Randy's.

We were sitting in Randy's driveway when Craig said, "A grown man shouldn't be in danger with a man who goes after little girls."

"I think that too, so what are we missing?"

"Billy is sure the man is gay?"

"Yes. Gay guys have a secret code, I guess. If he's not gay, then what would be his interest in Billy?"

"That's where I'm getting stumped. If he is gay, then how likely is it that he raped a girl?"

"Not very," I said.

"If he's not gay, why Billy? Billy has no children or access to children. He has no interest in children. He's a waiter, not a teacher."

"True," I agreed. "The only way Billy makes sense is if Randy is gay, in which case he might be innocent of the crime he did time for. Imagine going to prison for a hideous crime you didn't commit."

"Since you're in law enforcement, I'm sure you know that happens. What does your gut tell you?"

"You mean the gut I can no longer trust?"

"Yes. What does it say?

"It says Randy couldn't have done such a terrible thing."

"Well," said Craig, "I have faith in that gut even if you don't. But the bottom line here is that we need to find Billy. I know you won't rest until we do."

"Where do you suggest we look?"

"I suppose they could be just about anywhere. Pick a place and let's get on it. We're wasting daylight."

We drove through the Ghost Town in its entirety and over to Lajitas, then every other place in the Terlingua area. I showed Randy's picture to everyone, and Billy's to the people who didn't know him, but no one had seen either of them.

It was after both dark and dinnertime, so we went to my house for something quick to eat, and there sat Billy on the porch alone.

As I walked towards him he said, "Randy's the most incredible man I've ever known."

"This one is yours," Craig said under his breath.

Craig and Billy greeted each other. Craig was reserved, Billy enthusiastic. Craig went to make sandwiches, and I sat down next to Billy.

"Are you okay?" I asked, trying to keep my voice calm.

"I've never been better in my life." His blue eyes shone in the muted light coming through the window.

"Where were you, Billy?"

"We had breakfast in the Ghost Town. Then we went into the national park, and I showed him the places you've shown me. We hiked and ate a late lunch at the lodge in the Basin. Then he brought me back. I'm on the work schedule for early tomorrow, or I'd be with him now. We spent a long time kissing at a picnic table in a campground and, well, have I answered your question?"

"Yes, Billy."

"Something is wrong."

"Yes, there is."

Billy's hand went to his heart. "Are you going to tell me what it is?"

"Randy is an ex-con."

"I know that."

"Did he tell you why he was sent to prison?"

"No, we never got to that. And you know what? I don't care, because I see who he is."

"Billy, he served seven years of a ten-year sentence. He was convicted of raping a nine-year-old girl."

The hurt look on Billy's face made me regret telling him, but somebody had to. He would know anyway the minute the news hit the "streets" of Terlingua, and the gossip would be worse than the truth.

"He couldn't have done that," Billy said.

"You don't know that, Billy."

"But I do know it!" He took a deep breath that was more of a sob. "He's gay, Margarita. He's known he was since he was five. Gay men don't rape people."

"I know the statistics show that in general, but there are people of all persuasions who are twisted."

"Randy isn't one of them! I can't believe you'd say that about him. You met him first. For heaven's sake, you were interested in him before I was!"

There was no arguing with that.

"I hate you for saying these things," Billy said.

"I hope you don't hate me. I'm only telling you because I love you."

I'd had a hard lesson about loving the wrong man, and I didn't want Billy to have the same one.

Billy sniffed. "Well, I don't hate you, of course. I hate what you're saying." He reached over and took my hand. "You could prove he didn't do it."

"How would I do that?"

"You're the detective in this family. You got that mesa gifted to you because you're so good at what you do."

"Wait a minute, Billy. This is a totally different thing."

"No, it's not. It's just a different case, but it's still a mystery to be solved."

"I'm on vacation."

"Did you leave your brain with the sheriff?"

I shrugged. "No, but I misplaced it." Then I said, "I'm going to see Randy and hear what he says."

Billy jumped up. "I'm going with you."

"No, you're not."

"I don't see how you're going to stop me."

Billy is taller than I am and weighs more. He can be intimidating, even though I know how kindhearted he is.

"I want you to listen to reason," I said. "I need to talk to Randy without you there. He needs to speak freely, and I don't know if he'll do that in your presence. In you, he's obviously found someone he likes, and he might not be as truthful in front of you. If you want me to help him, then I need to know the unvarnished truth about a few things."

"Well..."

"It's human nature to want someone we're interested in to think we're perfect, even though none of us are. Please understand what I'm saying. If you go and he won't tell the truth because of your presence, then how will I get it?"

"I hate it when you talk like a professional."

"It's a good thing I don't do it often."

He sat down. "Don't be gone long. I'll be dying here."

"I know that, and it won't take long."

"Were you looking for me today?"

"Yes. I was afraid something was going to happen to you. When I got the news about Randy, I was terrified for you."

"Something did happen to me. Randy swept me off my feet. I'm in a lot of trouble, Deputy Means-Well, and I don't think you can save me."

Oh man, I had been there before.

"I know, Billy. Maybe everything will be okay. I just have to talk to him."

Craig came onto the porch. "I made sandwiches, but I covered them with plastic wrap because I don't think any of us can eat right now."

"You've got that right, General," Billy agreed with a salute.

"I'm not a general," Craig said, dead serious, and then he returned the salute. "I was a—"

"Let's go, Craig. He was just messing with you."

"Oh, I forgot how you two like to do that."

Billy jumped up again, incredulous. "*He's* going with you? Why?"

"He's moral support, since I can't take you."

"That's bullshit! If you two kick Randy's ass, I'll—"

Craig frowned at him. "Sit down, young man. I don't look for trouble, but if someone brings it to me or to someone I love, I'll do what I must. I'm going along to protect Margarita because she's like my own blood kin. If there's no trouble, I won't even open my mouth. I'm old and I don't look for reasons to fight. That's a promise you can take to the bank." He saluted Billy again and went to my car.

"Okay then," Billy said, "ten points to the old guy."

"We'll be right back."

"If you're gone too long, I'm coming there."

"Give me an hour."

Billy looked at his watch. "Not one second more."

CHAPTER 10

When we got to Randy's, Craig had to pep-talk me or I wouldn't have left the vehicle. I did it for Billy.

Randy came to the door and smiled when he saw me. Then he looked stricken. "You already know."

"May we come in?"

"Why is he with you?"

I introduced the two men.

"You didn't say why he's here," Randy said.

I started to speak, but Craig said, "I'm here because Margarita is here. I mean you no harm."

"Oh, I get it. You're here to protect her." Randy looked unbearably sad. "Do you really think I'd hurt you, Margarita?"

"I insisted," Craig said. "I didn't give her a choice."

"Please let me speak with you, Randy."

"Okay but stay out there. I don't trust anybody anymore."

Randy wore the same green ball cap on his head but was dressed in a t-shirt and cut-offs. His casual sex appeal made me remember Billy's stake in this, and I felt like throwing up.

"I'm sorry I have to be here at all," I said.

"I'm innocent of what they said I did."

"Will you tell me what happened?"

"They accused me of raping my nine-year-old neighbor. I would never have hurt her. She was like a younger sister to me. Somebody was abusing her, but it wasn't me. I tried to protect her, and for that I was charged with the crime and put in prison."

"What about your trial?"

"It was a joke."

"In what way?"

"I had a public defender who was terrible. I think he was part of it."

"Part of what?"

"The conspiracy that put me away."

I nearly groaned at the mention of a conspiracy. I glanced over at Craig, but he had an unreadable expression on his face.

"May I look at the transcript of your trial?"

"You could if I had it, but no one gave me a transcript."

"It may have gone to the prison, and they would've put it with your things. It would most likely be thick."

"Yes, so I would know if I had it."

I sat down on the rocky ground in front of the door and indicated to Craig he should do the same. Randy stood on the other side of the screen, looking like a man about to be crucified. He took the cap off and twisted it one way and then another. He folded it, unfolded it, then stuffed it in his pocket, took it out again and crushed it into a ball, then crammed it back into the pocket of his shorts.

"Did you tell Billy?"

"Yes. He wants to believe you're innocent."

"Goddamn it, I am innocent!"

"Then keep talking."

"Carterton is a backward little town. It's the kind of place where you could still be lynched if you're the wrong color or for any other reason that's acceptable to those rednecks. They don't like homosexuals, blacks, or Mexicans, in that order. Intolerance is a way of life there.

"I was friends with a neighbor named Sarah who lived with her father. He left her alone a lot. I was a loner and ignored by my father, too. When Dad was home, he'd watch TV and drink himself into a stupor. He could be abusive, but most often he'd just pass out in his recliner." Randy swallowed hard. "My mother died a long time ago."

He cleared his throat and continued. "I'd see this child watching from her porch across the street. When I'd wave at her, she'd wave back. I was always in the yard working on vehicles or taking care of the lawn or just hanging out. I don't like being inside."

I glanced at Craig and, though his face told me nothing, I thought Randy had just scored a few points with him.

"I worked at a garage," Randy continued, "but I did work on the side for people who couldn't pay garage prices. I also worked non-stop on my truck. I had the best-running truck in the state of Texas." He laughed a bitter laugh. "Every day Sarah moved closer to my house until one day she crossed the street and came up to me. I was raking leaves, and she offered to help. I invited her to sit down and talk. She was only nine, but she was funny and sincere, and I loved hearing her unique young take on things."

He took a deep breath and continued. "Sarah and I became close friends, and I thought of her as a sister. I looked forward to seeing her. When her father was home she didn't come over. Also, I was in love by then and spent less and less time at home. It got so I only saw her once or twice a week."

"Keep talking," I said when he faltered.

"Sarah became withdrawn and moody. I asked her what was wrong, but at first, she wouldn't tell me. Finally, it came out in a big jumble. A man came to her house at night. He went to her room and talked filthy and touched her and rubbed himself against her. She didn't understand what was going on, but it made her afraid. I knew exactly what was happening. I offered to talk to her father, and I did speak with him. He bullied me and called me names and accused me of putting sick ideas into her head. He threatened to call the sheriff, and I backed off."

"What happened then?"

"I began watching the house, looking for some sign of the pervert. If I could figure out who he was, I would put a stop to it. The first thing I noticed was that he never came in his own car. Sarah's father brought him to the house. He had to be aware of what that man did to his daughter, and that realization made me sick.

"I got the idea to wait for the man to leave Sarah's. I'd get his name if I had to beat it out of him. One thing I'd seen while spying was that he was small. I was larger and strong."

"What happened?"

"I waited for him to come out, and I jumped him. He wouldn't say anything or give me his name. It was dark, so I couldn't see his face. I was whaling on him when Sarah's father came out with a rifle and told me he'd called the sheriff. He said I'd be taken to jail if I didn't go home. He also threatened to shoot me and pointed out that in Texas it's legal to shoot an intruder."

"What happened next?"

"I went home and watched from my window. Sarah's abuser ran off on foot, and the sheriff came. He disappeared into Sarah's house and was in there a long time. Then he came over to my house and arrested me for raping Sarah. He said he'd interviewed her and she had identified me."

Randy stared at his hands. Neither of us spoke. I glanced over at Craig. He looked at me also, but his face was still unreadable.

"The sheriff took me to jail," Randy said, "and I haven't been free since, until my release a few weeks ago."

"Why would someone frame you?"

"They framed me because they could. I'd been seen with Sarah, and her father testified he'd caught me in their house. I'd never been inside their house. The man abusing her was wealthy and powerful; that was my impression. I went to prison in his place."

"What about the DNA evidence?"

"It was never brought out in the trial."

"How can that be? That's the most effective way to prove guilt or innocence."

"Yes, I know. What I mean is that they claimed my DNA matched the semen found on Sarah, but they didn't ever prove it in court."

"Were you examined? What DNA evidence was taken from you?"

"A cheek swab and fingerprints were taken, and a few of my hairs. I wasn't given any kind of exam. In fact, nothing was taken until late the following day. It was like an afterthought."

"And the rape kit exam on Sarah? What did that show?"

"It had to show I didn't rape her, but they said it showed I had. I didn't rape her, so my semen was not on her. Do you understand? I loved her, and I would never have hurt her." His voice broke and he quit talking.

I took a deep breath. "But at the trial, didn't they call in experts to testify? It seems as though the longest part of the trial would have been about the DNA evidence."

"No experts testified. The D.A. claimed my fingerprints were in her bedroom and my semen was on her. End of story."

I gaped at him. "No way. There couldn't have been a trial without the testimony of at least one expert and certainly not a conviction without DNA evidence or some other compelling evidence that proved you were guilty. Surely the jury would have questioned it."

"There was no jury, Margarita. I had a bench trial. My attorney said it would go better for me to put the facts before the judge only. By the time I saw what was happening, it was too late to change it." Randy looked down at me from where he stood and spoke slowly and distinctly, as though speaking to someone not proficient at English. "I am telling you that I was not given a fair trial. It was decided by powerful people that I was going to go to prison, and I went."

"Tell me about your attorney."

"He was court-appointed. I doubt if he's a stupid man, but he acted stupid at my trial."

"I don't know what to tell you. You're registered here now, and your presence will be public knowledge. Everyone is going to know. Life will be hell for Billy if you continue to see him."

"I'm trying to tell you that I never raped anyone. My attorney didn't even try to prove my innocence."

"I can't do anything about that."

"I didn't rape her!" he snapped. "I could never do something like that to anyone."

I had no idea what to say.

"You say you like detective work and helping people. Can't you find out what happened to my transcript? If you could get it, you'd see that I'm telling you the truth about the trial."

"Where were you tried?"

"It was at the Freeman County Courthouse in Simpson, Texas. That's the county seat."

"I'll call them in the morning."

His face brightened. "You believe me?"

"I don't know what to believe, but I'm willing to look at your transcript."

"Please believe me. If you could only have enough faith in me to help. You don't know what it's like to go to a new town and be forced to register as a sex offender. Nobody wants me, so I'm still being punished, and I never did anything wrong. I'll never have a life. I just can't keep moving from place to place forever."

"For now," I said, "I'm giving you the benefit of the doubt."

"Oh, Margarita." He stepped outside and hugged me.

When he did, he felt the firearm stuck into my pants and stepped back. "You brought a weapon? Were you going to kill me?"

"Of course not, but I didn't know what to expect."

"But you've been alone with me."

"Yes, I know."

"Oh." He looked sad and hurt. "You didn't know about my conviction then."

"I'm sorry, Randy. I didn't know what to expect."

"Do you think Billy would see me again?"

"He'd be here now, but I asked him not to come."

His face twisted with the effort of holding back tears. "I see."

"You'd better not be lying to me, Randy. You could hurt me and get away with it, except for Craig here, but if you hurt Billy—"

"I'm not a liar," he spit, "or a rapist. I would never hurt Billy."

Randy took out the crumpled cap, studied it, and then twisted it some more. "I'm afraid this'll never be over," he whispered, "no matter what you turn up. Someone won't like it that you're investigating, and he's powerful. I'm terrified of going back to prison. I'd rather die than go back."

***

Craig insisted he could walk home from the bottom of the mesa, so I agreed to leave him there. He'd been silent and stone-faced, and I had no idea what he thought.

"That man needs your help if anybody ever did," he said. "I hope you're going to help him."

"You believed his story?"

"Are you going to tell me you didn't?"

"I don't know what to think."

"You said you were going to give him the benefit of the doubt."

"I will, but even if he's innocent, what can I do about it?"

Craig's expression was incredulous. "What can you do about it? You can investigate it! It's not like you don't have time."

"I have plenty of time, Craig, but no resources."

He reached over and tapped me gently on the head. "This is the only resource you need, Margarita. I have the good fortune to live on a mesa that you only have because of this resource." He frowned when I started to speak. "Don't you dare open your mouth to argue with me!"

"Wouldn't think of it," I mumbled.

"If you need money, well, you know I have some."

"Thank you, Craig, but money isn't the problem."

"If you need my help, you know where to find me."

"Yes, sir."

"Don't hesitate to ask."

"I won't."

"Good night, then." He touched my cheek with the tips of his fingers.

"Buenas noches, Craig."

As I watched my friend head up the hill, my cell phone rang.

"I don't want to live here anymore," Cissy said in a sob. "I want to live with you."

"I'm sorry I didn't get to say good-bye. Why are you crying? Are you okay?"

"No. I'm not okay. My parents are outside fighting. If they come back in, I'll have to hang up. I hate them!"

"Parents can be difficult."

"Normal parents are difficult; my parents are assholes."

I agreed, but no way would I say that. "Keep in mind that you have special gifts, and you're going to escape Terlingua by getting a good education."

She laughed. "You never give up, do you?"

"Well, I'm a stubborn woman."

"I had a great time with you, Margarita, and my teachers are amazed."

"Why are your teachers amazed?"

"Duh. It's because I'm doing my homework."

CHAPTER 11

The next morning, Billy went to claim his old job in Lajitas, along with an apartment, so I went to speak with Randy. He came to the door wearing nothing but sleep lines and cut-offs.

He smiled sleepily. "Hey, Margarita."

I smiled, but nothing came out of my mouth.

"Did you call the court?" he prompted.

"No one's there yet."

"And you're here for—?"

"Uh..."

"You better come in." He held the door open.

"I thought we could look for your transcript to be sure you don't have it. Maybe it's not as big as I think."

He shrugged. "Just let me put on a shirt."

While he made coffee, I went through his few possessions. Even though I'd already been in his house, it hadn't hit me how little he owned. He had one beat-up suitcase and a box of clothes, two rusted folding chairs left by previous occupants, a small camp stove, a few pans, plates, and utensils, and that was it.

Even though it was a long-abandoned rock structure, Randy had gotten his home sparkling clean. It even smelled nice. In various locations around the room, thick bunches of brilliantly-colored wildflowers stuck up out of old bottles. It was difficult to picture a man who'd harm a child gathering wildflowers.

I didn't find a transcript, but I did find a copy of a sworn statement by the alleged victim, Sarah Jones. I read it twice, thinking, "No way."

"I hope you don't think a young girl dictated that," Randy said. He stood by a window too scratched and full of duct tape to let much light into the room.

"I don't, and it should've been obvious to anyone reading it."

"Sarah would never have accused me of anything except kindness towards her."

I sat on one of the rusted folding chairs. "Randy, explain again about the DNA. You're positive an expert from the crime lab didn't testify?

Were you ever absent? Could you have missed it somehow?"

"I was there every day and couldn't have missed it. I was waiting for it because I hadn't raped Sarah. At the trial, only the D.A. spoke about the DNA evidence, and he claimed it was a match."

"What did your attorney say?"

"He said he wasn't going to fight it because it would make things worse for me. How could it have? Whatever semen was found on Sarah couldn't have been mine!"

I called information for the Freeman County Courthouse, dialed the number, and asked to speak with the Clerk of Court. When she came to the phone, I identified myself as Deputy Ricos from Brewster County. She had never heard of my county, and I had to spell it for her, but I pressed on. I told her I wanted to obtain a copy of a trial transcript and gave her the case number stamped on Sarah's statement, the date, and the defendant's name.

She hesitated so long I asked, "Is there a problem? The transcript is public record. I'm prepared to pay for it."

"Yes, yes. Of course, it's public, but why do you want it? Is Randall Green causing trouble in your county?"

"Why I want it doesn't concern you," I said pleasantly, but I thought she was too nosy to be a court employee.

"I'm sorry, but I can't comply with your request. Our courthouse burned to the ground five years ago, and the old records were destroyed. We lost everything."

My heart sank.

"The courthouse was a complete loss," she continued, "and a new one had to be built."

"Were you there when Randall Green was tried?"

"Oh, yes. I've worked here twenty-five years. I remember it well. We don't have many cases like that one, thank the good Lord."

"What do you remember about the trial?"

"Only that Green was guilty of raping that poor little girl. It's hard to imagine how twisted and cruel some people are." She gave a long-suffering sigh. "I'd have thought he'd still be in prison. It's scandalous how they let people out because they behave well while incarcerated. How else could a person behave in prison?"

"He served his time."

"That's the thing I can't understand. He should have received life. I don't know what he's doing now, but he should be watched."

"I appreciate your help, Mrs.—"

"Halverson," she said, "Ruby Halverson."

"Thank you, Mrs. Halverson."

I snapped my phone shut. "She says the courthouse burned down five years ago, and all the records were destroyed."

Randy looked despondent.

"I'm going to check that story. She was weird."

"How will you do that?"

"I'll check the archives of newspapers." A courthouse burning to the ground in a small town is front page news. "Let's go to my house. I need my computer and Internet."

I looked up *The Simpson Weekly Report* and *The Carterton Reporter* and found that their online archives only went back two years, so I called them to inquire about the fire, starting with *The Simpson Weekly*.

"What fire?" The receptionist was shocked. "Our courthouse dates back to the early 1800s. Look up Simpson online and you'll see it. It's picturesque." She seemed proud of it.

"Please give me the name of the district judge," I said.

"Our judge is Joseph Washburn."

"How long has he been there?"

"About a year, I think."

"Who was the judge before him?"

"It was Judge Carter. He was here a long time."

I thanked her and hung up.

When the photo of the Freeman County Courthouse came up, I asked Randy if that was the courthouse where his trial had taken place. He said it was. I called Ruby Halverson again and demanded to know why she had lied to me. She sputtered and stalled, clearly flustered. Then she hung up. That told me what I needed to know about the trial of Randall Green without reading a transcript.

I repeated what I knew to Randy and then asked, "Who was on your side during your trial? In other words, who knows you're not a rapist?"

"An old girlfriend came forward on my behalf. I tried dating girls for a while, but that didn't take. Even so, we became close, and she knew I would never rape someone."

"Did she testify on your behalf?"

"At first, my attorney said she didn't make a convincing witness. In the end, they did let her testify, but they twisted everything she said. They made it sound like I was a sex addict, going after anyone still breathing. That became the 'proof' they needed that I would rape a little child."

"What's your old girlfriend's name?"

"Maryann Trousdale. She tried to say I was quiet and sensitive. She admitted that we had sex a few times but explained that I was not attracted to her in that way. They tore her apart on the stand."

"Who else knows you're not a rapist?"

"The man I worked for, Buddy King, knew it. I got a letter from him when I went to prison."

"And he said he believed in you?"

"Yes, that's basically what he said and that he was sorry he hadn't stood up for me more than he did."

"Do you still have that letter?"

"If you didn't find it, I don't have it."

"What about Ellen Miller?"

"What about her? She's not part of this."

"I saw a reference to her in your file. She sent you money and wrote love letters to you over the years. Shouldn't I speak with her?"

"No, she's—she moved away."

I pressed him because I thought he was lying. "So, a woman who wrote you love letters on a regular basis and sent you a lot of money over the years just moved away, and now you don't know how to reach her? Are you hiding something?"

"I can't talk about Ellen."

"Why?"

"I'll tell you one day, but I can't talk about her right now, okay?"

"You can't hold things back because it makes me suspicious. If I'm going to help you, I need to know everything."

Randy's eyes filled with tears. "Then, you're going to help me?"

"I'm going to see what I can do. I'm not making any promises, but I'm going to get that transcript."

"I don't know how I'll ever thank you."

"Don't thank me until I accomplish something."

I asked him how he'd survived in prison.

"I got involved in everything they offered. I went to therapy groups, participated in work details, and sports. I played basketball on the prison team. I gained some respect that way and a few privileges. I began jogging around the yard when I was allowed out. At first it was only a mile or so. Eventually I ran around the yard so many times I lost track. I worked out and read. Somehow the time passed. I tried to occupy my mind. Otherwise, I'd have gone insane."

"I think you're amazing."

"No, I'm not amazing. I just did what I had to do."

"It would help if you made a list of people I should talk to in Carterton. Let's think about going there soon. I need to get a feel for the place and talk to people who could help you."

Randy looked as if I had slapped him. "I can't go back there. Please don't make me go."

"I guess I can go without you," I said, thinking this was not what I had in mind for a vacation. No sunscreen needed.

***

I called Randy's former court-appointed defense attorney, Jacob Rawlings, and introduced myself to his secretary.

"He's out of town," she said. "I'm sorry, but he'll be gone at least thirty days."

"No way can this wait thirty days!"

"I'm sorry, ma'am, but that's all I can tell you."

"But this is urgent."

I pushed, prodded, and resorted to begging.

Finally, she told me that her boss had checked himself into an alcohol and drug rehabilitation center in Midland, Texas. She gave me the address and phone number for Midland Recovery, a private treatment facility where Jacob Rawlings had lived for two weeks. She thought he might speak to me if I called and explained my mission.

Next, I called Judge Washburn's office. His secretary was friendly at first and said her name was Jeanie. When I insisted on speaking with the judge, she became less friendly.

"Judge Washburn is a busy man, and his afternoon is full. I'm sorry to say he's not accepting any phone calls until next week."

"I only need five minutes of his time. I'm investigating a case that was prosecuted there. I'm a deputy from Brewster County."

That didn't impress her, of course. A deputy is low on the justice system ladder. Still, I never take crap from rude secretaries.

After trying unsuccessfully to woo her with my sweet nature, I tried bitchiness. "You can let me speak with him or relay a message to him to return my call right away; or I'll get a subpoena for him to appear in district court in Brewster County to answer my questions."

It was a bluff, big talk from a little liar, but it got her attention. She put me on hold and said she'd speak to him.

Gotcha! I thought, but I felt less haughty as I waited a long time for His Honor to come to the phone.

"Judge Washburn." He sounded gruff and impatient and like every other judge I'd known. "What's this about a subpoena?"

Oops. "I'm trying to find former Judge Carter. I have questions regarding a rape case from seven years ago."

"Tell me your name again."

I gave it, but by then I didn't want to.

"Well," said the new judge, "you should have been in touch sooner, Deputy Ricos. Judge Carter died a year ago. I've only been here since then. I wasn't here seven years ago."

"How can I get a copy of a trial transcript? I tried calling Mrs. Halverson. She told me the courthouse burned down five years ago."

"Is this a joke? Who is this?"

"I'm not joking. It's not true that the courthouse burned down, is it?"

"Certainly not. Why would Ruby tell you that?" He seemed genuinely puzzled more than angry, but he was that, too.

"For some reason she doesn't want me to have it, Judge Washburn. I wonder if you could get it for me."

"Well, sure; I can get it." He was confident, as any powerful man would be. "I'll have my secretary go and get it right now. Let me have your phone number and she'll call you back."

I gave him the same information I'd given Ruby Halverson.

I suspected that Randy's trial had been erased from the official records of Freeman County, but I didn't see how they could have erased the attorney's records, or the D.A.'s. Or maybe they had. Either way, the screwy case of Randall Green had captured my full interest. By then, I couldn't have turned away from it.

If I wanted to succeed, I had to have Randy's help, so I invited him to dinner. Billy had to work until ten that evening, so we'd have plenty of uninterrupted time before he arrived.

"I need to tell you about Ellen Miller," Randy said as he walked up the few steps to my porch.

"Wow, just like that."

He sank into the chair next to me. "I don't know why I was trying to keep it from you. I guess because of Billy."

"What does Ellen Miller have to do with Billy?"

"Ellen is really Larry Mills. He was my first love, and the only person I've ever been in love with. He couldn't have written me love letters under his real name, could he? If word had gotten back to Carterton and Simpson, his life would've been ruined. He was the basketball coach at Simpson High School, which also serves Carterton."

"What happened to Larry?"

"He hung in with me a few years, but I was looking at a ten-year sentence, and eventually he fell in love with another man."

"What does Larry have to do with Billy?"

"Well, nothing. I freaked out. It was stupid. I thought it would upset Billy to know about him. Sometimes I say or do the wrong things. Prison sets a person back socially; it's a setback in every way. I really like Billy and don't want to lose him before I can even get to know him."

"I understand."

"I haven't had a relationship since Larry gave up on me. I want to move slowly, but I don't know how long I can hold myself back from Billy. I don't want to mess this up. Do you understand what I'm saying?"

"Yes. I think you should speak honestly with Billy. He might seem flighty, and he plays around a lot, but he runs deep. Also, he's had his own difficult past. It wasn't as difficult as yours, but more so than most."

"Yes, I already see who he is. I'll talk to him."

"Have you spoken to anyone about getting work?"

"I spoke to the owner of the auto repair place, but he's not interested in hiring an ex-con. I hung around after he left for the day and helped one of his employees diagnose a problem that had him stumped. It impressed the hell out of him, but I doubt if he carries any weight with his boss."

"He might; you never know."

"It felt good to work on a vehicle again. Diagnostics was my specialty, even when I was a teen. People say it makes a funny noise, and I love figuring out what it is. I haven't touched a motor in seven years, but today it felt like no time had passed."

He watched me with serious eyes. "Hope is the best thing you can give a person. How can I ever thank you for that?"

"You don't have to thank me. I haven't done anything yet. Did you talk to any other places about work?"

"I spoke with all the restaurants. Somebody may trust an ex-con with the dishes. When I mentioned your name, the woman at the Chili Pepper Café seemed to perk up about hiring me. Of course, she didn't ask me why I'd been in prison, so when that comes out, who knows?"

"Did you talk to your parole officer? Maybe he could help."

"I'll call him tomorrow."

"Tell me about Judge Carter. Do you think he could have removed your transcript or had it removed?"

Randy nodded. "He sat at that 'trial,' and he knew I wasn't guilty, but he let me be sacrificed. I figured he was connected to the man who was abusing Sarah. It wasn't him because he was too tall, but he was protecting whoever it was."

"Do you know how to locate Sarah?"

"I don't know where she is, but someone in Carterton will know. I know Sarah never said I raped her."

"Do the people of Carterton know you're gay?"

"Yes, Margarita, it was at least partially about that. I don't want to go back to Carterton. I was terrorized there."

"Please tell me everything, Randy. I can't help you if you don't level with me."

"Are you sure? It's ugly, and I don't feel right telling you."

"You handicap me if you hold things back."

Randy studied his hands and finally began to tell his tale. "While I was in jail waiting on my trial, I took a lot of verbal abuse from the Freeman County deputies. They called me 'Baby Fucker' and 'Baby Raper,' and other nasty things."

"That must have been horrible."

"It was."

"Now I understand why you said what you did about deputies."

"This story gets a lot worse. This is your last chance to opt out of hearing it."

"Please continue."

"The food tasted so awful it was hard to eat. I got unsweetened oatmeal in the morning, stale bologna sandwiches at noon, and watery soup or stew at night. Larry sent me money under the name of Ellen Miller, so I could pay for anything I wanted. I just couldn't get anyone to bring me what I wanted.

"After a while, I made friends with a new deputy, and he started bringing me decent food. After several weeks, this man came to my cell one night and said, 'I want you to suck my dick.' I laughed. I swear I thought he was kidding. I never saw that coming.

"When I laughed, he got angry and came into my cell and unzipped his pants. I told him no, I wasn't going to. He said, 'but you're queer. You'll enjoy this.' I refused to touch him, and he finally zipped up his pants and left."

Randy grimaced. "I don't like telling you any of this, Margarita."

"I know, and I don't want to hear it, but I need to know everything if I'm going to help you."

"Damien—the deputy—came back and brought the sheriff. He told him I'd exposed myself to him. Together they beat the shit out of me. I had to be taken to the hospital. The sheriff told the nurses I'd attacked his deputy for no apparent reason."

"I want the names of those people."

"We'll get to that. After three days, I was released from the hospital, and Damien kept bringing me food and books like nothing happened. One night when we were alone, he came back to my cell with the same demand. Again, I refused. And again, he and the sheriff beat me."

"This is hard to hear."

"It's hard to tell it, too, and I don't like telling it to you. After that beating, I feared for my eyes and teeth, so I finally did what I should have done in the first place. When he came into my cell, I went somewhere else in my head.

"Fortunately, many nights we weren't alone, so he couldn't make his demands. Once, I asked him if he was gay. I figured he was if he was getting a man to suck his dick instead of a woman. He went ballistic. He told me to shut up, that at least I should be grateful for the sex. I wasn't getting any sex! It was all about him and he never touched me.

"The sheriff overheard us. The next day, Damien was gone and never came back. The other deputies told me he'd been fired for being a queer. Not fired because he'd abused me, but because the sheriff thought he was gay. He didn't want to work with no queers, they said." Randy let out a long, shuddering breath.

"I'm sorry, Randy."

"During the time of Maryann Trousdale's testimony, I began having sheriff trouble of a different nature. Her testimony made him horny, I guess. He said if I'd have sex with her and let him film it, he'd give me special privileges."

"I don't like this sheriff."

"I promise you, you wouldn't." Randy studied his hands again before he continued. "I told the sheriff I'd never ask Maryann to do what he asked and besides, she was my friend and neither of us wanted to have sex. By then, of course, I might've changed my mind, but that was never going to happen. He was only teasing me or teasing himself. I was afraid he'd beat me up again, but he didn't."

"I don't know how you survived."

"Sheer will," he said. "Can you understand why I don't want to go back?"

CHAPTER 12

"Help," Billy sob-whispered into the phone. "They're killing him."

I bolted upright and felt around for the lamp. "Where are you, Billy?"

"Randy's."

"I'm coming."

On the way, I called the dispatcher to say I was answering a call for help at a private residence.

"You're on vacation," he said.

"True, but I haven't forgotten how to respond to an emergency."

"What I meant is—"

"I know what you meant, but I have a situation here. Please notify whichever one of my partners is on call. Tell them I'm at Randall Green's house in the Ghost Town. They know where it is."

As I skidded to a stop near Randy's house, the headlights swept over the word "PERVERT" spray-painted in giant black letters across the front wall. It was disheartening that the news was out so soon and had probably morphed into something even worse than it was.

Randy's truck sat solo in the yard; I saw no others and no movement. I crept closer. The door stood open and the screen door was unlocked, so I slipped in holding my Beretta in front of me. Two ski-masked men held Randy upright while another one whaled on him. They were so intent on what they were doing that they didn't hear me. I didn't see Billy but didn't have time to think about him, either.

"Stop! Sheriff's Office!" I yelled, and the surprised men turned to gape at me.

Randy slumped between them, blood dripping from above one eye and from his mouth and nose. I couldn't tell if he was conscious.

"Well, well, if it isn't the female deputy," said a man attempting to disguise his voice. I felt sure he was Tom McAfee.

"Stay out of this," growled another. Rod Florence, I thought.

They shoved Randy at me with so much force that his big body slammed into me, I stumbled, and we crashed to the floor. While I struggled to regain my breath, the attackers made a mad scramble for the door. I jumped up and followed but slammed into Billy charging out of the bathroom. By the time we untangled ourselves, the masked men had escaped into the night.

An unseen man yelled, "Stop right there!" Buster had arrived. A minute later, he burst through the front door, breathless. "I pulled in," he panted. "I saw. Three dark shapes. Running from the house."

"Don't worry, Buster. Get your breath."

Meanwhile, Billy had scurried to Randy and dropped to the floor beside him. He tried to rouse him.

"Billy, please go get my mother." My mom is a doctor, and I thought it best to leave the Terlingua Fire and Rescue out of this for now.

"Do you want me to get her?" Buster asked.

"No. I want you to stay in case those men return. Billy will go."

Buster ducked back outside to watch for trouble.

Randy tried to sit up. "Lie still and don't move," I said as I placed a pillow under his head. "Help is coming."

To Billy I said, "I'll call Mom, so she'll be ready by the time you get there. Can you go for her, Billy? Now?"

"You should get her, and I'll stay with Randy."

"Billy! Pay attention. Go get my mom, right now! Here are my keys."

"But I can't leave him."

"I know first-aid, and you don't."

My mother would come without question to help anyone in trouble. If that person was me, she'd put a real hustle on it.

"But—"

"He needs medical attention. Now stop arguing and go!"

Billy left in a huff, but he left.

***

Dr. Stephanie Ricos stood in her bathrobe and took command of the situation. Give her an injured person, and she'll put the earth out of its orbit to help them. I stepped back when she entered the room because I knew better than to get in her way. I tried to tell Billy, but he wouldn't listen and learned the hard way.

"Young man," Mom said in exasperation, "please boil some water."

I had to bite my lip not to laugh when he went to the kitchen to do it.

She gave Randy a shot for pain and then a deadening shot above his eye, so she could stitch the wound there. As Mom worked, I told her what little I knew. She listened but didn't comment. She cleaned and dressed the cuts and bruises, and then softly assured her patient that he would be sore for a few days but ultimately fine.

He thanked her, shut his eyes, and didn't re-open them.

"Can he be moved to my house?" I asked when she finished.

"Probably so; are you thinking of his safety?"

"Yes."

"It'd be better if you stayed here. The less he moves around the better. I want him to go to bed and rest. After the shot I gave him, that's what he'll want to do."

Randy lifted one finger as if to agree but didn't open his eyes.

Billy came in carrying a steaming pan of water.

Mom took it from him. "Thank you so much, Billy. Now you may hold his hand if you wish." She set the pan on the floor.

"What's the water for?" Billy asked.

"It was to give you a focus and keep you out of Mom's way," I said.

He started to say something but thought better of it.

"Billy, are you injured anywhere?" My mom asked.

"No. I'm fine."

"Are you sure?"

"I'm sure; thank you for asking."

The three of us got Randy into bed and settled comfortably, to my mother's exact specifications. Then I took her home while Buster stood guard outside the house.

"Thank you so much, Mom."

"Not so fast, Margarita. I have some questions. I assume I've just treated the registered sex offender, Randall Green?"

"Yes, Mom."

"Barney spoke with me about him yesterday. Do you think that young man was guilty of that horrible crime?"

"I don't think so, but it's hard to know what to think."

"I guess we aren't going to figure it out tonight."

I thanked her again, she leaned across the seat, and we hugged.

"You don't need to thank me," Mom said, "but I would like you to do something for me."

"You got it. What?"

"Find out who did this and prosecute them. We can't have vigilante terrorism in Terlingua. First an ex-con, next it'll be an immigrant. Nobody will be safe."

"I'll do that, Mom."

"And somebody needs to get that word off the front of his house."

"I'll take care of that, too."

"And you should tell the sheriff about this."

"I will, Mom. Buster and I will make an assault report."

***

I took Missy back to Randy's with me. She would not intimidate anyone, but she would never let anybody sneak up on us, either.

Buster was happy to see her, and the feeling was mutual, to say the least. Missy was beside herself to find Buster already seated on the ground, where she could show him the love she felt he deserved.

"Those men won't be back, I bet," I said.

"I think you're right."

"Missy will let us know if they come anywhere near."

"Yes, she will," Buster said in a puppy-talk voice, loving on her as he spoke, "because she's the best, bravest little girl in Texas."

My pup ate it up.

"I'm going inside to check on the guys. You can go home if you want to, Buster."

"I think I should stay a while."

"I appreciate it."

I had a hundred questions about what had happened at Randy's house, but he was asleep. Billy was curled against him, but he struggled to open his eyes when he heard me come in.

"Go to sleep, Billy. We'll talk tomorrow."

"But where will you sleep?"

"I'm going to sit by the door in case those men come back. I'll sleep tomorrow. Don't worry about anything."

I joined Buster and Missy outside for a while. The pup ran around sniffing, while we leaned back on our elbows and watched the sky. It was a twinkling wonder, as usual, and so quiet we could hear the stars whisper to each other. On a clear night, which is most nights, our desert sky gives new meaning to the phrase, "All is bright."

When the men didn't return after a couple of hours, Buster went to sleep in his truck. Even though we pegged them as cowards, we thought it was a good idea to keep a Sheriff's Office vehicle in the driveway.

I got two blankets from the trunk of my car and laid down beside the door. Missy thought that *at last* I had figured out where to sleep. She was comfortable; I wasn't, but I was too tired to notice for long.

* * *

Early the next morning, I went home to shower and change my clothes, and Buster left to do the same.

After I fed Missy, I called Sheriff Ben because I didn't know what he'd have heard, and I thought he should know the straight scoop.

"I was surprised to learn you responded to a call last night," my boss said. "I thought you'd be on a beach by now."

"I have a lot to tell you, Sheriff."

"What's going on?"

I told him about meeting Randy and becoming friends before I knew he was a registered sex offender. Then I explained that he and my friend Billy had become a couple. The sheriff expressed surprise that a gay man would rape a little girl.

"He claims to be innocent of rape," I said, "and I believe him."

"Since rape is most often less about sex and more about power and control, it's still possible that he's guilty. You know that, right?"

"Yes, sir. I do know that."

I gave him details about the incident last night and explained why I'd been called instead of 911. He was upset that Randy had been attacked but had no problem with the way things had been handled. Of course, he wanted a full report right away.

When I said I planned to do research on Randy's case, he didn't have a problem with that, which surprised me. But he said, "I think working on a case is a poor way to spend your time off."

"I know, but the guy needs help, and my friend Billy is counting on me. It's hard to explain, but I couldn't say no. I'm going into this with some skepticism, but if you met Randy you'd understand why I believe his claim of innocence."

"If you discover that he really did rape that little girl, that's just going to add to your stress and aggravation. I want you to return to your job, not become more disgusted with it."

"I understand what you're saying, Sheriff, but I got myself into a position where I couldn't say no."

The sheriff felt sure that I would probably be disappointed in the outcome. I didn't argue with him because I didn't want to be on the phone all day. I was relieved he wasn't against what I planned to do and decided to be satisfied with that.

His final comment on the subject was this: "Margarita, I want you to listen carefully. If you wish to help this man, then go ahead, but please think of yourself as a private investigator and not a sheriff's deputy. To represent yourself as a deputy would imply that I sent you on this mission, and I'm not doing that. Do you understand?"

"Yes."

"Are you sure?"

"Yes. I understand."

I understood, but I didn't like it. I was accustomed to investigating as a deputy with the weight of the sheriff behind me, and I didn't have a clue about being a P.I. I'd have to figure it out as I went.

***

When I returned to Randy's, I called Barney.

"I'm coming there now," he said.

"You don't need to. I can handle this."

"Aren't you on vacation? I'm coming, and you can go home."

I didn't argue with him. What good would it do? I waited for him outside because I knew he would give me a hard time.

"What do you know about this incident?" Barney asked as he climbed out of his truck.

"My mom came here last night to treat Randy Green for injuries received in a beating by some local men."

"And?"

"He's going to be fine."

Buster pulled in behind Barney. After we greeted each other, Barney continued his interrogation.

"Ricos, it's great that he'll be fine, but what else do you know?"

I gave him a brief synopsis.

"Did you do something wrong?" Barney asked.

"Not that I'm aware."

"Then why the guilty face?"

"I don't have a guilty face. I have a nice face, don't I, Buster?"

"Oh, yeah," Buster said in an exaggerated way that made us laugh.

Barney held the door. "I sure have a lot of questions."

"I do too," I said.

Barney introduced Deputy Mayhew to Randy and Billy without referring to him as Buster.

Randy sat propped up in bed. He looked pathetic but said he felt a lot better. Billy sat next to him holding his hand. I indicated the folding chairs to the two deputies and sat at the end of the mattress.

"Randy, please tell us what happened," Barney said. "Billy, since you were a witness you can corroborate his story or add to it, but please wait for him to finish."

Billy nodded his agreement.

"Billy worked in Lajitas last night," Randy said. "Afterward, his car wouldn't start, so I drove over to pick him up at ten-thirty. When we got back, Billy went to shower. I was in the kitchen trying to figure out how to reheat some food he brought. I haven't bought a microwave yet. Three men burst in through the front door."

"Had you locked it?" Barney asked.

"No, only shut the screen door. Even that wasn't latched."

"What happened next?"

"They attacked me. Billy was getting out of the shower, and he heard what was happening and called Margarita."

Busted—and so soon into the story.

Barney's head whipped around to glare at me. "I see. Why did you call her instead of 911?"

"Because I knew she'd come fast," Billy said.

"That's the point of calling 911. It's fast."

"She's my friend. And she already knew about Randy and me."

"So, you and Randy and Margarita are friends?"

Billy nodded. "Yes, we are. Margarita is going to prove that Randy is innocent."

Crap!

Barney turned to me but changed his mind. "Tell me about the men who attacked you," he said to Randy.

"They wore masks, and I probably wouldn't have recognized them anyway, but I think one of them was the man who gave you trouble in the canyon, Margarita."

"What made you think that?" I asked.

"I recognized his voice."

"Someone gave you problems in a canyon?" Barney was incredulous and gaped at me. "How come I don't know about this, Ricos?"

"He's talking about Tom McAfee. Randy made him back off."

"When did this happen?"

"A few days ago."

"When were you planning to tell me?"

"I wasn't because he hasn't bothered me again."

Barney gave me a look that was more hurt than anything and returned his attention to Randy. "What made you think it was Tom?"

"It was his voice and some of his mannerisms. In prison, I learned to be observant. Also, he mentioned to his friends that *she* wasn't here, so he might think Margarita and I are sleeping together."

"But you're not?"

"No, sir, we're not." He held up Billy's hand entwined with his, in case the deputies had missed the obvious. I didn't think they had.

"Was there any other talk?" Barney asked.

"They called me a sick freak, and a fucking pervert, and a stupid prick, and a lot of other things, but they were beating me up; I stopped hearing or caring. They demanded I leave Terlingua or I'd get worse next time. I think I would've been more seriously injured if Margarita hadn't arrived when she did." Randy turned his attention to me. "Thank you for coming so fast and for everything you've done for me."

"You're welcome, Randy."

"I believe Billy is right about you, Margarita."

"I don't know what Billy's been telling you, but I'm glad I could help."

Barney asked Randy, "Do you remember anything else that might help us identify the men?"

"One of them walks with a significant limp. One of his legs is shorter than the other. Someone called him 'P.W.' His initials, I guess."

"Billy," Barney said, "what do you remember? Do you have anything to add to what Randy has said?"

"I was in the bathroom. I thought they were going to kill him." He sniffed at the horror of the memory. "I was terrified to come out because I thought they'd kill him if they knew he was gay and maybe kill me also."

"You two are gay?" Buster sounded clueless, but he's not. It made him nervous to work with Barney. They'd gotten off to a rough start, and Buster hadn't forgotten it. "Together, I mean," Buster added, which just made him seem worse.

Barney sighed and raised an eyebrow at me.

"Yes, we're gay together," Billy admitted, "and separately."

I had to chew on my lip to keep from laughing, while Barney had one of his loud choking, coughing attacks. Buster blushed a bright shade of red.

"Maybe this was a gay bashing," he said to Barney.

"They didn't know Billy was here," Barney said patiently. "I think this was an ex-con bashing. How long have you guys been together?"

"We met at the store three days ago," Billy said, "but we've never been anywhere together except the national park. This is the first time I've been in Randy's house. I don't think anybody could've figured it out yet."

"There's one more thing," Randy said. "I got a good punch in on that Tom guy before they grabbed me. If you can find him, I think he'll have a shiner."

"I have something to add," I said, earning a scowl from Barney. "I made note of the clothes since I couldn't see faces. One man wore black boots, jeans, and a black jacket. Another was wearing black cotton pants and a denim jacket and combat boots with a camouflage print. He was the one with the limp. The one we think was Tom wore nice loafers, expensive slacks, and a brown leather jacket."

"Good job, Ricos!" Barney smacked me on the back and then stood. "Buster, please get signed statements. That's assuming you'll press charges, Randy. When we figure out who to charge, I mean."

"Yes, I will," Randy said.

"Ricos, come with me."

I knew it. I followed him out the door and over to his truck.

"Lu-u-u-cy," he said in a perfect imitation of Ricky Ricardo, "you got some 'splainin' to do."

"Sí, Ricky. What do you want to know?"

"Everything you know about this, starting with how you met our ex-con and coming forward and leaving out nothing."

I told him almost everything, and it took a while.

"Let me recap this," Barney said. "You ran into Randy while running, and he saved you from Tom. You thought you'd make a play for the brave rescuer, him being a handsome sort, but Billy stole him right out from under your nose."

"That's not even close to what I said."

Barney continued as if I hadn't spoken. "Then, for reasons that are mysterious to me, you offered to help exonerate him of the crimes for which he has just done time and for which he is still on parole. You haven't mentioned any of this to our sheriff or to me for that matter."

"The sheriff does know about it, but I'm investigating on my time, not his. As for you, I didn't want to tell you because I figured you'd ride me unmercifully."

"Were you ever going to tell me?"

"Someday I would, probably, when we're old."

"And I can't outrun you," Barney said.

"You can't outrun me now."

"Is that a challenge?"

"I'm stating a fact."

He shook his head. "I don't know whether to kick your butt or give you a hug."

"If I have a say, I'd rather have the hug."

"Not so fast, Lucy." He shook his head, tut-tutting. "You're a real sucker for a sad tale, aren't you?"

"I guess so. It just can't hurt to look around. That's all I'm saying."

"Why can't you show this kind of compassion for poor Jupiter?"

"He's a jerk. He kisses and tells like a teenage boy."

"Speaking of teenagers, I better go get Buster."

He started to walk back to the house, but he returned to give me one of his bear hugs.

***

I went in search of Tom McAfee, not that he's a hard man to track. His Jeep sat in front of the Big Bend Café, as it often did in the morning.

When I walked in, the gossiping cluster of bad examples got quiet and stared at me. Rod Florence was slurping coffee with the rest of them, and I felt even more certain that he was the third man in the attack on Randy. He was wearing the same black boots and, unless I was mistaken, the same slept-in jeans. Tom had a nasty-looking shiner and wore leather loafers, nice pants, and a brown leather jacket.

My intention had been to jump on Tom with both feet and accuse him outright, but I decided not to. My papi taught me not to blab everything I know, and I thought this might be one of those times. We would bust him, but we'd do it when we could make the charges stick.

Tom jumped up and pulled out a chair for me. "Hey, Margarita! Will you have some coffee with us?"

I wanted to grab that chair and hit him over the head with it.

"Good morning." I addressed everyone as if I didn't have a clue they harbored wrongdoers among them. I wondered why the limping man was missing from the group.

I stared at Tom's black eye. "That looks painful."

"Yeah, it is. I, uh, I fell down some stairs."

"You should watch where you're going," I said, and then left them to talk about whatever numbskull things they discuss when I'm not there.

I went home to pack for a trip to Carterton, a place I'd never heard of before I met Randy, and a place I didn't want to visit.

CHAPTER 13

I left before dawn and ate yogurt and bananas on the road while I tried to organize the trip in my head. Topping Randy's list of people I should see was Larry Mills, his former lover. I'd tried to get a home phone number, but it was unlisted. By calling Simpson High School, I discovered that he still worked there. The school secretary had stated proudly, "Mr. Mills is our winning basketball coach, possibly the most loved man in this whole town."

When I checked online, I read that their team held six state championships in their division and had made it to play-offs every year since Larry had come on board ten years ago. That was impressive, for whatever it was worth.

With further research online, I discovered that the sheriff was still Gil Hancock, the same man who had arrested and abused Randy. Randy believed he would pose a "serious danger" and advised me to avoid him. I didn't plan to talk to him until I had solid proof of his wrongdoing, and even then, I thought the talking would be done by a district attorney and a grand jury, not by me.

Thinking of Sheriff Hancock led me to Sheriff Ben. My uniform hung in the back because I hoped if I got enough information, my boss would let me work on the case as a deputy under his auspices. I wasn't even sure people would talk to me as a "private investigator." What I needed most, even more than my badge and uniform, was my partner.

* * *

I called my mom to be sure she had picked up Missy from my house. She was insulted that I thought she'd forget her. I'd wanted to bring Missy with me, but I couldn't be sure she'd be welcome in hotels. For certain she wouldn't be welcome if she complained at the top of her lungs when I left her to interview people.

Billy called me in a stew because he and Randy had not had sex. I don't like giving sex advice to anyone and feel especially unqualified talking about it with a gay man, but Billy is Billy, and how would I get out of it?

"He's injured," I reminded him.

"Well, he's not injured *there*," he whined.

"How do you know?"

"Oh my God, do you think something is wrong with him?"

"How would I know that?"

"I don't know. You know things."

"Billy, Randy was in prison for seven years."

"I know," he interrupted, "that's why he shaved his head. He thought his hair smelled like the prison. It just seems like he'd be more anxious to have sex after being incarcerated for so long."

"If you'd let me finish, I was going to say that he wants to do things right with you. He cares about you. He feels socially inept because of prison and his self-esteem is shattered. You should be patient and let him set the pace."

"How do you know all this?" he asked accusingly.

"He spoke with me about it. And he's going to speak with you. Just give him a chance. Keep your clothes on for the time being. Can you do that?"

"I can, but I don't want to."

"I get that, but you're going to mess things up if you push him."

"Do you think he had a lot of kinky prison sex?"

"Billy, can you get your head away from sex for five minutes?"

"No; can you?"

"You called me for advice, right?"

"Right."

"Then here it is. Take your cues from Randy. Don't push him. Don't ask him about prison sex, for heaven's sake. Let him tell you about it as he is able. It's possible he was raped. Now don't get hysterical, just realize he's had some experiences you haven't. I'm sure he'll confide in you, but he might not until he knows you better."

Billy freaked out, of course. "Do you know if he was raped?"

"No, Billy, I don't know that. I know you'll be good for Randy, but not if you push him too hard. He's recovering from new injuries and yet another terrible experience. Give him time."

"Okay. What you say makes sense, I guess. To change the subject, Randy is worried about you, and he feels guilty for not going with you."

"Tell him to knock it off. If I took him out of Terlingua right now, my mother would hunt me down, demand an explanation, and probably try to ground me."

"Say no more."

Cissy called following Billy. "I'm at school," she whispered.

"If you're at school, you aren't supposed to be on your cell phone."

"Why can't you just say good morning like everyone else?"

"Good morning, Cissy. How are you today?"

"I just had a math test, and I made a perfect score."

"That's great!"

"Are you proud of me?"

"You know it! I'm about to burst."

She whispered even lower. "This morning I noticed small bumps."

"Where? Do you feel bad?"

"No. I mean my breasts started to grow."

"That's wonderful! I don't see how a girl could possibly have any more good news than you do this morning."

"Aren't you glad I called?"

"I'm happy you called, but aren't you missing classes?"

"Give it a rest for five minutes. It's just Spanish."

"Don't you think it'll benefit you to learn Spanish, especially considering where you live?"

"It's so hard, and why would I need it?"

"Porque yo hablo español y me gusta hablarlo. Es una lengua hermosa."

"What? What did you say?"

"I said, in answer to your question about why you would need Spanish, 'because I speak Spanish and I like to speak it. It's a beautiful language.' You'd better get yourself into that classroom if you expect to hang out with me."

"All right, all right. I'm goin'. Thank you for the book. It's good, but it's so sad."

"I know, but isn't it a powerful story?"

"Yes, it is. My dad didn't want me to read it."

"Is that because he thought it would be too adult for you, or because black people are portrayed as human beings?"

"Neither. He doesn't know what *To Kill a Mockingbird* is about. It's because you gave it to me. He says he doesn't trust you."

"But he let you read it?"

"Yeah, I told him it was about hunting."

I laughed. I had called her "Opinionated Little Girl" and "Perceptive Little Girl," but maybe the best name for her was "Resourceful Little Girl."

"When I get back, I'll pick you up from school, and we'll get ice cream or burgers or whatever you want and talk about the book."

"You're on a trip?"

"I'm doing a favor for Randy."

"Ooh-la-la," she whispered.

* * *

Since it was a school day, I thought Larry Mills would be at the high school. When I stopped at the office, the secretary was on her toes.

"Why do you need to speak with him? Are you a parent? I've never met you before."

"I'm not a parent. It's about a private matter."

"Is Coach Mills in some type of trouble?"

"No, but I need to speak with him."

"What's goin' on?"

"Nothing to cause concern, but I still need to see Coach Mills."

She looked at the clock on the wall. "He's probably in his office at the gym, if he's not on the basketball court."

"Thank you. I appreciate your help."

The odor of sweat dominated the gymnasium. A whistle shrilled, and rubber soles screeched against waxed hardwood. A tall, fit man stood on the basketball court. I assumed he was the one in possession of the whistle, but I didn't immediately assume he was Larry Mills. For one thing, he seemed too young to be 20 years older than Randy. That would make him 46. I'm not good at guessing ages, but the only hint that he might be over 30 were the bits of silver in his otherwise dark hair.

"No, no, no," he yelled in a good-natured way. "Everybody, come over here."

A group of sweaty boys wearing gym shorts surrounded him. I sat on a bleacher to wait for him to get a break. When the boys went back to playing, he walked over to me.

"Good morning. Welcome to ninth grade gym class."

"Good morning. Are you Coach Mills?"

"Yes. I am." He held out his hand. "I'm Larry Mills. Are you here about one of my students?"

I took his hand. "I'm Margarita Ricos, an investigator from Brewster County."

"How can I help you?"

"May I speak with you about Randy Green?"

He became flustered at the mention of his former lover's name and glanced around as if guilty of something. "Is Randy all right?"

"Yes, he's doing well."

He sat down next to me. "How do you know him?"

"We're friends. I met him about a week ago."

"I can't speak with you now," he whispered.

"Could I meet you later?"

"No. I shouldn't speak with you at all."

"I really need your help. I'm trying to find out the truth so that Randy can get his sex offender status removed."

"I wouldn't be able to help you."

"But you supported Randy more staunchly than anyone."

"I'll tell you this. He never raped anybody." Larry's whisper was heated, but I could barely hear him above the din of the boys.

"That's what I'm trying to prove. Please help me."

He thought about it while I tried to maintain a pleading look. Finally, he said, "I don't suppose you have shorts and athletic shoes with you?"

"Yes, I do. I'm a runner."

"That's perfect!" He glanced around again. "I have some free time at noon. Please meet me back here then, and don't mention it to anyone. You could put us both in danger by investigating Randy's trial. I'm only meeting you because you're a friend of Randy's." He leaned towards me. "I'm going to pretend to give you a basketball lesson. I do training with adults sometimes, so nobody will suspect that I'm talking about the trial."

"Okay, I'll be here at noon."

"Listen. Be careful who you speak with in this town."

"Meaning?"

"You don't want to get the attention of the wrong people."

***

Frank "Buddy" King was the second person on Randy's list. He had been his employer at Carterton Auto Repair.

The place looked like a typical mechanic's shop with partially dismantled vehicles and parts of vehicles everywhere. A huge pickup had been raised on a lift in a three-bay garage and sat awaiting attention while a burly older man worked under the hood of a different truck in the next bay. He stood on a step-stool and leaned into the engine. He wore a short-sleeved jumpsuit and his arms were covered with colorful tattoos and various oily smudges. He lifted his head, removed a grimy cap, and wiped sweat from his brow with the back of his hand, leaving one more smudge.

I got out of the Mustang and walked towards him. He looked my way and then buried himself under the truck hood again, unconcerned by the arrival of a possible customer.

"Hello," I greeted him. "Are you Mr. King?"

He raised himself slowly and looked me over. "Who wants to know?"

"I'm Margarita Ricos, sir. I'd like to speak to you a few minutes."

"Well, I'm not stoppin' you. Speak to me, young lady. You talk, I'll listen." He went back to working on the truck.

"I'm here to inquire about Sarah Jones."

His head popped out of the motor, and he leaned against the truck, studying me with serious brown eyes. He removed the cap and wiped his brow again.

"What do you want with Sarah Jones? She hasn't lived here for going on seven years, and I don't believe you ever lived here. I'd remember you, not to mention that blue car of yours."

"I need to speak with her."

"Is she in trouble?"

"No, I don't think so."

"Whaddaya want her for, then?"

"I want to talk to her about the rape."

His brow furrowed. "What do you know about that rape?"

"The case is being re-investigated."

"And you are what—an undercover detective?"

"I'm a private investigator."

"Who's paying for that?"

"I'm not at liberty to say."

Now he was interested but still not volunteering anything. Another man came into the bay from a side door, carrying a socket wrench in one hand, a soda in the other. Since he was looking me up and down, I waved at him. He tripped and dropped the wrench.

"Let's go in my office," said Frank King, "so nobody gets hurt."

He set his tools down and shut the hood of the truck. "Follow me. Would you like something cold to drink?"

"No, thanks, I'm fine."

"Have a seat, and I'll be right there."

His office was the temperature of a meat-storage locker. I sat in a beige plastic chair next to a dirty, disorganized desk. Greasy fingerprints covered everything: the desk, the tan filing cabinets, and even the front of the air-conditioning unit. His prints would be easy ones to lift. *That's always the case when they're not needed for anything,* I thought, entertaining myself.

He came back into the room with an orange soda, sat behind the desk, and took a long drink from the can. "Why?" he asked.

"Why?"

"Why do you want to bother that poor girl about her rape, especially after such a long time? What's to gain from dredging all that up?"

"I want to prove Randy's innocence."

"That's never going to happen, not here."

"What do you mean?"

"Randy Green is the best mechanic I ever knew." He changed the subject, but I let him roll. "He's even better than me and I'm good." He winked. "He started working here at age fourteen, just helping out and running errands on his bicycle and such. Then I put him to fixing flats and by the time he was fifteen, people asked for him by name to fix their tires.

"One day I had a hell of a time changing out a truck part and Randy took over. He said, 'Here, let me do that for you, Boss.' Damned if he didn't do it perfect. I asked him where he learned, and he said he picked it up from tinkering with vehicles for most of his life. Most of his life? He was only fifteen!

"Anyway, by the time he turned sixteen he was my best mechanic, and I could give him anything. He was careful and would always re-check his work so nobody ever had to bring back something Randy fixed. He was an impossible guy to hurry, too. He took his time, but he could fix things that made other mechanics throw up their hands and cuss."

Randy hadn't lied about even that small detail.

"I think he's a mechanical genius. He could practically just touch the hood and know what was wrong, like a second sight."

"Mr. King, do you think Randy raped Sarah Jones?"

"What I think don't matter."

"It does to me."

"Look here. You get away from my business and call me. I'll tell you what I think, but not here. The wrong people might get ideas."

"Who are the wrong people?"

His eyes narrowed. "Do what I say or get out."

"Okay, Mr. King. I'll call you in a few minutes."

He handed me his business card. "Here's the number, but I don't know anything that'll help."

"I'd like to speak with you anyway."

"As far as anyone is concerned, you came here about a job. I advertised for a secretary-bookkeeper. Got that?"

"Okay. I understand."

As Barney would say, *What in lawman's hell?*

I stopped at a roadside park and called Buddy King.

He coughed and sputtered. "I changed my mind 'bout talking to you. "I'm sorry I can't help."

"Wait! Please. I won't ask you for names again. I only want to know if you think Randy Green raped Sarah Jones."

"Hell no! He wasn't a rapist. That boy was kind and timid and kept to himself. He never caused trouble."

"Randy just got out of prison. He did seven years of his ten-year sentence. Now, wherever he goes he's forced to register as a sex offender, so in some ways, he'll always be doing time. That's why I'm determined to help him."

"Who is Randy Green to you?"

"He's a friend."

"And what causes you to believe in him?"

"I see who he is. He claims to be innocent and asked me to help prove it, so I asked to read the trial transcript. We tried to get it from the court and couldn't."

He didn't volunteer any more information, so I asked again about Sarah Green.

"Her father took her to Phoenix. He transferred there to get her away from here. He was a friend, but I started to think he was moving so Sarah wouldn't know what happened to Randy. I know that little girl wasn't raped by him. It was someone else."

"Why do you believe that?"

"I already told you; that boy is not a rapist! And the trial—there was something wrong about it."

"What do you mean?"

"It was all hush-hush. Barely any news from it leaked to the public. It got around that it was for Randy's protection, as if the details were so sordid the townspeople would've come after him with pitchforks." He let out a long breath. "Maybe they would have."

"Was there ever any talk about the physical evidence?"

"Nah, except to say it proved his guilt. Then the rumor went around that Sarah would not be brought in to testify. I understand that to a point. She was only nine." He drank from the soda and then, "What little news they published in the paper was what the judge gave permission to leak."

"Such as?"

"They said Randy's semen was all over the girl, but they didn't quote any experts or anything. That would lead a person to think there weren't any experts testifying."

"Randy says that no experts ever testified."

"My wife is a nurse at the hospital, and she said Sarah was taken to a hospital in Midland instead of to the county hospital in Simpson, which is closer. It didn't make sense. That news was never in the paper, either. They printed a lot of editorial-type claptrap that boiled down to a bigoted hatred of homosexuals."

"How did people know for sure he was homosexual?"

"They didn't know for sure, but the kids he went to school with thought he was. Let's just say he had that reputation around town, and he never denied it. He might have denied it at the trial, but we can't know that, can we? I sure never asked him because I didn't care if he was or not."

"Is Sarah still in Phoenix?"

"I don't know, but her old man lives there, I think."

"Can you call him for me or give me his number?"

"I don't have his number. The last time I spoke with him he said it changed, but he forgot to give it to me. I don't think Sarah lives with him now anyway."

"Did she go back to her mother?"

"I don't know. You can probably find her through the school system if she's in Phoenix, unless you know a better way."

"What about her mother?"

"Her mother lives in California, last I heard. She lost custody of Sarah when she and Leroy split up. I don't even know where in California she is, so that doesn't help you. Sarah could be back with her for all I know."

"You've helped me a lot, and I appreciate it."

"Look here. I never spoke to you about Randy Green. Remember that you came to my business to ask me about work. You got that?"

"Yes, but I wish you would tell me who you're afraid of."

"You seem like a bright girl. Think about it." He hung up.

***

I drove around for a look at Carterton. It was laid out like many small towns with businesses at the center and residential areas surrounding that. A pint-sized mall, a Wal-Mart, and a Dollar Store were set away from the center of town, as were the churches. Carterton had some interesting small businesses, too. One was Polly's Palace for the Plus-Sized and another, a honky-tonk called Forever Five O'Clock. A mile from that stood a rickety, unpainted wooden building that looked like it had been lifted out of a Louisiana bayou and set down hard in west Texas. The sign read, *Bo's*

Beer, Bait, Boots, and Ammo. Seriously. I made a mental note to return.

Carterton was a nice enough place on the surface, but an unknown evil lurked in the shadows. It seemed like the kind of town Stephen King would make up so that he could keep his readers awake all night.

I drove through Randy's old neighborhood, noting where he had once lived and where Sarah had lived across the street. A young family now lived in Sarah's family's old place, judging by the toys scattered throughout the yard and cluttering the sidewalk. A colorful swing set sat in the backyard. It looked too new to have ever been Sarah's. I got out and walked around, but being there made me sad.

As I was about to get back in my car, an old man came towards me from Randy's former home. He carried a shovel and had been working in the yard.

"What are you doing here?" he yelled, not in an unfriendly way, but not friendly either.

As I walked towards him, I noticed a strong resemblance to Randy. He was handsome in an old-man way and had the same eyes, the same questioning expression I'd seen before on Randy.

"I'm just looking around. A friend of mine used to live here," I said.

He leaned against the shovel and stared at me. "I think you're mistaken, young lady. I've owned this house for almost thirty years. Maybe your friend lived next door."

"His name is Randy Green."

"Don't know anybody by that name," he grumbled and headed back to his house.

"Your loss," I called after him and got back in the Mustang.

I stopped at the now-familiar roadside park and called Midland Recovery Center to ask if I'd be allowed to see Jacob Rawlings if I came there later today. Yes, they would allow it but only if Mr. Rawlings agreed to see me. They took my number and promised to talk to him and call me later.

Next, I called Judge Washburn to see if he had located the missing transcript, but I couldn't get past his secretary.

"Do you know if anyone has located Randall Green's trial transcript?" I asked.

"No, it hasn't been found. The judge is having the records section turned upside down."

"May I have an appointment with him this afternoon?"

"Ms. Ricos, the judge is a very busy man."

"I'm aware of that, but I drove all this way, and I need his help."

"He wasn't here seven years ago. How will he help you?"

"I don't know that yet. That's why I need to see him. I have questions about court procedure and the responsibility of judges."

"Judge Washburn is a responsible judge."

"I'm sure he is, but I have legal questions I believe he can answer."

"You need an attorney to answer legal questions."

"Please, Jeanie. Why are you fighting me so hard? I need help from the district judge and that's Judge Washburn." Damn it, I was tired of pleading with snotty secretaries, but at least it worked.

"Very well, he has a free moment at two-thirty this afternoon."

"That's fine; I'll be there then."

"I mean a moment *only*, Ms. Ricos."

"I got that."

After that battle, I called Barney. First, I asked him to let Randy know things were going fine, although that was technically not true. So far, I had nothing that would stand up in court; it was all hearsay. The day had to get better. Or, if I was in a King novel, it was going to get a lot worse.

"Have you found out anything about the man who limps?" I asked my partner.

"All I know is that he's not from here. He's been in several of the local businesses."

"I don't suppose he used a credit card anywhere?"

"No, I checked already. He paid cash for everything. There's one thing, though. He visited the Starlight Theatre earlier on the night he went to Randy's house, assuming it's the same man. He drank beer and chatted up Darcy." Darcy is a bartender at the Starlight Theatre, a restaurant and bar located in the Terlingua Ghost Town.

"What did he say to her, Barney?"

"In the course of the conversation, he mentioned that he needed to get back to Austin. She had the impression he works there."

"Austin?"

"That's what he said. She's sure of it because they talked about this small piano bar on Sixth Street she likes, and he knew the one."

"Why would a man from Austin care about Randy Green?"

"If I could answer that question for you Ricos, then maybe all of this would make sense. Right now, nothing does. I'm still asking around."

"Maybe he's the wrong limping man. Other men limp."

"Yes, but you said he wore a blue denim jacket and camouflage boots, and so did this man. I don't think that's a coincidence, do you?"

"No."

"Maybe you should ask Randy what a man from Austin has against him. Carterton is not near Austin, is it?"

"No. It's as far from there as it is from Terlingua."

"Maybe it's the man who molested Sarah Jones," he said. "Maybe he moved to Austin."

"Maybe so," I said, but I doubted it.

I still had a long way to go before I understood the significance of the limping man and his connection to Randy and Austin.

CHAPTER 14

I rented a hotel room near the Interstate. It was closer to Simpson than to Carterton, but it didn't matter because I still had interviews to do in both places. I changed into running gear and headed back to the high school gym. It felt weird, but I didn't think Larry Mills had switched over to the dark side. Randy had loved him, so I'd give him the benefit of the doubt.

Quiet prevailed at the gym, but the smell of adolescent sweat and stinky feet lingered. The coach dunked balls from the free-throw line and scored each time. He was not even trying, or maybe it looked effortless because he was so good at it.

"I'm here for my lesson, Coach," I said in a voice too loud for the acoustics.

He grinned, caught the ball, and dribbled it over to me. Then he indicated we should sit on the bleachers. "Did you play basketball in high school?"

"I played for fun, but there was no girls' team back then."

"You didn't go to high school that long ago."

"I went to a small school. They spent all the money on boys' sports."

"I bet you didn't think much of that."

"I didn't. I complained to the superintendent, but it didn't do any good. All I got out of it was the number one position on her list of troublemakers."

He laughed at that.

"This isn't a good place to talk in private," I whispered. "Our voices echo and seem overly loud."

"Let's go into my office."

His office was glass on three sides, so it wasn't as though anyone would sneak up on us if anyone wanted to sneak. I wasn't sure what to think. These paranoid people had started to get to me.

Coach Mills lifted a book from a shelf near his desk and pretended to show me something in it.

"How can I help you clear Randy's name?" He pointed to a diagram of a basketball play as he spoke in a whisper. It almost made me laugh.

"I want to check some facts."

He leaned closer to me. "Tell me about Randy. How does he look? Is he happy? Is he healthy?"

"He looks great and seems healthy. I met him running."

"He's still running?"

"Yes."

"I guess Randy told you about us."

I nodded. "He says he met you when he was sixteen. The two of you fell in love and would've lived together had things been different in Carterton then."

"That's true. He fixed my car and delivered it to me, and I seduced him. We fell hard for each other. I'm twenty years older than Randy. I hope you don't think I'm a pedophile, but Randy was mature for his age. I had no idea he wasn't in his twenties until it was too late to back out."

I held up my hand. "What's important to me is what you have to say about the trial, the charges brought against Randy, and anything else you think I should know."

"The trial made a mockery of the law, Ms. Ricos."

"Please explain."

"The defense attorney and D.A. decided that a bench trial would be better than a jury trial. That kept witnesses out. I didn't like it, but I couldn't be vocal about it without losing my new coaching job at the school. Randy and I couldn't take our love for each other out of the closet without risking our lives and our careers. We were caught up in lies. It was the most terrible time of my life."

He stood and walked to a small refrigerator. "Would you like water or juice?"

"I'd like water, thank you."

He got two bottles and handed one to me. Then he sat and continued. "The court appointed an attorney who was worthless. When he advised against a jury trial, Randy didn't know what else to do. It was evident from the beginning how it would go. A lot of attention was put on Randy being homosexual, not as much on the rape. I couldn't even visit him in prison without news of that traveling back here to haunt me. Also, it would've made things infinitely worse for him, I think."

"Randy told me you wrote to him."

"I had to get a post office box in another name in a different town so that I could send and receive his mail."

"Randy says you're the main reason he lived through his ordeal. Your love helped him survive."

Larry's eyes filled with tears. "I know how hard it was for Randy when I fell in love with another man. I continued to send him money, and I hope it helped, but money is only money and not the same as love."

"He understands and has no hard feelings."

Larry wiped his eyes. "That's a relief."

Next, I told him about Mrs. Halverson and her lie and what Randy had said about Judge Carter.

"I always thought it was the judge," Larry said. "Somebody powerful pulled the strings. I suspect that everyone important to the case was paid off or received favors of one kind or another. Carter was in charge, so he was either behind it or was one of the ones bought off."

"Randy says a DNA sample was taken from him, but DNA evidence was never properly presented. Is that true?"

"I'm sure it is, but how could I prove it? The only honest person at that trial was Randy. They made sure nobody else would see what they did to him."

"Would you be willing to make a formal statement?"

"No; I can't do that."

"Have you been threatened?"

"I *feel* threatened. People here are afraid of the Randall Green trial, of what happened to him, so you aren't going to get much cooperation."

"But the judge is dead."

"Then it wasn't only the judge, was it?"

"Do you know something you're not telling me?"

"No. If I knew for sure who sent my Randy to prison, I would kill him."

"You don't have any suspicions?"

"No. All the powerful people are suspect and yet none of them are. Sarah would be the one to talk to. She's sixteen years old now, so maybe she'd help you."

"Do you know how to find her?"

"No. She was sent to live with her mother during the trial. Afterward, she returned, but her father moved away with her. He said the horror of what happened was too vivid for her."

"Does anyone in town know where she is?"

"The man who owns the mechanic shop where Randy used to work was friends with her father. He's Frank King, but everybody calls him Buddy."

"I spoke with him and he doesn't know, or he's afraid to say."

"Nobody is going to help you. I'm sorry, but that's the way it is here."

"I have to try. I'm already convinced that Randy is innocent, but I have to prove it. Once I get his case before a judge, people can be subpoenaed, but I need a lot of proof to even get a judge to talk to me."

"You could talk to Maryann Montgomery. She was Maryann Trousdale when she dated Randy. She tried to help him after he was arrested. She would tell you about the way she was treated when she testified, but she's out of town right now. I can't think of anything else that would be useful."

I made a note of the name. "Where does she live?"

"She lives in Carterton but teaches here. She'll tell you what a joke that trial was. Or she might not, but you can try."

"If you think of anything else, would you call me?" I wrote down my personal cell number for him.

"Wait. I have something you should have. While Randy awaited trial in the county jail, he sent me an odd letter. It was formal and said something like 'Dear Mr. Mills, I'm returning the handkerchief you loaned me. It's valuable, and you'll want to keep it.' It was just a standard handkerchief, so I was curious. I thought the wording meant he wanted me to guard it. Later, when he went to the state prison, I asked about it in a letter. His response was that it was important, and he asked me keep it safe, which I've done."

He unlocked the bottom drawer of a file cabinet and pulled out a sealed plastic bag with the letter and handkerchief inside. "Perhaps you'd give it to him for me."

"Of course."

"Will you give Randy my best? Tell him I wish him well."

"I'll do that. Thank you for the basketball lesson, Coach Mills, but I might need another."

He winked. "Let me know."

***

I went back to the room and changed into my street clothes.

Curiosity lured me back to Bo's Bait. Maybe Bo knew something useful. His store was bound to be entertaining, at least. When I parked in a slanted slot in front of it, I noticed a small, sloppy sign taped at the bottom of the glass door: XXX Books & Mags! Just Ask!

How could a bonafide Texan go wrong in a place that sells beer, bait, boots, ammo, and under-the-counter XXX, all under the same roof? Even though I didn't need anything—new boots would be nice—I pushed through the door. I hoped the smell that greeted me was dead minnows or something like that, not the man seated behind the counter at the back of the room. Bo, or someone I assumed to be Bo, sat on a stool, absorbed by a magazine. As I walked towards him, the floor creaked, and he shoved whatever it was under the counter and stood.

"Well, well," he said. "What can I do you out of?"

"Hello. Are you Bo?"

"Bo's my daddy. I'm Junior."

He smiled big, proving he still had about half his teeth. Junior looked more than 40 but less than 60, impossible to say exactly.

"You're not the law, are you?" he said with a laugh.

"No. Why would you ask that?"

"I don't really know. I've been half-expecting an undercover lawman to come about our magazines." He glanced around. "Somebody in this town always has to go and make trouble. As far as them magazines go, we don't sell nothin' with children or animals. Daddy's real strict about that. What we got is legal, just not for ever'body; that's why it's under the counter. We don't want nobody gettin' insulted at Bo's."

"Junior, the truth is that I'm a deputy sheriff, but I'm not here in that role. I must have 'deputy' stamped on my forehead."

He grinned at me. "You sure don't, but sometimes I pick up on things. I guess it's because I've been working with the public all my life."

"I don't care about your magazines, so don't worry."

"Good."

"I'd like to look at your handguns," I said to change the subject, and because I like them, but more because it would give us some common ground.

"Yup," he said with enthusiasm, "just step right over here, little lady."

His best ones were in a glass case that had seen better days. The guns were great, though; shiny, brand new, and alluring in their cold, potentially lethal way.

"It's okay to touch 'em," Junior said. "None of 'em is loaded."

I didn't need a handgun, but this wasn't about needing anything except information. I held them anyway and appreciated each one for its lines or its light weight or for whatever I could see to appreciate about it. My enthusiasm for and knowledge of them impressed Junior.

"Don't get many women in here that knows weapons," he said. "Course you bein' the law..." His comment trailed away.

"Don't Texas women have a reputation for being gun owners?"

"Yup, but around here the men buy them for the ladies." He was quick to add, "But I bet you'd want to pick it out your own self."

"Yes. A weapon is personal and should fit the person who's going to use it, don't you think?"

He nodded in solemn agreement. "What county you serve?"

"Brewster."

"Oh, you're way down by the Rio Grande. Do you have a lot of trouble with drugs and wetbacks and such?"

"Do you know Sheriff Hancock?" I asked to get him away from that.

"Well sure. Are you thinkin' about workin' for him?"

"What's he like?"

"Aw, he's a good ol' boy, one of our best customers."

I wondered which of the items the sheriff bought the most often.

"Is he a fair guy, you think?"

Junior considered. "Well, *fair* ain't exactly the word. For example, he wouldn't hire you because of you bein' a female, especially such a young female. No offense to you, sugar. We're talking 'bout the sheriff, not me. I have diff'rent views on things."

"What about being Latina?"

Junior blushed scarlet. "Well, I didn't want to say that, but yes, if you're talkin' about the sheriff. He don't care for Mexicans or blacks or mixed races of any type. You might notice we don't have a lot of them people here."

"He has a reputation for not caring for gay people, either."

Junior shook his head in wonderment. "Lord, don't get him started on that subject. He'd shoot homosexuals if he could get away with it. Now me, I don't care what people do, long as they're adults and have a say about what they're doing. But Sheriff Hancock, he—he thinks—different."

"Do people here fear the sheriff?"

"To some extent, I suppose." Junior looked around. "I don't badmouth him, though. I don't want my business burnt to the ground."

Just when I was getting somewhere, a customer came in and Junior had to leave me to wait on him. I set the handguns back in their display stands or boxes and wandered over to the boots and hunting clothes. All I saw in footwear were steel-toed boots for work, hunting boots, and cowboy boots with no style selection. He had nothing for women, or not this woman anyhow.

While I perused the boots, a man about my age sidled up to me.

"Finding anything?" he asked.

"I was looking for something a bit more stylish."

He laughed. "Not much here for women, unless ya hunt."

I moved down a way and he followed. "Dang, you're beautiful," he said as he looked over the boots with me.

"Thank you." *Go on, now.*

"You don't live here, do you?"

"No, I'm passing through."

"We could go for a drink."

"No; but thank you."

"I'd love to see what the rest of you looks like."

"Seriously? You get much action with that line?"

"Well, not much."

The other guy called, "Eddie!"

"Comin' Earl," he yelled. Then he turned back to me, "Gotta go. Last chance to drink and dance with a local boy."

"I have to pass this time," I said.

I sat on a faded red plastic chair and wondered if Sheriff Hancock was who people feared; it had to be. He'd had a major role in what happened to Randy, so he'd have a reason to keep the trial and everything surrounding it under wraps. Perhaps he still protected the guilty man, and that's what made people afraid.

Junior had more visitors, but they didn't stay long, mostly beer and bait customers, and they knew what they wanted. Eventually he found me at the boots try-on area.

"Do you have any sexy boots in the back, Junior?" I asked.

He reddened. "No. Sorry."

"What about under the counter?" I asked just to mess with him.

He became flustered and a shade darker. "No, no boots under there."

"Back to the sheriff, then."

"Let's drop that."

"But you were saying something about businesses burning down."

"Nuh-uh, little lady, I didn't say that."

"Is he who everyone is afraid of?"

"You should meet him." Junior's brow wrinkled in thought. "Hey! Ask him for a job. For all I know, he's had a change of heart." He said it, but he didn't believe it.

"Yes, I will." *As if.*

He scratched his head thoughtfully. "I hope you do get hired. Come back here if you do, and I'll give you the lawman's discount on anything in the store. I could order some of them sexy boots if you show me a pitcher of what it is you want."

"Thank you, Junior, I'll keep that in mind."

***

It was a few minutes after one-thirty. I felt hungry, which made me think of Barney, who always wants to eat. I called to see if anything new had developed in Terlingua.

"How are things going with you?" he asked.

"The people here realize that Randy was innocent, but they're afraid to talk."

"What's that about?"

"I wish I knew. I don't know if they're scared of the boogeyman or somebody real. Did you find out anything else about Limping Man?"

"No, but he seems to be gone from here."

"Did you talk to Rod Florence or Tom?"

"They claim innocence and neither admits to knowing a limping man. I could drag them in and beat the truth out of them if you want."

"When I suggest using rough tactics, you always throw the sheriff in my face, or the law, or even human decency."

"That's because none of those things support the use of violence."

"Unless you're doing it."

"I can't do it, either. But for the record, I want to."

"Oh yeah; I'd like to shoot a few people here."

"I hope you don't have a weapon."

When I failed to reply immediately, he said, "Aw, hell. I should've assumed that you do."

We signed off, and then my phone rang again. The rehab center in Midland was calling on behalf of Jacob Rawlings. He didn't feel up to seeing anyone today. They were sorry and blah, blah, blah.

* * *

I rode into the heart of town, looking for a café with home cooking or at least something that looked interesting. I spotted a place on Main Street called "Minnie's Main Street Diner," and in front of it sat a Sheriff's Office vehicle. Deputies, I felt sure. I wasn't ready for a run-in with the sheriff, but deputies might be helpful.

I parked my car a couple of blocks away. When I entered, I headed for a booth near the back because it would take me right past the deputies. Two young, uniformed men sat together with no sign of a sheriff.

I stopped at their table, all smiles and friendliness. "Hello, Deputies. I thought I should stop and say hello because I work as a deputy, too."

"No kidding?"

"No kidding."

"Would you like to join us?"

"That would be nice," I said with a smile. I took his extended hand and introduced myself. The other man also stood and shook my hand, and then they indicated I should sit. I slipped into the booth beside the one named Ronald James Strait or 'Ronnie Jim' to his friends.

"What brings you from—?"

"Brewster County," I said.

"Brewster County," he repeated softly.

A waitress appeared, and the guys suggested the special, which was meatloaf with mashed potatoes and green beans. I ordered iced tea and a special with no meat and extra veggies. That flustered her and my dining companions for a few minutes, but everyone recovered.

"So where is Brewster County?" asked the deputy sitting across from me, Nick Findley.

"You know where it is, Nick," said Ronnie Jim. "It's down there on the border. It's the largest county in the state. It sits right up against the Rio Grande, doesn't it? And Big Bend National Park is down there, too."

"Yes; you're correct on all counts."

"That's the most beautiful place in Texas. My family used to go there to camp sometimes when I was a kid."

"You didn't say why you're here," Nick reminded me.

"I'm here doing some private investigating for a friend. I didn't come as a deputy."

"Do you need help?" Ronnie Jim seemed eager and then, "What kind of investigating?"

Both guys were around my age, so they probably weren't deputies seven years ago. Still, they might be able to help me find whatever evidence there was from the trial. It had to be in storage, and they might be convinced to let me look for it.

Instead of answering Ronnie Jim's question, I asked him one. "Who is your sheriff?"

"Gil Hancock. He's been here for a hundred years."

"Careful, Ronnie Jim."

"He's not here," said Ronnie Jim with a big grin. "He's gone for the week, but we could help you with whatever you need."

"That'd be great. I'm working on an old case of rape."

"How old?"

"It happened seven years ago."

Nick leaned across the table and whispered, "Was Sheriff Hancock involved?"

"I don't know. I only know he was the sheriff then."

"Are you thinking he did it?"

I hadn't considered that.

"I didn't say that," I said. "Do you think he would rape someone?"

"Prob'ly not, I was just asking."

"Maybe he could still get it up seven years ago," mused Ronnie Jim.

"Ronnie Jim! You're talking about our sheriff."

"Sorry. I didn't mean to be crude," Ronnie Jim said.

"Don't worry about it." I leaned in close. "What I need is to see that evidence, which I feel certain would be in storage. I don't know if the prosecutor's office would have it or if your office has it."

"The old evidence files are kept in our basement," said Nick with pride, as if it had been his idea.

Ronnie Jim leaned closer. "If you're not here as a deputy, then what are you here as?"

"I'm working as a private investigator."

"We'll do what we can to help you, okay?"

"Thank you," I said. "Thanks a lot."

Whatever had everyone else cowering didn't seem to faze the two deputies. Were they fearless or clueless?

Our food arrived, and our attention turned to that for a while. It tasted delicious, but I gave half of mine to the guys because in addition to what was mentioned, the meal came with a salad, a homemade yeast roll, and the diner's specialty, pecan pie. I wanted to have room for that pie.

"When do you want to look for the evidence?" asked Nick.

"I'll come by later this afternoon. Would 3:30 work?"

"Sure. Just come to our office when you're ready. We'll be there unless something exciting happens."

The men looked at each other and laughed.

"Do you have a lot of excitement here?" I asked.

"Not really," said Ronnie Jim. "You're the most exciting thing that's happened since I've been working here."

I laughed, thanked them, and got out of there.

CHAPTER 15

Judge Washburn's office was on the second floor of the picturesque 19th century courthouse in Simpson, 15 miles from Carterton. I felt every bite of the Minnie's Diner homemade lunch as I climbed the stairs.

I expected to speak with the snarly secretary, but a man stood behind her desk, looking out the window. He wore pressed blue jeans with a sports coat, not an unusual sight in West Texas courts. However, a ponytail of pitch black hair stuck down the back of his clothes *was* unusual. As if a ponytail wasn't non-conformist enough, a tiny silver hoop glinted in one ear lobe. It was so tiny I wouldn't have noticed it if I hadn't been checking him out so diligently. He looked around as I approached and turned to face me. His severe expression softened when I smiled at him.

"Are you Deputy Ricos?"

Uh-oh. I'd forgotten that I'd given the judge, his secretary, and Ruby Halverson the name "Deputy Ricos" before Sheriff Ben spoke with me about not using that title.

I swallowed hard. "I'm Margarita Ricos, and I'm here to see Judge Washburn."

"I'm Judge Washburn." He offered his hand. "Glad to meet you."

I took his hand. "I'm serious," I said with a laugh, "I'm here to see the judge."

In rural west Texas, I expected a grumpy old white man in a black robe and with a bad attitude, not pierced ears. And no ponytail or high Native American cheekbones.

"I'm Judge Washburn," the man repeated, intent on his little joke.

I smiled big. I'd play along for now.

He indicated we should step into the adjoining office and invited me to sit in a chair across from a large desk. He sat in a leather chair that was surely the judge's. He had cojones, this joker.

He clasped his hands on the desk and stared at me. "Are you the woman who threatened me with a subpoena?"

My face got horribly hot, and I've never wanted so much to disappear into thin air. "I hoped you'd forget that, Your Honor."

"I haven't forgotten it. I don't like to be threatened, Deputy Ricos."

His look was fierce and intimidating. Give me an old, grumpy white man any day.

I coughed and false-started, but I couldn't form a complete sentence.

"Under what authority would you subpoena me?"

"I don't know, Your Honor. I apologize for threatening you. Your secretary gave me such a hard time that I..." My voice trailed away.

"Jeanie went to bring Ruby Halverson," the man said, appearing to let me off the hook. "I'm sure she has some answers for us by now."

"Yes, sir, I hope so, but I think the transcript has been purposefully removed."

"What makes you think that?"

"Mrs. Halverson lied to me about a fire."

"That's what you said on the phone. We'll ask her about that when she gets here."

"I need the transcript because I think it'll prove my friend had a bogus trial and went to prison for someone else's crime. Then someone covered up the whole mess."

Anger flashed in his black eyes. "Oh, so that's what you think?"

I nodded. Why can't I just keep my mouth shut?

"And you came to this conclusion how? By talking to the ex-con?"

"Well, yes, but I believe him."

His look softened. "Maybe you've been misled."

"If Ruby or anyone else finds that transcript, then we'll see how misled I am."

"It's early to presume someone removed it."

"It's still missing, isn't it?"

"I'm afraid it is," he admitted.

"No matter how long you search I don't believe you'll find it. The trial was a joke, and someone didn't want anyone to be able to prove it."

He leaned towards me, his gorgeous skin reddening with anger. "That's a serious accusation. You're in a courthouse speaking to a judge."

"I know, and I don't mean any disrespect to you, Your Honor. I think Judge Carter manipulated the trial and had the transcript removed. I know I have more work to do, but I believe I can prove that."

"Ms. Ricos, you weren't at the trial. You're not investigating based only on the convict's word, are you? You know those guys lie, right?"

"I know they lie, but I don't believe he's lying. So far, I've spoken to two people who corroborate his story."

The judge rose. "Please excuse me for a moment. I'll be right back."

I watched him leave. His hair was beautiful, and I thought it was wrong to hide it. But he was a judge in Redneckville and probably had to. Once he was out of sight, there was nothing to look at except for a frightening number of law books and the courtyard. I could see it from the window behind his desk. Roses bloomed in every imaginable shade of red and pink, commanding attention, like the judge.

My mind wandered, but it soon came back to Judge Washburn's long, shiny, black hair and stern, native face. *Ay Dios,* was he really the judge?

He spoke to me, and I might as well have been in Terlingua.

"I'm sorry, sir. I was thinking about something else."

"Your look was far-away."

"I apologize." For a moment I was afraid I'd sighed or drooled on myself.

"I said that when—oh, Jeanie—" He greeted someone I couldn't see. "Here they are now."

Two women entered the room. One was mid-30s in age; the other was at least double that.

"Ms. Ricos, this is Jeanie Wilson, my assistant, and Mrs. Ruby Halverson, our Clerk of Court."

I stood and shook their hands. Mrs. Halverson barely grazed my hand and didn't look directly at me, the old biddy. They sat when the judge invited them to.

"Ruby, what happened to that file?" Washburn asked. It was obvious she wasn't carrying it.

Ruby picked at her wavy gray hair. "I don't know, Your Honor. We've turned the records section upside down looking for it, and we've found nothing."

"Files don't just walk off. There's a system in place, which you know better than anyone. It must be there somewhere, Ruby, if it's not checked out."

"It hasn't been checked out. It's just not there, sir."

"Mrs. Halverson," I said, "when I called you to ask for a copy of the transcript, you informed me the courthouse had burned to the ground five years ago, and all the old records were destroyed. Why did you do that?"

She looked at me because she had to. "I apologize. I panicked when you asked for it."

"Explain that, Ruby," ordered the judge.

She looked from me to him several times. "Okay. I've known for a long time the transcript was missing. I always hoped nobody else would find out. I didn't want to be blamed for it."

"You don't think it could simply be misfiled?" asked the judge in a gentle voice, and with a quick glance in my direction.

"No, sir, it's not misfiled. It was taken by someone soon after the trial ended. I noticed it missing and never said anything."

"That makes you an accessory to whatever miscarriage of justice happened here, Ruby. You should have reported it."

The old woman looked stricken. "I know that, Your Honor, but we had another judge then, and he was—he was different from you."

"Different in what way?"

"He did things during the Green trial as if he had the final say, no matter what the law said. I became afraid of him. Nearly everyone who worked for him was. I knew he was doing wrong, but I couldn't afford to lose my job because my husband was sick. He couldn't work for almost a year, and I had to work, sir."

"You suspect Judge Carter took the file?" Judge Washburn asked.

"Yes, I know he did, or he had it taken."

Ah hah!

We all stared at Ruby. "There was something wrong about the trial, Your Honor," she said. "I don't doubt that boy's guilt, but his trial wasn't right. He was a known deviant and certainly not a Christian man, but according to the law, everyone should have a fair trial, even homosexuals."

The judge and I exchanged a glance. I had the impression he didn't care for that comment, either.

"Ruby, would you be willing to make a sworn statement that you had nothing to do with the removal of the file? And that you suspect Judge Carter took it?"

"Yes, sir, I'd swear to it on the Bible."

"Good. Well, you may have to before this is over."

The judge turned his piercing eyes to me. I expected—something.

"Ruby and Jeanie, you may go," he finally said. "Thank you both." He got up and shut the door behind them. Then he took out a handkerchief. "Let me wipe the egg off my face, and we'll talk."

I laughed at that.

Judge Washburn took a deep breath. "Please start at the beginning and tell me everything you know about this case, starting with how you got involved in it."

"I'll do that, but first I need to say that I'm not here as a deputy from Brewster County."

"You do work as a deputy, though?"

"Yes, but my sheriff didn't assign me to this investigation. I'm doing it on my own because I believe in Randall Green. And I believe in justice, Judge Washburn."

"All right. Go ahead."

He sat back in his big chair and gave me his full attention. The man seemed intelligent and thoughtful and only interrupted with perceptive questions. He understood the grave wrong that had likely happened if half what I said was true.

"What's your next move, Ms. Ricos?"

"I'm going to look for the physical evidence in the county's storage. It may be futile, but I won't know until I try."

"I'll get a full statement from Ruby. Jeanie will notarize it, and it'll be ready for you to pick up later in the day."

"Will you call me when it's ready?" I handed him my card.

"Sure, I'll have Jeanie call you. Did the sheriff mention whether or not he has the evidence?"

"I haven't spoken with him. He's out of town."

"I think you should be careful doing anything behind his back. He can be—difficult, our sheriff."

"Yes. I've heard that."

"Don't step on his toes."

"No, sir. I won't. Thank you for your help, Your Honor."

"You're a hell of a friend to have. I hope Randall Green appreciates you." He started to say something else but changed his mind. "Adiós, Margarita Ricos," he said instead.

***

I headed over to the Freeman County Sheriff's Office, where my new buddies hurled spitballs at each other and otherwise goofed off.

"About your evidence," said Nick when I walked in, "the sheriff called, and we asked him about it. He says the evidence from that trial is stored somewhere else."

"Did he say where?"

"No, he didn't. He's angry that a deputy from another county has asked for it."

"Why would he be angry? Anybody in law enforcement should be able to access old evidence."

"You don't know our sheriff. He doesn't like other law enforcement people to meddle in his county."

"I'm not meddling. Also, I'm not here as a deputy. Please remember that. I'm an investigator trying to clear an innocent man. Did you mention that?"

"Yeah, but he 'bout took my head off. He thinks you're insulting his integrity."

Ronnie Jim hadn't said a word, and I wondered why. "Why are you so quiet?" I asked.

"I think we should help you anyway. The sheriff's not even here."

Nick whirled around. "If you want to lose your job then go ahead; but leave me out of it."

"I don't want either of you to lose your jobs," I said.

"I know the box is in the basement," said Ronnie Jim sulkily. "We could let her look at it. Nobody has to know."

"Do you know that for a fact, or is it a guess?" I asked.

"Every other file for the last ten years is down there. Older files are stored in the courthouse basement. It'd have to be in our basement."

Not necessarily. If the evidence proved Randy's innocence, it was probably removed the same time as the transcript. I thought of a new tack and then dropped it. These guys provided a direct line to Sheriff Hancock. I had no reason to rile him over something I could check out with the good-looking judge.

"Thank you for trying to help me," I said. "I hope I didn't get you in trouble."

"Naw, you didn't," said Nick.

"Keep in mind that *I* would've helped you look for it," said Ronnie Jim.

"Thank you, Ronnie Jim."

"What did you think of our Injun Judge?" asked Nick.

That slur made me angry, but I was about to get out of there and would probably never have to see them again. Since Nick asked, I answered him. "I think he is too young and interesting to be a judge. I love his hair."

* * *

I sat in my car trying to figure out what to do next. Jeanie Wilson called from Judge Washburn's office to say that the signed statement from Ruby Halverson was ready for me to pick up. I asked if I could see the judge, and she said of course, but I needed to make an appointment.

"That's what I'm trying to do." She meant in advance, more advance than ten minutes, I guess. "I know this isn't far in advance, but it is in advance."

"He's busy," she said with enough snip to shorten my hair. "Couldn't you speak to him by telephone?"

"I'm coming over there anyway. Will you please ask him if he'll see me?"

She huffed as though my time with him would come out of her pay. "I'll see what he says about it."

After making me wait a long time, she came back on the line. "He says to come on. Can you be here in fifteen minutes?"

It wouldn't take that long. I was sitting in front of the sheriff's office next door.

Jeanie was cordial in an aloof way. Now that I had seen her judge, I figured she had a thing for him, and I couldn't blame her. She handed me Ruby's signed statement and led me to her boss's office. "Ms. Ricos is here, sir."

He looked up from his desk and smiled at me.

I forgot why I had come.

"Would you like to sit down?"

I sat, but I didn't know what to say.

"Ms. Ricos?"

"I want to ask you something." Whatever it was, I'd lost it. In the nick of time, I made an acceptable save. "It's about the crime lab."

"What would you like to know?"

"Which crime lab does local law enforcement use?"

"They use the Texas DPS lab in Midland and sometimes the one in El Paso. Why do you ask?"

"I spoke with two deputies this afternoon. They intended to let me hunt for the evidence from Randy Green's trial, but the sheriff called. When they mentioned it to him, he said it was kept in a different location. He didn't like it that I was there asking about it."

"Are you here for a warrant?"

"No. I guess the evidence has been removed, and I don't want to tip off the sheriff that I suspect anything. I can ask the crime lab to look up the results on Randy's DNA test."

"That's true, but they move slowly."

"I didn't think I could get a warrant because I don't have proof of anything yet."

"That's true. I didn't offer you a warrant, only asked if that was why you came."

"That's mean. You dangled it in front of me and then jerked it away."

"That's not so. I didn't offer you a warrant, therefore I never dangled one."

"Oh, it was dangled all right."

"No, it wasn't."

I chewed my lip. "I'm not going to win this, am I?"

He laughed. "Probably not even worth trying."

Jeanie put a stop to kidding around with her judge. She appeared in the doorway and sucked the humor from the room. "Mayor Tillman is here,

Your Honor."

I stood and extended my hand. "Thank you, Your Honor."

He took my hand. "I hope I'll see you again."

"You will when I come back for that warrant you dangled."

He laughed and then went back to looking stern.

***

I sprawled on the bed in my room. I didn't want to do one more thing, but I called the crime lab in Midland to ask about seven-year-old evidence. I spoke with three people before I got to one who thought he could help me.

"You should be able to get that information from the files of the prosecutor's office, if you know which county."

"I know that's true, but they claim the file is missing. You retain copies of your findings, don't you?"

"Yes, but it'll take me a while to locate them."

I explained again what I needed and thanked him, made sure he had my phone number, and fell back against the bed. I missed my puppy. She never failed to lift my spirits with her enthusiastic and unfailing love.

I tried to call Billy, then Randy, and got no answer from either. So, I did what I often do when confused, frustrated, or bored. I went for a run.

I felt nearly tired enough to quit when a Sheriff's Office vehicle pulled onto the highway from a side road. I kept running and expected it to pass but, when I glanced back, it crept along behind me. I figured it was one or both deputies out for some fun.

After a while, I decided to bring their game to a halt. I stopped, turned back, and walked towards the vehicle. It pulled up next to me.

"Don't you have something better to do?" I blurted before I realized the driver wasn't either of the deputies.

"No, ma'am, I don't. Not right now," drawled a menacing old man. I assumed he was Sheriff Hancock. "As a matter of fact, I was looking for you."

"Oh?"

He didn't explain and instead stared rudely. It made my skin crawl.

"Who are you, and why are you looking for me?"

He still didn't answer, so I gave him the look-over he was giving me.

The nametag on his uniform read *Hancock*, so that much was settled. An impressive gut challenged the waistband of his uniform pants, and one cheek bulged, chipmunk-style. His pudgy hand held a small coffee cup that he occasionally spit brown goo into. In short, Sheriff Hancock lacked the sharp, professional look I was accustomed to in a sheriff. And for the record, he wasn't wearing a seatbelt.

When he smiled, it was not reflected in his hard, brown eyes. "Deputy Ricos?"

How did he know that? "Yes, I'm Margarita Ricos."

"Get in." It was more of an order than an invitation.

I didn't want to get into a vehicle with him, especially since I was underdressed. "I need to get cleaned up. Could I come see you in the morning?"

"You're seeing me now. I want to talk to you before tomorrow."

"What's happening tomorrow?"

"You're leaving."

"Oh?"

"You brought me back from a fishing trip," he said. If he was trying for ominous, he hit the mark.

"I hope you didn't have to come far."

"Get in, or would you rather I sent a deputy to fetch you after a while?"

I got in.

"I was over at the lake," he said and made it sound as though *the lake* wasn't far. A lake would explain Bo's Bait—sort of. Regardless of the distance he had come to "see about" me, he wasn't happy about it. "We'll go to my office," he said. "We can speak more comfortably there."

"That's fine." I doubted it would be any more comfortable.

"So, you're a deputy in Brewster County?"

"Yes, sir, but please understand that I'm not here as a deputy."

"How long have you worked as a deputy?"

"About five years, but I'm not here as a deputy."

"Who is your sheriff?"

"Benjamin Duncan."

"He's been there quite a while, hasn't he?"

"Yes."

"I don't know him, but I've heard his name mentioned. He has a good reputation."

"Yes, he does. He's a great sheriff."

He nodded and spit into the cup.

Once we settled in his office, Sheriff Hancock lost all semblance of friendliness. "It's come to my attention that you were trying to coerce my deputies into breaking the law today." His voice sounded normal, but his look was dark and made me nervous. This, I thought, is the man making everyone afraid.

"I didn't break any laws," I said.

"You showed up without a warrant and demanded to see evidence that my deputies don't have my permission to show you." He practically growled at me. "I'm not sure what you expected, but I called in before harm was done."

"First of all, I never demanded anything. Secondly, what harm?"

"What reason do you have to see seven-year-old evidence?"

"In my county, we cooperate with other law enforcement agencies."

"In my county, there's a certain protocol."

"I understand that. I did ask permission. You're acting as though I broke in and stole it. I spoke with your deputies, and at first they agreed to let me see it."

"My deputies don't speak for me."

What? The point of deputizing is to bestow the powers and responsibilities of the sheriff to others who can help. But he knew that.

Hancock shifted his weight in the chair, making it groan. "I have it on good authority that you've been consorting with our new judge." His tone was accusatory, and he stared at my legs as he spoke. It was as if he dared me to make him stop and, believe me, I wanted to.

"Of course," he drawled, "a woman like you can get things done."

"What are you implying?"

"I'm not implying anything. I want to know what you want here, what you took from here, and how you got my men involved."

"I didn't take anything! I asked your deputies for help and they offered it. They didn't think they were doing anything wrong. To answer your question about why I'm here, it's because I'm trying to help a friend. He went to prison for a crime he didn't commit."

"I know that's what you told my men, but I take offense at that."

"I don't see why the truth would offend you."

"Your friend Mr. Green was judged in a court of law and found guilty. There was nothing unfair about his trial, no matter what he may have said to you or what you may believe. I've been working in law enforcement a long time, Ms. Ricos, and I resent you coming here to make accusations that indicate I didn't do my job. And worse, you made these claims to my employees."

"All I said was that justice hadn't been done in Randy's case."

"And you don't consider the county sheriff a part of the justice system?"

"I do, of course. What I mean is that I never said you'd done anything wrong."

"But you thought you could sneak around in my basement to look for seven-year-old evidence that does not concern you."

"I had no intention of sneaking, and I never went in your basement, so what harm has been done?"

"None, I suppose."

"Do you have the evidence from that case or not?"

"I don't. The file box has been misplaced."

"The trial transcript has also been misplaced."

"I don't know anything about that."

"Do you have a copy of it?"

"No, I don't, but I'm sure it's there. It's probably misfiled."

"Ruby admitted that someone removed it shortly after the trial ended. She knew it but was afraid to tell the judge. Do you have any idea who took it?"

"Ruby is lying to cover her butt. She's become more and more forgetful the last few years. All of us hope she'll retire soon."

"She says someone took the file seven years ago, Sheriff. Judge Washburn seemed to believe her."

"Frankly, I'm not impressed by our judge. What he believes or doesn't believe doesn't matter to me."

"He's still the judge, though, and he doesn't have to impress you."

His eyes narrowed and grew cold as glaciers.

I changed the subject. "I wish you would tell me why DNA evidence wasn't presented by an expert during the trial."

He rose, making his knees creak instead of the chair. I prepared to run. Instead of attacking me, he asked, "What makes you think it wasn't? You've already said you don't have a copy of the transcript."

"Sheriff Hancock, what are you saying?"

"Green's semen was all over that poor little girl."

"If that's true, why wasn't it presented by an expert from the crime lab?"

"You weren't there, and you don't know anything about it. If you'd been there, you would've been as horrified as the rest of us."

"You didn't answer my question."

"How the hell am I supposed to remember the details of a trial from seven years ago? A lot has happened in the last seven years."

The old liar was about to make my hair stand on end. As I watched him, I could only think of the beatings and abuse he had heaped on Randy.

I decided to speed things along. "Why don't you tell me your view of what happened?"

"The semen belonged to Randall Green. We didn't make it public because people were incensed, and we feared for his life. You can only protect a prisoner so far, even when he's in custody."

"Randall Green was in your jail awaiting trial, wasn't he?"

"Yes, that's right."

"And you and your deputies abused him."

"I don't like your tone. I'm a man of the law, no matter what false things you've dreamed up in your head. I protect all my prisoners, no matter what they've done or how I feel about it."

"You didn't protect Randy Green from sexual abuse by a deputy, and you beat him so badly he had to be taken to the hospital twice."

"He exposed himself to my deputy, who was only trying to do his job. You probably haven't been around queers much, but they go by a different set of moral standards than you and I."

If he hadn't been such an old man, I'd have jumped him. "I know Randy was abused by your deputy. You fired him because of it."

"You have been lied to, little lady."

"We're finished here."

"We're done when I say we're done." He groaned as though I was stressing him out. He collapsed back into his chair and began drumming a pencil on the desk. "I want you to go back to your county in the morning. I intend to file a formal complaint against you."

"Sheriff Hancock, I'm not here as a deputy. My sheriff will tell you that." There was nothing else to say, so I got up to go.

"Hey. Aren't you Mexican?"

"No; I'm an American, born in Alpine, Texas. I prefer to describe myself as a human being."

"Ooohwee, you got a mouth on you." He spit a brown glob into the cup. "I'd like to knock you down a peg or three."

And I wish you would try. I had my hand on the door by then.

"I don't want you to come back here for any reason," he snarled. "You think you can come here and shove people around? This is *my* county. I expect you to return to yours. You have no business here. Your friend raped that child no matter what fanciful scenario you've come up with. Randy Green raped her, and it ruined her life."

"My friend did not rape anyone, and you know it."

"If I was your sheriff, I'd get shed of you today."

"If you were my sheriff, I'd have found another job by now."

"Damn, that mouth of yours will get you in trouble. Listen. Don't bring that queer back to this town. We don't want him. I hope that's clear enough for you, *little lady*."

CHAPTER 16

I jogged back to my room, pulled the curtains shut, and checked my Beretta. I wasn't going to shoot the sheriff, but it made me feel better to know I could.

My phone rang, causing me to jump. The man from the lab said he couldn't find anything regarding the trial of Randall M. Green. He thought I'd given him the wrong case number. He suggested calling the El Paso lab, but it was after five o'clock, so that would have to wait.

I took a shower and felt better, less like killing people. To quote Barney, "You can't shoot a person just because they're an asshole, or there'd be a lot of dead assholes."

I called Sheriff Ben to warn him about a call from Sheriff Hancock, but I had to leave a message.

After that, I dressed in blue jeans, a purple blouse, and brown leather boots. Dancing was on my mind, and mingling with the locals.

And maybe one beer, I thought as I entered Forever Five O'Clock. Loud cry-in-your-beer music played on the jukebox. Couples danced, laughed, and drank. The smell of sawdust and stale beer mixed with the clinking of glasses and bottles screamed "bad idea." I stood for a few seconds arguing with the obstinate part of me that still believes, after all the proof to the contrary, that I can have one beer and go home.

I wheeled around and practically flew out the door. I smacked head-on into Judge Washburn. He grabbed me and staggered backward but made a nice save.

"Oh, Judge, I'm so sorry! I nearly knocked you down."

"It's my fault."

"I had to get out of there."

"Is the place on fire?"

"No, but I had to leave."

"But you just got here."

"How do you know that?" I had no trust for anybody in Carterton. Judges can be just as evil and twisted as anyone else.

Before I got far along that line of panic, he said, "I, uh, well, you see. It's that—"

"What?"

"I saw you running."

Was everybody in this town following me?

"I went to turn around and came back, but you had disappeared. So, I've been looking for your car."

"Why?"

"Because I assumed you'd be driving it."

"Is there a problem?"

"I hoped to find you."

"Is it because of the sheriff? He stopped me, not the other way around. Why not call my cell phone if you need to talk to me?"

"Frankly, I didn't think of that." He glanced around. "Could we move this conversation out of the doorway?"

I pointed to a bench in front of the building. "Should we sit?"

"Yes." Judge Washburn took me gently by the arm, and we moved a few feet to the bench and sat. He took a deep breath. "I was looking for you because I wanted to ask you out."

I didn't see how anything in Freeman County could surprise me, but that did. "You mean like on a date?" I sounded like a teenager and not even a smart one.

"Yes. Would you go out with me, Ms. Ricos?"

"Um. Well. Yes."

"Would you like to go in and dance?" He indicated the country joint.

"Yes—I mean—no."

"It has to be one or the other."

"I'm sorry. No, I don't want to go back in there."

"Why did you run out?"

"Oh. Well. I had a bad feeling about the place."

"Meaning you don't want to tell me."

"Could you forget it for now? We could do something else. What do you like to do for fun in this town?"

"I like to restore old trucks and cars."

"Okay, not that."

He laughed. "We could start with dinner. Have you eaten?"

"No."

"Do you like Italian food?"

"I like all food."

"I know a nice place that's just a short drive from here."

"Should I change my clothes?"

"No. You look great, Deputy Ricos."

"Hold on. You can't ask a woman on a date and call her "deputy." My name is Margarita. Deputy Ricos is—well, half the time I don't know who she is, and besides, I'm not here as her."

"Oh, true. You said that before. Please call me Joe."

"It seems weird to call a judge by his first name."

"Don't think of me as a judge. I'm also a man."

"Right; I figured that out already. I'm sharper than I seem."

He laughed. "I'm only Judge Washburn at work. At home I'm more fun. You'll like Joe better than the judge, trust me." He took out his phone and said, "Excuse me for a minute while I make a reservation."

His hair hung outside his shirt in a thick braid. He was dressed casually in jeans and a yellow, long-sleeved cotton shirt. He also wore silver wire earrings that were so delicate as to be barely noticeable. You had to look closely to see them.

He led me to a spotless, restored, green Ford truck from the fifties or sixties. I wasn't sure.

"This is what I do in my spare time," he said when he opened the door for me.

"It's beautiful."

"It's a 1956 model. We'll go in this or, if you'd rather, we could stop at my place and get the Lexus."

"I like this a lot," I said.

"That's good, because I think of the Lexus as the judge's ride."

"How did you get to be a judge so young? I thought judges were old and mean."

"I guess it depends on who you talk to you about the mean part. About the young part, I'm forty. That's not young compared to you."

"I'm not as young as I look."

"Really? How old are you?"

"Twenty-eight."

"In that case, I have bad news. You look younger."

He moved us onto the Interstate and picked up speed.

"I guess you became a judge by working hard and excelling in your work."

"That's true. I like to apply myself."

"I'm guilty of that, too."

A short time passed in silence.

"You have a beautiful name, Margarita."

"Thank you, Joe."

"I want to tell you something I haven't told anyone in a long time. My birth name is Joseph Redhorse. I took 'Washburn' in college because of prejudice against native persons by people who'd never even met me. And to me, Wash-burn sounds like an acceptable Comanche name, but not as in-your-face as Redhorse."

"So, you're Comanche?"

"Does it show?"

"It explains your hair."

He looked doubtful. "What do you know about the Comanche?"

"Not enough to impress you, I'm sure, but I know that traditionally the males don't cut their hair, and they wear multiple sets of earrings and paint their bodies."

"It's amazing you know that much. The history of my people is being lost and rewritten by the—wait. Don't get me started. Let's talk about you."

"The Comanche were fierce warriors. They used to make raids into Mexico and take horses and women. I guess they took anything they wanted."

"Are you going to hold that against me?"

"No; you didn't let me finish. The Comanche and Apache mixed it up with the native peoples in Mexico, for instance the Aztec, as well as the Spaniards that had settled there. What I'm trying to say is that Mexicans are a mixture of all kinds of native peoples and a few tough white guys."

He laughed. "I like your version of that better than any I've heard."

"As over-simplified as it may be."

"Well, at least it's true."

"My point is that, for all I know, I have some Comanche blood. When I'm angry, my father says the Comanche comes out, which used to seem funny, and I was proud of that, but now I feel I've just put my foot in my mouth."

He glanced over at me. "I sure do like you."

That stumped me. At least it got me to quit talking.

"Do you enjoy being a deputy?"

"Sometimes, but let's talk about something interesting."

"I find you interesting. The fact that you're in law enforcement is only a small part of it."

"I noticed there are no female deputies here."

"I know, and it's a shame."

"Your sheriff has some old-school ideas and not just regarding women."

He laughed. "You're not kidding."

"You need women to balance things out."

"Maybe you'd come to work here and straighten out these bubbas?"

"Are you kidding? I could never live in such a repressed place. There's too much backward thinking. I don't know how you stand it."

"Things are changing, albeit slowly."

"Could my friend Randy move back to Carterton and be accepted?"

"I don't know. It's a small place and things are slow to change. Simpson would be better, but even there, it's tough to be different. They're suspicious of me because I'm not sixty years old. I'm not from an old Freeman County family like the last judge, and my skin is too dark. Also, I've been seen in gym shorts, Great Spirit help us. I like to play handball and basketball, but worse than all that is my long hair and pierced ears. It's too much for them."

"Yeah, I thought you seemed a little untrustworthy."

"I'm not kidding. People think I can't possibly know the law unless I've been in it for forty years and have short hair and white skin. It's ridiculous." He breathed a long breath. "I'm sorry. I didn't mean to get into that."

"It's okay. I understand how you feel."

"Let's talk about something else."

"Do you know Larry Mills?"

"Sure. We play basketball together. How do you know him?"

Oh, crap. My mouth had opened before my brain had a chance to say *not that*.

I stalled for time. "I met him today."

"Did you just run into him or what?"

"No; you're the only man I tried to knock down today. I know him because of Randy. It's complicated."

"I know he's gay, if that's what's making you uncomfortable."

"Oh. That's a relief. I had the impression he was still in the closet."

"No, he came out several years ago, according to the gossip. It put the town on its ear for a few days until people realized he's their beloved basketball coach. They weren't about to give up their winning streak over what he does in his own bed."

"That's big of them."

"Yeah, they're broadminded like that."

"What do you think of Coach Mills?"

"He's a great guy and a superb coach. Not to mention his basketball playing skill is phenomenal."

"I saw a sample of that today."

"Why are we talking about Coach Mills?"

"He was Randy Green's lover until Randy went to prison."

"Oh. I had no idea. I had the impression Green was a much younger man."

"He is. He's twenty years younger than Larry. But with love, do you think age matters?"

"Well no, I'm quite sure it doesn't."

* * *

Gino's Ristorante Italiano was about ten miles outside of Carterton. It occupied a large brick house that sat alone on a lot surrounded by small oak and mesquite trees. It looked busy, with a packed parking area to the side of the building.

The aromas of basil, garlic, and cheese hit us at the door. I felt transported right into the heart of Italy. The main dining room was full of round tables for two and larger ones for four. Red checkered tablecloths covered them, and a candle burned at the center of each one. Other rooms stood to the side of the dining area and held larger tables and more people.

"I have a reservation," Joe said to the young host. "My name is Washburn."

"Yes, sir, right this way." The young man was dressed in a European style, with tight black pants, a black vest, and a blousy white shirt with puffy sleeves. He spoke in rapid Italian to an older man who passed us.

The host seated us at a table for two at the back of the room that was dimly lit and romantic. Almost immediately, a waiter brought two glasses and a bottle of red wine.

Nobody knows me here, I thought. It was only wine, and I wanted to drink it. Alcohol addiction is a sneaky, devious master. The last time I drank with a man I'd gone to bed with him, and I regretted it and would continue to regret it as long as state troopers continued to live and breathe in Brewster County.

"Joe, I don't care for wine."

"Would you prefer white or something else?"

"I'd like iced tea."

"Make that two, please," Joe said to the waiter.

"I can't drink wine," I said when the waiter left, "or anything else with alcohol. It's okay if you do, though."

"Truthfully, I like iced tea better than wine."

"I'm an alcoholic, Joe. It's hard to admit that to someone I just met. When I drink, I get in trouble."

"Is that why you fled Forever Five O'Clock?"

"Yes."

"Had you gone there to drink?"

"Apparently so."

A waiter brought tea and set a basket of warm Italian bread between us. The fragrance made my mouth water. I'm a breadaholic too, but a woman can't confess all her faults at one time to a man she barely knows.

"Are you involved with someone, Margarita?"

"No; I wouldn't be here if I was. What about you?"

"No. I'm not seeing anybody. Have you ever been married?"

"Yes, but my husband was killed in an accident a few years ago."

"Oh, I'm sorry. Do you have children?"

"No. What about you?"

"I was married, but my wife died of breast cancer seven years ago."

I hated this part of getting-to-know-you.

"I haven't dated much since Ruthie died, and I'm not good at it. The truth is I wanted to ask you out when I met you, but I was nervous you'd say no. I bring shame to my ancestors."

"Your ancestors would just grab a woman and ride like hell."

"Yes, but nowadays that's kidnapping and rape."

"It was kidnapping and rape back then too, but who was going to stop them and point that out?"

"Good point." He smiled and then took a sip of tea. "Let's ignore the ancestors before they give you the wrong impression."

"I hope you don't think I'm insulting your people. Sometimes my brain can't keep up with my mouth. Anyhow, I was joking. I'm no good at dating, so if you think you're nervous, double it."

***

The waiter returned, and since I hadn't looked at the menu, Joe suggested the vegetable lasagna. They made it with five different cheeses, but I only had to hear "lasagna," and I let him order it for me.

"Why don't you tell me about yourself? Who are you when you're not being a deputy?"

"First of all, I'm a woman."

"That, I know. I'm sure that even in a uniform that holds constant."

"It does, yes. At no point have I ever been a man."

He laughed.

"This is going to be a tough evening," I said. After a short pause, I blurted, "Could I touch your hair?"

Joe didn't say anything. Instead, he took my hand and touched it to his hair. It felt incredibly soft. Then he held my hand against his cheek. It was so affectionate I felt like crying. Then he barely touched my hand to his lips and set it back on the table.

I couldn't have spoken if my life depended on it. Someone came to refill the tea and left.

"Well? What do you think about my hair?"

"It's stunning. Your hair was the first thing I noticed about you. I guess you think I'm forward or crazy or both."

"I think you're amazing."

"But—"

"There's no *but* in my sentence, so please don't add one." He sounded so stern I tried to keep my mouth from opening again.

The waiter brought our food and it caused a momentary distraction.

"Since you're a judge, I assume you're an attorney?"

"That's true, but I hope you won't hold that against me, either."

"I don't have anything against attorneys," I said, "but I do know some great jokes. I won't tell them, though. I asked because I wondered how a person goes from working as an attorney to working as a judge."

"In my case, I was appointed to fill Judge Carter's term when he died. When his term runs out, I'll have to stand for re-election if I decide I want to. I have about as much chance of winning as a gay black man. They call me the Injun Judge."

"Yes, very clever, these local boys."

"You already heard it?"

"Yep; I'm sorry."

"You've been here *one day,* and you already heard it?"

"Keep in mind that I spent part of my day with the deputies Nick and Harry Bob or whatever his name is."

"The sheriff encourages their disrespect. I'm a Democrat and he thinks that's radical and subversive. And I don't go to any of the local churches, so I'm a heathen. Well, hell, I guess being Comanche makes me heathen. Around here, if you haven't accepted Christ as your personal savior, they think you're evil. I'm spiritual, but I'm not a Christian—and the way some Christians are acting these days it's a wonder regular people admit to being Christian. I hope I'm not stepping on your toes."

"You're not."

"I was coerced into going to the First Christian Church by a woman

I thought I wanted to date. I heard more hate coming out of there than if I'd gone to a Klan rally. I asked my friend 'where is the love?' I'm not an expert on Christianity, but I do know that Christ taught love and tolerance. Who did he hate? She had bought into all that 'Christ hates fags' crap. I didn't go out with her again." He took a deep breath. "You asked me a simple question and I ended up in church. How did that happen?"

"It's all right. I blame the sheriff since we were talking about him."

"He'll get his. He's trying to undermine me, but I have a few friends in high places. I'm going to cause some problems for him."

"Good. I want to see that. This dinner is delicious, by the way."

"I've had nearly everything on the menu and it's all good, but this is my favorite. The other thing I appreciate about this place is that Sheriff Hancock never comes here, nor do his deputies."

"They hate Italians too, I bet." I took a sip of tea, which I like, but wine would've taken the edge off. It was too late to ask for it, though.

"I feel sorry for people like them because they're missing the richness of life," Joe said. "Diversity makes things interesting, and we all have so much to learn from each other. Ah, well, enough of that."

"It's hard to feel pity for them, even though I know it's fear that keeps them so hateful and ignorant."

"The thing that irks the sheriff the most is my hair," Joe said. "He can't understand why a grown man wants a ponytail. I don't want one, but if I wore my hair down as I'd like, he'd call me a savage, a woman, or some other ignorant rant. I wear it inside my clothes out of respect for the white man's custom. But why should I? Nobody respects my customs, or even knows them."

I felt shaky just thinking of him with his hair down.

After speaking about many other things for a while, I asked, "What were you doing before you became a judge?"

"I worked in the Texas Supreme Court as a legal research consultant."

I put my head in my hands. "Please don't ask me what I did before I became a deputy. I think you asked out the wrong woman."

"I invited exactly the right woman. Don't question my taste because it brings out the Comanche in me."

I laughed at that.

"Do you like to dance, Margarita?"

"Yes."

"Do you care what kind?"

"No. I like every kind of dancing."

"I wish you'd teach me to Two-Step sometime. I can do a rain dance or a war dance, a wedding dance, or even a fertility dance, but I don't need any of that for dating Texas women."

"The Two-Step is easy. How did you escape learning it? Aren't you a Texan?"

"No," he whispered, "I was born and raised in Oklahoma, but I don't want that getting around. It'll bring me more grief than my hair."

"I won't tell anyone."

"I was raised on Comanche Nation lands. We were poor, so I never went any place where I could've learned to dance the Two Step until I went to college. There, I experienced culture shock and would've been mortified to dance in front of people. I married a woman who didn't like to dance, so I still didn't learn."

"How did a boy raised in poverty on a reservation in Oklahoma get himself to the Texas Supreme Court?"

"It started with books. After I'd read all the books in the library on the res, I started on the library in the nearby town." He took a sip of tea. "It's a long story, but the short answer is that I was a determined boy, and my grades were good enough to get me a scholarship to Oklahoma State University. After that, I went to the University of Texas School of Law in Austin."

"Who appointed you judge?"

"The governor appointed me." Joe took my hand. "May I take you dancing, Margarita?"

"At Forever Five O'Clock?"

"We won't go near the liquor, I promise. I'll hold you so close you won't be able to make a move towards the bar."

I took a deep breath. That sounded pretty good.

CHAPTER 17

We got as far as the parking lot of Forever Five O'Clock and the kissing started. It began with his hair, and I accept the blame. I have nothing to say in my defense. I reached to touch it and Joe pulled me close and kissed me, and then we didn't stop kissing for a long time. I learned something important that evening. Sometimes I blame alcohol for things that aren't its fault.

When we got to my hotel, I freaked out. Joe invited me to come to his condo, but my panic wasn't about where. It was about trust more than anything. I had none, and it wasn't even on backorder.

"This isn't easy for me," Joe said, "if that's what you're thinking."

It wasn't.

"If you think I'm a run-around-Joe, think again."

"That's not what I think at all."

"Well what *do* you think?"

"I've been through hell, and I can't do this right now."

"Did your husband hurt you?"

"No, but I do have trust issues."

"Not all men are liars and cheats—or violent."

"I know that in my head, but my gut hasn't gotten it yet."

Thunder rolled, and a flash of lightning illuminated his rugged native face. *Take a chance on this man,* my sane voice begged. But I wasn't sure if the sane voice had spoken or my libido.

"So...what are you saying, Margarita? Is this good-bye for us?"

"I don't know. I'm a mess. I just need some time."

He wrote down the address of his condo and explained how to get there. He gave me the telephone number and his private cell phone number in case I changed my mind. It didn't take a genius to see his anger. I had led him on and then backed out, which is the black and white way men think when it comes to sex.

***

I got into a hot bath and cried. I had made a man mistake *again,* and it was the opposite of the mistake I'd made with Jupiter. I shouldn't have had sex with him and should have had sex with Joe. I cried harder because I was never going to get anything right again. Yes; it was pitiful.

The lights blinked out.

At first, the thunder made me think the lack of electricity had been caused by the storm. Since the bathroom door stood open, I could see that the rest of bedroom was dark also. We lose power all the time in Terlingua, and it wasn't a big deal until I heard movement. I groped around, tried to turn the radio down, and the bathroom door slammed shut. I wasn't alone, but in the pitch black, I couldn't tell who'd entered. You can't bathe with a firearm, so my Beretta was in its holster in the bedroom, useless.

I ventured a, "Who's there?"

Not a sound.

"This is not funny."

Out of the blackness came this, "You're right it's not funny, but scream, and I'll be forced to strangle you."

I was too terrified to scream and nearly jumped straight up out of the tub and through the roof into the storm.

The toilet seat slammed shut with a loud crack. "I'm going to sit here and have a talk with you, so I want you to listen carefully."

Naked, wet, and alone with no weapon, I was in no position to argue.

A tiny light flashed, but the unknown menace extinguished it so fast all I saw were starbursts.

"Nice," he said, and my heart skipped a beat.

"Who are you?"

"If I threw something electrical in there, you'd cook." His tone made my stomach roll, and I shivered uncontrollably.

"I hope you won't do that. What do you want?"

"I've come to talk some sense into you since the sheriff probably failed at that. I won't throw anything into the water unless you start fucking with me."

It's horrifying when a man you can't see starts talking about fucking.

"I'm listening."

"Let's talk about Randall Green."

"What about him?"

"How are you related to him?"

"Why does that matter?"

"I'm the one asking the questions."

The voice was gruff, but I didn't think he was the sheriff, and I was sure he wasn't either of the deputies. Had I heard that voice before?

"He's my friend," I said in answer to the question about Randy.

"Are you willing to die for him?"

"I'd rather not."

The menace laughed. "Maybe we're on the same page, then. I'd rather not have to kill you. It seems like such a waste."

"It does to me, too."

"I guess it would." He took a deep breath. "Here's the deal. This Randall Green thing is over and done."

"It's not!"

"You're going to piss off, have pissed off, some powerful people. Green is out of prison, so I don't see what you hope to accomplish. He already did his time."

"I'm trying to help him clear his name."

"That won't be allowed, Ms. Ricos. The people in this town believe that Green raped Sarah Jones, and they don't want him here."

"But he didn't rape her!"

"You might believe that, and it might even be true, but nobody cares about the truth now."

"I care about it, and so does Randy. He doesn't want to live here. He just wants his name cleared so he doesn't have to go through life known as a child rapist."

"There are things we all want. We don't get everything we want."

"Did the sheriff send you?"

He chuckled, but it held no humor; it was sinister, and right next to me. Terror gripped me by the throat.

"No. The sheriff is only a pawn in this game and is moved around at the whim of the king. He didn't send me, and he doesn't know I'm here."

"Who are you, then?"

"I'm a man paid to do a job."

"You don't have a name?"

"You can call me Mr. Pro if you like. I hope you don't think this is personal."

"You're threatening me in the tub in the dark. That feels personal."

"It'd be personal if I fucked you."

That again.

He touched me with a gloved hand. A gloved hand on a stranger in the dark is the stuff of horror movies. I jumped straight up and kicked at him as hard as I could. My foot connected with something, his shoulder maybe, or his neck. A groan escaped him, and he started cursing.

"You bastard! Son of a bitch! You bitch!" He couldn't decide which curse fit me, and then his language became uglier and more menacing.

I managed to grope and crash my way past him into the bedroom, but like all bullies, he didn't play fair. A small light flashed, and he was on me in seconds. He grabbed me from behind, but I struggled so hard we crashed to the floor. I tried to roll away from him, but he had the upper hand because of his size. Soon he straddled me. He was out of breath but not enough for me to get away. I couldn't breathe beneath his weight. Wet, naked, and cold, I felt even more vulnerable. The only positive thing was that I pulled out some of his hair in the struggle. If he didn't crush the life out of me, I would find him.

He shifted his weight and I could breathe again. He grabbed me by the shoulders and shook me hard. I clung desperately to the hairs in my hand. "Listen, you bitch. You're gonna force me to kill you if you don't calm down."

I stopped fighting him. "I'm calm."

"That's better." He stood, pulling me with him, and sat on the bed. "This could be fun but sadly, I'm not here to play. What I need to know is if you're going to get out of here in the morning."

"Yes."

"And you'll not come back?"

"No."

"And we won't hear anything more from you?"

My Beretta lay on the dresser, but I was too turned around to tell where that was in relation to where I sat.

"Ms. Ricos? I need an answer right now."

"No, you won't hear from me again. You people are too unfriendly."

He laughed and pushed me up off his lap.

"You walk with a limp, don't you?"

That surprised him, and his hesitation answered my question. "I'm the one asking the questions here," he reminded me.

"Why did you beat up Randy when you know he's done nothing wrong?"

"Are you suddenly deaf?"

"Why can't you tell me? I'm cooperating with you."

"I gotta go." He shone the light on the dresser and found my Beretta. "Sweet," he said and pocketed it.

"Please don't take that."

"I don't want you to shoot me in the back when I leave here."

"I would never shoot someone in the back."

"I believe you, sort of, but just in case you get a wild hair."

"You could take the ammo and leave the pistol."

"We don't get everything we want."

While he checked the gun, his tiny penlight shone with enough light for me to see his large size and that he limped. He kept his back to me, so I couldn't see his face.

He extinguished the light. "Want to fool around?"

His remark came as a terrifying surprise.

"Please leave. I thought you were leaving."

"There's one more thing."

"What is it?"

"You're not safe here, and I don't mean just me."

"Then what do you mean?"

"Things are rotten in Freeman County, from the ground up." He paused and then dropped his bomb. "That judge you were playing kissy-face with? I bet he invited you to go to his place, didn't he?"

"I want you to leave."

"He did, didn't he?"

"It's none of your business."

"He's not who he claims to be. Hell, he's not even a judge."

What?

"Look, all I'm saying is that my boss is not the only reason you need to scram. Serious harm is going to come to you if you stay and keep poking around in this sore spot." He took a deep breath and let it out. "You're an innocent woman; I know that. You mean to help your friend. You're not hard to look at, either. For all those reasons, I hope you'll listen to what I'm saying."

"What would Judge Washburn, or whoever he is, have against me?"

"He has nothing against you. It's that you're getting too...close to some things. He has reason to stop you from going further in your investigation."

"Are you saying he was going to kill me?"

"Do you know a better way to stop someone?" He let that sink in, and then added, "I'm going to open the door, but don't try any funny stuff."

"I won't." If I tried anything, it wouldn't be funny.

When he slammed the door, it popped back open a crack. He had dropped a key card to my room on his way out. I was relieved to see he had set my Beretta against the wall on the opposite side of the hall; so relieved that I made a naked dash for it. It was expensive, registered to me, and comfortably familiar in my hand.

I tried to switch on the lights, but he must have cut them at a breaker. Likely someone had cut them for him, since he'd come in when the lights went out. That and the key card meant someone at the hotel had served as an accomplice.

A motor started, and I looked out the window. A small truck, black maybe, pulled away. I gave him ample time to get down the road. Then I slipped into a robe the hotel had provided for my comfort. It was a lot more comfortable with my Beretta in the pocket. I ran to my car. Rain poured down by then, but lightning flashed, and I could not see anybody lurking in the parking lot. I grabbed my laptop, shoved it under the robe, and ran back to the room to put on dry clothes. By then, the lights had come back on.

I felt frightened and sad and, more than anything, angry. Sometimes the best thing to do is nothing, so for a few minutes, I sat immobile on the bed. I tried not to wonder, think, obsess, cry, imagine, scream, crave a drink, or feel sorry for myself. I took a few deep breaths and tried to make my mind a blank.

After a while, I got up, dried my hair, and then opened my laptop and did some research online. Peter Adams had been the D.A. during the time of Randy's trial. He was now in private practice in El Paso, at a firm called Adams & Singleton. I wrote down the address and phone number.

Next, I looked up all the high schools in Phoenix and the surrounding area, and I made a list of their phone numbers.

And, of course, I looked up Joe Washburn. I didn't believe Limping Man, but, on the other hand, how would it hurt to look? I got a lot of hits, from newspaper articles about his involvement in the Texas Supreme Court to a photo of him with Governor Cardenas when he was appointed District Judge of Freeman County. I thought it likely that since Limping Man had lied about him not being a judge, he had lied about everything regarding Joe. I believed Joe was as innocent in all this as I was. Still, there was that empty place in me where trust had lived. Suspicion and doubt had rushed in to fill the void, and they nagged.

After my research session, I sprawled on the bed and thought about, of all people, my mom. She has said, since I was small, that when you aspire to do good, the Universe conspires to help. I was counting on that.

I changed into a blouse, a skirt short enough to cause either of my fathers to frown, and suede, open-toed pumps with four-inch heels. Then I packed my bag and waited for the rest of the state to wake up.

* * *

My birth father, Zeke Pacheco, rises before the sun. I called him because he's a Texas Ranger, and I thought he could get my hair evidence through their Midland crime lab fast. He lives in Austin, but he's known to all the Ranger units across the state because he and his team work their unsolved crimes.

I explained, as concisely as possible, what I was doing. He was intrigued, and I think a little proud, that his daughter was working on behalf of an underdog. Being a die-hard investigator himself, he used his position and reputation to get my hair evidence into the lab with a rush on it. I only had to get it there.

Zeke reminded me that if I needed his help, I only had to call. I assured him his number was near the top of the emergency contact list on my phone.

***

Craig answered his cell phone on the second ring, proving that miracles happen. He had vigorously fought having a phone, and even though I won that battle of wills, I was afraid he would counter by not answering it.

"Come up for coffee," he said in place of hello.

"I'd love to, Craig, but I'm not in Terlingua right now."

"Oh, I—how did that slip my mind? How's it going there?"

"I've proved to myself that Randy is innocent, but I still need to be able to prove it to a judge. I've run into trouble, and I need your help."

"What do you want me to do?"

"Would you pack a bag and join me? I'll come get you."

"You know I don't like to travel."

"I know, and I wouldn't ask if it wasn't important. You can bring Marine if you want. He can stay in the hotel room while we work. I need someone to have my back while I check out a few things."

"Well...since you put it like that."

"That's why I'm calling you."

"I'll be ready before you can get here. What do I need to bring?"

"Bring a change of clothes for a couple of days and all your combat gear, including those black fatigues you have. And your black boots, too."

"We're going to do battle?"

"I hope not, but I want to be prepared. I've shaken up things here, and now I'm being threatened off Randy's case."

"And you're digging in."

"Yes. Now I know for certain that I'm on the right track."

"Who's threatening you?"

"He's just a goon."

"Like those others?"

"Yes, but he's not a cartel goon. But a goon is a goon is a—"

"Coward," Craig finished my sentence.

"Yes."

"When are you leaving there?"

"I'll be on my way soon. I'll call you and pick you up at the bottom of the hill. I'm going to rent a car, so don't expect the Mustang."

"What should I expect?"

"Expect anything, Craig. I don't know where this will lead."

***

After I loaded my car, I returned to the room to be sure I had everything. I stood in front of a full-length mirror, examining and pep-talking myself. All right, I even admired myself. In spite of no sleep, no sex, a lot of crying, and a harrowing night, I looked pretty good.

I had a game plan, and I felt ready to work it. Do not tell me to back off a gross injustice. Not happening.

Sheriff Ben had said he wanted me to rest and come back to work. Well, I had big news for him. Deputy Ricos had returned, in spades.

***

My reason for dressing up "bimboesque" was to get the attention of the men who wanted me to leave. Nothing says *Look at me* like a short skirt and slut pumps. I didn't want them to miss the fact that I was on my way out of there, so they could let down their guard. *Back off, boys.*

Men in law enforcement like to gather and gossip over coffee in the morning, if Brewster County lawmen are any example. And, hello—I found them at a Simpson diner called Wanda's Good Eats.

I strutted in and then paused, as if wondering where to sit. The looks on the faces of Nick and Ronnie Jim were priceless. They stood and flailed their arms, yelling for me to join them. Perfect. I slipped into the booth next to Nick.

After we greeted each other, I said, "I hoped to see you guys."

"You did?"

"I wanted to say good-bye."

"Aw, why are you leaving so soon?"

"I spoke with Sheriff Hancock yesterday. He says the evidence I need has been misplaced. Anyway, it looks like I'm wasting my time. The DNA testing proved my friend guilty of the rape, so I guess he lied to me."

A waitress came and filled a mug of coffee for me without asking if I wanted any. I didn't. I was wound too tight to drink coffee.

When she left, Nick leaned so close he was practically touching me. "The Sheriff told you that?"

"Yes, yesterday afternoon."

"We found the evidence," he whispered, and my heart started galloping.

Ronnie Jim stared at the table and suppressed a grin.

I tried to stay calm. "You found the evidence in your basement?"

"Yes, we did."

"Below your office?"

"Yes. It's supposed to be filed under the accused's name, but the box reads 'Jones' instead of 'Green.' It's filed in alphabetical order, like it's supposed to be, but it's in the wrong name. It's filed in the wrong year, also—two years ahead of where it should be."

"How did you find it?"

Ronnie Jim leaned across the table and whispered. "Last year I found the box in the wrong year and mentioned to the sheriff that I'd put it back where it belongs. I had no way to know the name was wrong, too." He glanced around. "A few months later, I was looking for something and found it again. It had been moved back to the wrong place. I kept my mouth shut about it, but I didn't forget it, either."

"You're amazing!"

He blushed scarlet and continued. "After you left yesterday, I told Nick I could prove to him that the sheriff is doing something hinky."

"We don't know why he'd move an evidence box unless he's hiding whatever's in it," Nick said.

"Did you look at the evidence?"

"No. We were afraid the sheriff would come in and catch us."

"He's been in a bad mood since he found out about your visit," Ronnie Jim said.

"I'm going home, so maybe he'll lighten up."

"You don't want to see the evidence first?"

"I'd like to see it, but I know the sheriff won't allow it."

"Maybe you could get a court order."

"I could if you'd tell the judge what you know. But I'm not asking either one of you to do that. It would mean the end of your jobs."

"You mean the sheriff would have to know we told?"

"Yes, you'd have to testify before Judge Washburn, and it'd become part of the record to back up the warrant."

Both men looked stricken.

"I'll try to think of another way," I said. Truthfully, I knew a way, but it was illegal. "If my friend wants to pursue this," I continued, "he'll have to get someone else. I have other work to do, paid work."

"Yeah, working for a living sure gets in the way of other things," Nick said.

I agreed that it did. We ordered breakfast and talked about law enforcement in general and being deputies in particular. I bragged about my sheriff while they complained about theirs. Then Nick began talking about a recent arrest they made of a "dangerous meth producer."

That was the "in" I needed to obtain some delicate information. "Does anybody ever break out of the county jail?"

"Naw, it hasn't happened yet," Ronnie Jim said.

"How about the office?"

"We don't hold anyone in the office except during questioning."

"That's what I meant."

"That hasn't happened, but I guess it's possible."

"Our office doesn't have an alarm," I said. "Of course, there's no alarm service in Terlingua."

"We don't have an alarm, either. The jail does, but it's one of those old-fashioned siren alarms."

"Your office doesn't have an alarm system?"

"Naw. Who'd want to break into a sheriff's office?"

We laughed about that, but inside, I did a happy dance.

***

Making Ronnie Jim and Nick think I was leaving was great and all, but what was I thinking? The sheriff needed to hear it from me, as much as I dreaded seeing him again. He would be the one to inform the limping terrorist of my compliance.

The sheriff wasn't in yet, but when I stepped out of his office, I spotted his unmistakable physique standing on the courthouse steps next door. I walked over slowly, forcing myself to go.

Sheriff Hancock looked just as unsavory as I remembered. He busied himself reloading his cheek. He looked up as I approached, but it was a while before he bothered to look at my face.

"I'm just saying my good-byes," I chirped. *Bite me.*

He held a pinch of tobacco in mid-air and gawked at me. It made me uncomfortable, but I was still glad I had worn the skirt. He would think I was a flighty female, nobody to worry about, exactly as intended.

"Good-bye, you say?"

"Yes, sir. It looks like my friend Randy lied to me. I'm going home, but I didn't want to leave you with a bad impression of the Brewster County Sheriff's Office."

Since I was *in my place* and dressed like a female is "supposed to" dress, and even showing some leg, the old codger's attitude changed one hundred percent. He positively glowed with charm and charisma.

He droned on, but I ceased listening because Joe Washburn walked onto the courthouse landing and stood transfixed, wearing a black robe. The look on his face said murdering me was not even a remote thought. It was also plain that he was not in cahoots with the sheriff. Like me, he wasn't paying any attention to him. Sheriff Hancock was a troll standing between me and a prince.

Take a chance on this man. That voice again.

The prince held the door open wide. "May I see you a moment, Ms. Ricos?"

"Yes, Judge Washburn."

"Well, good luck to you, little lady," the sheriff crooned.

"Thank you, Sheriff." I gave his hand a record-fast shake.

When I entered the courthouse, Joe pulled me into an empty office and shut the door. "So, what's this about?" He indicated my mode of dress.

"Can't a girl dress up?"

"Oh yes, and you look ravishing, but I think you know what I mean."

"I'm saying good-bye to the people who want me gone, and I'm doing it in a way they'll notice and remember."

"Were you planning to tell me good-bye?"

"Are you one of the people who want me to go?"

"You know better than that."

"You're not angry about last night?"

He looked away from me for the first time. "Oh, hell, maybe I should be, but I'm not." His eyes met mine. "You know, you were the one who started—oh, never mind. I'd like to accept your offer to get to know each other if the offer still stands."

"It does. And no, I hadn't planned to tell you good-bye because I hoped to see you again."

"How is that going to happen if you're leaving?"

"It will happen, but you'll have to trust me."

"Okay, since I don't have much choice."

"You need to know that I was terrorized last night. The lights went off in my room, and a man came in."

"What man? Did he hurt you? Why didn't you call me?"

"He didn't hurt me, but he threatened me off Randy Green's case. Among other things, he said you're not who you say you are, and not even a judge. He said I shouldn't trust you, and that you want me dead."

"WHAT?"

"Shh, Joe, you don't need to say anything. I didn't believe him."

"What does the man look like?"

I described Limping Man and explained that he was one of the men who attacked Randy in Terlingua. I didn't mention the hair evidence because he took my hand and that train of thought derailed.

"Where do you want to go from here?" he asked gently.

"It's better if these people think I've been scared away. And I don't want to drag you into it any further. I'll be back soon, but I have to go now and work my plan."

"You have a plan?"

"Yes, and please don't ask me about it. The less you know about it the better." I took a deep breath. "All I'm saying to you, Joe, is this. If you need to kill me then go ahead, but I want you to kiss me again first. Then it would be worth it."

He pulled me into him, and kissed me, a long, sweet, hungry, no-doubt-about-it kiss. "If you're not back soon," he whispered into my hair, "I'll go down there, grab you, and ride like hell. Understand?"

CHAPTER 18

I drove to the Department of Public Safety crime lab in Midland while constantly checking the rearview mirrors. I didn't think anyone had followed me, but if Limping Man had, he would find out where I was going but not why. He would never get anything out of the lab, especially after I gave them his description and explained that he was a wanted criminal. Any questions, call me or Zeke Pacheco. Zeke's name was like a magic key at the Rangers' lab. Use it on any door.

***

I decided not to rent a car in case Limping Man followed me away from Carterton/Simpson and right to a rental company. Instead, I had another idea.

As soon as I arrived in Terlingua, I went to the nonprofit clinic where my mother works as director and doctor. She looked up from her desk and smiled when I walked in. "Hi, sweetheart! I thought you were working out of town."

"I was, but I came back to see if you'd trade cars with me. I need something less attention-grabbing."

"In that case, you should put some clothes on."

"I needed to draw attention to myself this morning."

"And you succeeded, I bet."

"Mom, what do you think about trading cars?"

She was only too eager to do it. She loves to drive the Mustang. I handed over the keys, accepted the keys to her white Nissan Murano, thanked her, hugged her, and nearly escaped.

"Hold up a minute." She got up and shut her office door.

I gave her a questioning look.

"What's going on with you? Come here and let me get a good look at you."

"Don't, Mom. I'm fine."

"You seem… I can't put my finger on it. Have you had a check-up lately?"

"Mom, I feel great."

"Something is going on with you."

"What's different about me is my new outlook. I started doing something for somebody else, and I began to feel better."

"Well, I won't say I told you so, but—"

"Good." A beat or two passed. "Also, I met an interesting man."

"You met a man in that backward town where you were?"

"Aren't you the woman who claims there are good people everywhere?"

"Huh." She looked surprised. "Who knew you were listening?"

"I don't know one-hundred percent if I can trust him with my heart. I want to, but—"

"You're afraid of getting hurt again."

"Yes."

"You're going to run into a good man one day, one who is exactly who he says he is. You know that, right?"

"Right, I know that. I hope so."

"But this friend isn't a man like that?"

"I believe he is, but I need more time to get to know him."

"I think that's wise."

"On the other hand, I just want to jump on him." Two beats. "That came out wrong," I said, but she knew better. We started laughing.

"Sometimes I do worry about you," Mom said, "and with good reason, I think."

The nurse pounded on the door. "Dr. Ricos, there's an emergency!" Just like that, I was saved by some poor soul with a badly cut hand.

I went home, changed into blue jeans and a t-shirt and took my ATV up to the bluff to see Craig instead of calling him to meet me below.

"You didn't bring Missy with you?" Craig asked after he greeted me, and we settled into chairs on his porch.

"She's at my mom's house. I hated to get her for a few minutes and then leave her again."

"I thought you said you'd pick me up below."

"I've changed my mind, Craig. I don't want to take you. If I get into trouble that's one thing, but I don't want to drag you along."

"Nobody's dragging me. I'm willing to go."

"I know, and I thank you for that."

"What is it you plan to do?"

"I'm going to break into the evidence storage basement of the Sheriff's Office."

"Are you sure?" Craig looked horrified. "That's so risky."

"The sheriff was part of a conspiracy that knowingly sent an innocent man to prison and left him marked for life. He has evidence I need to see. Do you want me to walk away from Randy?"

"No."

"That's good because I can't. I don't want to break in, but I don't see another way to protect that evidence."

"But anything you take out of there will be inadmissible in court."

"I know that. Not to mention that I'd go to jail."

"That's the part I don't want to see happen."

"I'm not going to remove anything."

"Please explain your thinking."

"If the evidence only proved Randy's innocence, Sheriff Hancock would've destroyed it already. But he kept it because it proves that somebody other than Randy was guilty. It's the sheriff's insurance that nothing happens to him. He hid it in plain sight by misfiling it. Only he knows where it is, or so he thinks."

"Not a bad plan overall."

"No, and it's worked a long time."

"What makes you think the sheriff would move it now?"

"I can't be sure he bought my *I'm leaving* drama, and if he thinks for one second that I'll continue investigating, he'll move the box out of there. I can't take that chance, so I'm going to misfile it again."

"And then what?"

"Then I need to legally find some evidence, anything, that will allow me to get a court order to search the basement."

"But what evidence?"

"That's where the rest of my plan comes in. I need to find the victim and interview her. I need to talk to the former District Attorney and to Randy's court-appointed attorney. Nobody in law enforcement ever questioned what happened because the law enforcement in that county is corrupt. This was a grand scale cover-up. It's difficult to keep something so big under wraps, so something has to give."

"That's true."

"The crime lab has hair that may be my first big lead. I should know more soon. I have to get in and out of every place fast because I have to bring this down before the man behind the cover-up knows what's hitting him. And so that goon of his can't stop me."

"You're talking about a blitz."

"Yes, exactly; why do you think I called in the marines?"

He grinned. Then his look turned serious. "But now you've changed your mind about taking me."

"I was going to have you stand by and warn me in case someone showed up, but I can't do that. I feel this will go better if I go alone. I thought about it all the way home. I'll go at two in the morning. The only way someone would come in at that hour is if there was an emergency, and even then, they won't come to the basement."

"How are you going to get in?"

"Through the back door. I can tell by looking at it that it's not used often."

"Won't there be an alarm?"

"No. According to the deputies, the only alarm is at the jail. People don't usually break into Sheriffs' Offices. I checked it out early this morning, and there's only one padlock on a chain. I can break the chain and replace it with another that looks like it."

I felt sure of my plan, but Craig was reserved, nervous that if the sheriff found the switched-out evidence, he would know who did it.

"He could have you grabbed," Craig said, "and demand to know where you put the evidence. How long do you think you'd be able to hold up under torture?"

"Well, jeez, Craig, I'd spill my guts at the first threat of it."

He laughed, but the thought made me cold.

***

I rented a motel room on the west side of Carterton and tried without success to sleep. Thoughts of Joe pestered me: the way he smelled, his silky hair, his sexy whispered "threat" in my ear.

I finally slept a short while and got up at two. I tied my hair close to my head and wrapped one of Craig's black bandanas around it. I dressed in dark everything and hit the road. I parked the car in a lot a quarter-mile away from the Sheriff's Office. Sticking to shadows as much as possible, I made my way to the building.

When I reached the rear door, I set down my tools and put on gloves. Only a yellow insect light illuminated the back, so I loosened the bulb but left it in the socket. Then I cut the padlock off the chain, trying not to damage the door. I would replace the old chain and lock with a set that looked the same and hope nobody would notice anything different. Thankfully, Ronnie Jim had let it slip that they rarely used the back door, so I was hoping they would stay true to pattern until I finished this case. If the back door had been locked with a deadbolt like the front door, my plan wouldn't have worked.

By the time I was ready to enter the building, my heart was pounding so hard I could barely hear my conscience.

I tiptoed through the hallway using a penlight, looking for a door to the basement. In the first pass, I missed it and got all the way into the main office, where there was enough light to get busted if anyone looked in. I retraced my steps and found the correct door not only unlocked but standing ajar. That indicated that the sheriff felt comfortable regarding the problem of the "little lady" deputy, or else he had already moved the box.

I crept down the stairs while the usual array of voices gave their opinions, the most insistent being, *you're gonna die!* At last, I arrived in the basement and flashed the penlight around to orient myself. It didn't take long to find the solved cases in the year two years ahead of Randy's trial, and then the box marked "Jones."

My hands shook as I opened it. Inside was a DNA profile of Randall McKinney Green, which was clearly marked as a no-match to the semen found on Sarah Jones. There was another DNA profile, but it was labeled *unknown donor*. That person hadn't been in the system then; maybe he would be in it now. The thought electrified me, but I still couldn't take the evidence.

The rape exam on Sarah had been called inconclusive, but the registered nurse who signed off on it made an opinion statement. She didn't believe a rape had taken place that night and furthermore, the child had never been raped.

There were other things in separate bags: Sarah's nightgown taken from her that night, underwear taken from Randy's bedroom, the so-called sworn statement made by Sarah, statements from neighbors who had seen Randy running from the Jones house, and so forth.

I laid out the things and photographed them one by one. Then I found a file box from the section that held the ten-year-old boxes. The name on it was Fernandez. I took the evidence out of it and put Randy's evidence into it. Then I put the Fernandez evidence into a file with the name Rodgers and the Rodgers evidence into the box marked Jones and put it back where the sheriff had stashed it.

I shelved the Fernandez box containing the Green/Jones evidence in a different year and wrote down everything I'd done so I wouldn't forget. If the sheriff happened to look inside the Jones box, he might know it had been compromised, but he wouldn't know how to find his prized evidence. Looking for it would take a long time, and he wouldn't have a lot of time. I hoped.

I sneaked back up the basement steps, left the door as I found it, and made my way to and out the back door. I stood for a moment in the shadows to scan the area. When I saw no movement of any type, I replaced the padlock with one that looked identical to the one I'd removed, and then I made my way back to the car.

Part one of my plan had worked. I still had a long way to go and not much time.

CHAPTER 19

I wanted to call Joe when I returned to the room. I felt excited and energized by the success of my mission and giddy with relief. The thought crossed my mind that I could have sex with Joe and leave my heart out of it, the same way I had with Jupiter. Yeah, and look how well that turned out.

Here's the thing: in my head I'm a slut; but in real life, not so much. I didn't call Joe, although I started to a dozen times. When morning came, I still didn't call him to have breakfast or anything else.

Sex and breakfast would be delicious, thought my inner slut, o*r no breakfast.* Anyhow, I couldn't be seen in Simpson, so I stayed sequestered in the room and worked like a good girl.

I made an appointment with the former District Attorney, Peter Adams, for the afternoon. Then I called Phoenix high schools looking for Sarah Jones. Not one of them had her registered. That was disheartening.

I drove towards El Paso a while, and then stopped in a roadside picnic area to eat fruit and yogurt. It was a far cry from sex and breakfast.

I continued my journey but stopped at a fast food chain to access their free Internet. Using my laptop and my Sheriff's Office password, I looked up Sarah on a law enforcement people-search website. No hits there, either. Maybe she had changed her name.

Buddy King seemed like my only hope.

"Mr. King, this is Margarita Ricos, the woman who came to see you about that bookkeeping job."

He was confused at first, and then he laughed good-naturedly. "Ah yes, Ms. Ricos. I remember."

"Well, sir, I hope you can help me. I need the full name of Sarah Jones's father."

"I don't know where he is."

"That's okay. I only need his name."

He hesitated. "You won't tell him I gave it to you?"

"Of course not. I have no intention of causing problems for you."

"Well—"

"Please, Mr. King. I'm trying to clear an innocent man. I'm begging you to help me do that."

He took a deep breath. "His name is Leroy Beaumont Jones. I guess anybody 'round here could tell you that much. His family called him Beau growing up, but he's used Leroy ever since I knew him."

"Do you know where he was born?"

"Anthony, Texas. Why?"

"Did he grow up there?"

"Yeah, he did, in a small house near Rainbow Lake. Are you familiar with the lake? Lots of bass and bluegill in there. It's right by Anthony. That's past El Paso, near the New Mexico border."

"Did you ever go there with him?"

"Why do you want to know that? Don't get me involved."

"I'm just looking for a lead to follow. Right now, I have nothing. There is no 'Sarah Jones' in any Phoenix High School."

"She must be with her mother in California."

"You were telling me about the lake place. Did you ever go there with him?"

"Yeah, once or twice we went to fish, but it was a long time ago. He still had his old family place back then. But what does this have to do with anything?"

"Do you remember how to get there?"

"Well, sure, but I doubt if he goes there nowadays."

"I doubt it, too, but I have to follow every lead."

He stalled as if forced to reveal personal secrets. "The lake is behind the Old El Paso cannery near Anthony. I don't recollect the name of the road, but it's dirt and heads right to the lake. It's a small frame house, painted white last time I saw it. It has an attached garage."

"How old is Leroy Jones?"

"Let's see, I reckon he's about thirty-nine or forty by now."

"Mr. King, is there anything else you remember that could help me locate Sarah? Do you remember her mother's maiden name?"

"No, but her first name is Sadie Lou."

"Anything else?"

"I don't reckon you'll find Sarah Jones, Ms. Ricos."

"Why do you say that?"

"Because certain people don't want her found."

***

El Paso glimmered on the horizon when Barney called. When I said, "Hi Barney," he said, "Let me guess. You have it all figured out and can't be bothered to call in and tell me."

"No, but I have a plan that I'm working."

"Uh-huh."

"Will you update Randy for me? I don't want to give him any details, but tell him it's going well, and I have a few leads."

"I'll tell him."

"Anything else I need to know?"

"Sheriff Hancock called Sheriff Ben last night about your unprofessional behavior. Among other things, he claims you did an illegal search of his records. Of course, our sheriff knows better than that, but he called the judge this morning to see if he had issued you a warrant."

"Sheriff Hancock lies, Barney."

"That's what the judge said in so many words. Hancock is also pissed that you're asking questions in *his* county."

"I know. He thinks he sent me packing, but that isn't happening. I might be getting somewhere. At least I've shaken things up."

"Yeah, that's your specialty."

"Have you seen any sign of Limping Man?"

"No. He's probably tailing you."

"That's not funny, Barney."

"I didn't mean it to be. You need to be extra careful."

"I will. I've already had a run-in with him."

"What? Did he hurt you?"

"No. He scared me in the dark, and I was naked, which made it worse."

"That sounds like something out of one of those Halloween movies."

"Well, it's not. He threatened to kill me if I didn't leave this alone. He said some powerful people are getting pissed off."

"Hell! Ricos, you should come back now."

"I'll know who he is soon, because a couple of his hairs are at the crime lab."

"How'd you manage that, Batgirl?"

"I yanked them out when we were fighting."

He groaned. "You need me with you, don't you?"

"That's true, but before you can get away, I'll be back."

"There's a plan. I feel all better."

"Good. I'll see you soon."

I'd barely hung up when Randy called. I told him everything I could, which wasn't much when I subtracted making out with the judge, and the visit of the late-night limping man.

He said he felt better, thanks to my mom. Then he said, "I'm never going to be able to pay you back for all you're doing."

"I haven't accomplished much yet. Please stop worrying about repaying me. I'm being repaid for anything I ever did for you."

"What do you mean?"

"I'll explain it when I get back."

"Margarita, you're not getting in trouble, are you?"

"I don't plan to."

"You saw Larry? How is he?"

"He's tall and fit, very good-looking."

He laughed. "Right, I know that. I've met him, remember?"

"He seems happy, and he wishes you the best. He gave me a handkerchief you asked him to keep for you."

"He still had that?"

"Yes, you told him it was important."

"I changed my mind."

"What is the significance of the handkerchief, Randy?"

"It'll have that deputy's semen on it. But I don't want you to do anything about him."

"Why not?"

"He's dangerous. Don't look for him alone, please."

"I won't look for him now because other things are more important, but I'd still like to know his full name. We might need that at some point."

"Please don't get hurt."

"I won't, Randy. Stop worrying."

I was pulling into the attorney's parking lot in El Paso when Joe called to tell me about his conversation with Sheriff Duncan.

"Where are you?" he asked.

"I can't tell you that."

"You still don't trust me, do you?"

"It isn't that, Joe. I don't want to listen to you tell me that what I'm doing is crazy or stupid or illegal or dangerous."

"It's all those things, isn't it?"

"I can tell you where my head is, though. It's with you."

"I can't stop thinking about you either, Margarita. Let me rephrase my question. If you're less than four hours from here, we could have dinner together tonight. I can drive towards you, and you can drive towards me, and we'll meet in the middle, so to speak."

"That's a sneaky way to find out where I am."

"Listen to me. I don't care where you are. I was making conversation when I asked. I want to see you again. And I'm not patient. Are you willing to meet me or not?"

"I'd love to meet you, but I have to decline for tonight. I have more to do here."

"What about tomorrow?"

"Could we talk about it tomorrow? It depends on what I find out today."

"Aren't you worried that the man who limps will get wind of what you're doing?"

"Yes, that's why I'm trying to move fast. If I can figure this out before he makes another move, then he loses."

"I don't suppose there's any point in telling you to be careful."

"Not much, no. If you think I'm the sort of woman to back off just because some thug threatens me—"

"Save your breath. I already know who you are."

I laughed. "And you still want to meet me somewhere?"

"Margarita, you're trying my patience. When are you going to stop running?"

"I'm not running. I'm working."

"Call it what you want. How about a phone date tonight? That's better than no date. And by the way, your sheriff is anxious to speak with you."

C'est la vie. I was way more interested in Joe than Sheriff Duncan, and I continued talking to him until I had to go in for my appointment.

***

I felt certain the former D.A. would never agree to a recording of our meeting, but I brought a small recorder anyway. Whatever I recorded without his permission wouldn't hold up in court—like everything else I had—but at least someone besides me would hear the truth or his refusal to tell it. It rode in my pocket, and I turned it on when I entered the office building.

I had made the appointment under the pretext of seeking a divorce. That was what came to mind when his secretary asked the nature of my visit. As she led me back to his office, I felt a pang of fear. What if Peter Adams was Limping Man? That hadn't occurred to me.

Adams rose from his desk and came around it to take my hand. I breathed a sigh of relief that he moved like a normal man. In addition, he was too small to be Limping Man. He was also doughy, going bald, and had bad skin, along with a nervous tic, but he deserved a lot worse from life than that.

He was cordial, seeing money signs. "Please have a seat, Ms. Wallace, and tell me exactly what you need."

I took a deep breath. "I'm not here for a divorce. I want to talk to you about the trial of Randall Green in Simpson seven years ago, and I want to record our conversation."

His mouth sprang open. "What the hell?"

"The hell is that Randy went to prison for a crime he didn't commit. He didn't get a fair trial, and you were part of it. You prosecuted an innocent man, and you knew all along that he was innocent."

"You've got a lot of nerve barging into my office and making accusations about a trial you know nothing about."

"I know enough about it to know what you did. How do you sleep at night?"

"Get out!" He fumbled the phone. "I'm calling security."

I stood. "There's no need for that. I'll leave peaceably."

"Who are you? What do you know about Randall Green?"

"Do you want me to leave or do you want me to answer questions?"

"Please sit down and tell me who you are."

"My name is Kim Wallace, and I'm a friend of Randy Green's."

"You're taking his word that he's innocent?"

"I know he's innocent. There was no rape, only a conspiracy to charge him with rape, and then a cover-up."

"Were you there? How would you know that?"

"I know it. That should be enough for now."

"What kept you from coming forward before?"

"Would you let me record our conversation?"

He flung his arms angrily. "No! Absolutely not!"

"Do you have a transcript of the trial in your possession?"

"No; why would I?"

"Will the current D.A. have one in his records?"

"You'd have to ask him."

"Why did you leave your position in Freeman County?"

"I went into private practice for better opportunities. But that's none of your damn business, like the rest of this."

"Are you the man who removed the Green transcript from the court records?"

"Who says it was removed?"

"At the trial, you made the statement that Randall Green's semen was found all over Sarah Jones. Yet you never brought in an expert from the crime lab to testify to the DNA findings."

"You're crazy if you expect me to remember every case I ever tried."

"Oh, you remember this one. This one keeps you awake nights."

He glared at me in silence, his pasty face turning crimson.

"Do you want to make a formal statement about your crucial role in the false imprisonment of Randall Green?" I asked with wide-eyed innocence.

"Are you out of your mind?"

"It might ease your conscience to come clean."

"What do you want? Are you after money?"

"I want to know who you're protecting."

"I'm not protecting anyone. You need to leave now!"

"Okay." I rose. "I'll call you tomorrow to see if you've changed your mind."

"You could call me every day for the rest of your life and it won't do you any good."

"Please think about it. Surely this wrong is weighing heavily on your heart. It would make you feel like a new man to do the right thing."

He glared at me.

I smiled at him, but it was forced. "Maybe you'll feel like talking tomorrow."

"Get the hell out of my office!"

***

I rented a hotel room and spent time searching for Leroy Beaumont Jones on the law enforcement search site. It yielded several last known addresses, phone numbers, and places of employment, all in Phoenix. The phone numbers no longer worked. One former place of employment was no longer in business, but the other, Big Jim's Auto Sales, was.

A man answered the phone this way, "Big Jim here! You've come to the right place for a fair deal on a used car or truck. Big Jim will always do you right!"

"Hello, Big Jim. I'm trying to find Leroy Jones."

"He doesn't work here, but I could get you behind the wheel of a good-as-new car or truck before this day is over!"

"Sir, I need Leroy Jones."

"Who are you and why do you want him?"

"My name is Kim Wallace, and I owe him money."

Big Jim laughed. "There's a new one. Everyone else calls because he owes them." Then he dove into another sales pitch without missing a beat. "I can put you into a brand-new-looking car today if your credit checks out. If it doesn't, it might take a day or two longer unless you pay cash."

"Thank you, but no."

"I take ten percent off a cash deal."

"Please help me find Leroy Jones. I have to repay him."

"I wish I could help you do the right thing, but ol' Leroy went back to Texas. El Paso, I believe."

"Do you have an address or phone for him? Do you know where he works?"

"Negative, my friend, nada. I don't have any of that. He left here—well, he left without saying adios."

"Oh, I see. Does anyone else there know anything about him?"

"I doubt it."

"What about his daughter, Sarah?"

"I wasn't aware that Leroy had a daughter."

"Would you ask around about her and him, and call me back? Please, Big Jim."

"Well, yes, since you ask so sweet, I'll call you back in a few."

"I can't thank you enough."

I flipped on the television, but no good news came from that.

When my phone rang, the caller's number began with Phoenix area code 602, so I answered, "This is Kim."

"Kim, my name is Rick. Big Jim asked me to give you a call."

"Thank you, Rick. Do you know how to find Leroy Jones?"

"Maybe I do. I have a cell phone number that might still be his."

"Would you give it to me, please?"

"What you want with Leroy?"

"I owe him money, and I'd like to repay him."

He laughed until he started choking. "I don't believe that for one second. More likely, he got you pregnant and you're tracking down his sorry ass."

Ha! That was a good one, so I laughed along with him. That must have convinced him, because he gave me the number. It had an El Paso area code. My heart sped up; Leroy and I were in the same city.

After a long time of ringing, a gruff voice answered the phone. "Beaumont."

Following a hunch, I asked, "Is this Leroy Beaumont?"

"Who wants to know?"

"I'm a friend of Sarah's."

"Sarah?" He hesitated. "I don't know a Sarah." His surprise at hearing her name told a different story.

"Please help me get in touch with Sarah, Mr. Beaumont."

"How did you get my name?"

Before I could answer his question, he hung up on me. When I called back, he didn't answer. I stewed but decided to wait until morning to check out the old family home of Leroy Beaumont Jones. With any luck, he was living there again.

***

My phone date with Joe was more fun than I expected. He told me about growing up on a reservation and how terrifying it felt to leave it for the drastically different world of the city and college, but he had kept his eyes on his life's dream. He said he loves the Comanche, and even the bleak land where he grew up, but has no desire to go back except to visit.

I recounted tales of growing up on the border with one foot in Mexico and one in the United States and a muddy river running between them.

We laughed and shared personal things about ourselves, and mentally had our hands all over each other—well, that's what the slut thought. The point is that by the time we finally said good-night, it was already too late to keep my heart out of it.

***

The small white house near Rainbow Lake was easy to find. It looked lived-in, but when I knocked on the door, no one answered. I walked around it, looking for a way in. I stopped short of picking the locks because someone might come home, and I didn't need any scrapes with Anthony's lawmen. I peered in the windows long enough to see that a teen girl lived there or visited there, judging by posters on the wall of a bedroom and the way clothes were scattered all over. My only option was to wait and see who came home.

I wandered down to the lake, but there was a fee to get in. It wasn't much, but the sun was hot now that it was late morning, and I wasn't tempted to sit around in it. My cell phone rang as I headed back to the house.

Billy called with alarming news: Randy had been abducted. My friend was so hysterical I could barely understand him. The gist of it was that a note had been left at Randy's that read: *Your friend will be returned unharmed when you desist, Deputy Ricos. He's hidden in the backcountry, so don't bother looking.* I thought it might as well have been signed *The Limping Man,* but it wasn't signed.

I had been followed to El Paso yesterday, or more likely, Peter Adams had notified Limping Man of my visit. Why hadn't I assumed he would?

Because your mind is consumed with Joe Washburn, the judging, know-it-all little bitch in my head sneered. Then she reminded me that most of the thoughts were not even repeatable, which didn't help.

I called Barney to tell him about Randy. He was upset by the news and promised to notify the sheriff. He also said he would check for forensic clues, or any clues, at Randy's house.

I headed back to Terlingua.

CHAPTER 20

Barney, Buster, and Billy were waiting at the office when I arrived. Billy had calmed down since our phone conversation. I thought it was Barney's influence since he has that effect on me as well.

"Tell me everything you know," I said to Barney.

He handed me the note, which he'd put into an evidence bag. "There'd been a struggle in the bedroom. Randy would've been hard to subdue, but I found a syringe in the bathroom sink that explains how they did it, I think. I also found a washcloth with blood on it. It could belong to one of the perps, but it may be Randy's."

"I picked up a piece of plastic from the bed," said Buster. "It was part of the syringe wrapper."

"If he was drugged, which I believe," Barney continued, "I still think it took more than one man to pull that off. Somebody had to hold him down, and I think it would've taken two or three somebodies."

"My gut says Limping Man wrote the note," I said. "I wonder if the same men who attacked Randy before helped relocate him. They might be holding him at Tom's."

"Tom is an idiot, but he's not that stupid. They're probably holding him in the backcountry, as the note claims, but I'll go to Tom's to check it out."

"What they call the backcountry is probably accessible by vehicle," I said. "Those three couldn't haul Randy and supplies way back in there where there're no roads. That limits the possibilities to several hundred locations rather than thousands."

"Well there's a cheery thought, only hundreds."

"Yeah, I know. Also, I think there would be a shelter wherever they put him, maybe an abandoned building or a hunting camp. Anyhow, it won't be far from Terlingua and is most likely even closer than we think."

"Who do you think the third man is?" Barney asked.

"I think it's Rod Florence. He would be easily led to bully someone perceived as an outsider and a 'sinner.' The third man at Randy's was large with dirty clothes, which is how I best remember Rod."

Barney nodded. "That's possible. He's another card-carrying jerk.

But if we round up all the jerks in Terlingua, it'll take a few days."

"Why don't you just round up those two for now? I'm going to talk to a man who knows more about the backcountry than anybody I know."

"Craig?"

"Right."

"What do you want me to do?" asked Billy.

"I think you should wait at Randy's in case he comes back."

"But how will he come back?"

"He might escape. As Barney said, he isn't an easy man to subdue. I think he'd be hard to control, too. And he's a survivor. He's smart."

"But what if they keep him drugged, or what if they kill him?"

"Try to stay calm, Billy. Whoever is behind this only wants me to stop because I'm getting somewhere. If they kill him, they know there'll be a full-scale investigation involving a lot more than one lone 'girl deputy.' I don't believe they'd take that risk."

That made Billy feel better, and I left him at Randy's. I wasn't convinced what I'd said was true and only prayed it was.

* * *

Craig agreed to help and had a few ideas about where Randy could be. We left his cat with my mom, who also had my dog. She never complained because she was livid that her new patient had been drugged and dragged off where she couldn't monitor his progress.

My mother blames Zeke for my save-the-world genes, but she's loaded with them, which is what led her to study medicine.

"You find that young man," she ordered.

Craig snapped his heels together and saluted her. "Yes, ma'am!"

* * *

Craig prepared a backpack with supplies for a couple of days. He had once lived in the backcountry, so if Randy was there, Craig would find him. He knew enough about sneaking around in enemy territory to move without being seen. My only hesitation was his health. I didn't dare mention it because I'd already endured several of his lectures about how a grown man could look out for himself. I kept my worries to myself.

When Craig and I went by my house, Billy was pacing the porch.

"I know you were just trying to get rid of me," he said, near tears.

"That's not true Billy, but I don't know what else you can do."

When he saw the way Craig was dressed, and that he carried supplies, he became suspicious. "What is he doing?"

"I'm going to look for Randy," Craig said.

"I want to go with you."

I opened my mouth to tell him it was a bad idea, but Craig asked, "Do you know how to be quiet?"

"Yes, sir."

"Can you hike long distances and endure discomfort without whining?"

Billy nodded solemnly.

"Can you sleep on the ground without falling apart?"

"Yes, sir."

"We have less than two hours before dark settles. Then we camp. You're not afraid of the dark, are you?"

"No, sir."

"We won't be able to carry a lot of food or water."

"That's okay. I don't feel like eating."

Craig mulled it over. "I'll take you if you can follow my orders to the letter."

In answer, Billy saluted him. I thought there were a lot of ways it could go wrong, but it was up to Craig. His expression was impossible to read.

***

I wanted to go with Craig and Billy or help Barney and Buster interview locals, but Barney said, "We can handle this. You need to finish what you were doing."

I stared at him.

"Go on, Ricos."

"We need to find Randy first and keep him safe."

"We'll do that; you can trust me. Can't you see that you need to keep doing what you were doing? You must be close for them to start taking chances."

"Limping Man said if I didn't quit he'd be forced to kill me."

"If he does that, I'll personally hunt him down and take him out."

"Great, but I'll still be dead."

"Huh. That's a problem."

I wanted to throw something at him. Instead, I said, "You're right. I am close."

"As soon as you know who he is you can go and pick him up."

"You make that sound as if it'll be a piece of cake."

Barney glared at me with his hands on his hips. "Are you gonna stand there whining about how hard it is, like—like one of those big-mouthed old guys at the café? If this job was easy, everyone would want it."

"Yeah, we've had that conversation before."

"Then don't make me repeat myself. Either you're gonna solve this case or you can stay here and work with Buster, and I'll go solve it."

"You don't even know what I'm doing."

"That's my point; now get out of here!"

* * *

I went home, re-packed my suitcase, showered, and crawled into bed early. My plan was to leave at one in the morning, so I could be at the old Jones home before its occupants left for the day. Before I fell asleep, I called Joe to say I couldn't call him later that night as we'd planned and to explain why. He was horrified to know Limping Man had taken Randy. He thought I should quit, at least until I had him in custody. How would I get him in custody if I quit?

I wasn't going to give up, and I told Joe that as gently as possible. He seemed to realize he was arguing an impossible viewpoint and got quiet. We talked about when we would see each other again and realized that no matter when that was, it wouldn't be soon enough to suit either of us.

CHAPTER 21

There wasn't even a hint of daylight when I left Terlingua. I wanted to go to Simpson and crawl into bed with Joe. I planned it out and fantasized about it. When I got to Alpine, I had a decision to make: west to El Paso or east to Joe. I chose Joe, but Deputy Ricos, that intrepid seeker of justice, mighty champion of the underdog, she made me go to El Paso.

I didn't have to wait around because lights shone in every window at the Jones home; someone was there. When I knocked, a woman came to the door wearing a raggedy bathrobe and carrying a cup of coffee. My alcohol-sensitive nose knew there was a healthy dose of whiskey in it. The woman's blondish hair stood up as if she'd been through a tornado. Eye make-up had gone off-duty sometime during the night, and the result made her look raccoon-ish. She smelled like a morning-after drunk and looked old and palsied, but at the same time, she was young.

Here is an excellent reason not to drink.

The woman was not pleased to see me at her door.

I greeted her in a sunshiny voice. "Good morning. I'm looking for Leroy Beaumont Jones."

Her brow furrowed. "Leroy doesn't live here."

"But you know him?"

"Sure, I know him. Why do you ask?"

"I want to talk to him."

"I'm not sure where Leroy lives. He's somewhere in El Paso, but I don't guess that helps. And he might've changed his last name again. When I say I know him, I mean not that well anymore. I'm his ex-wife, but it's not like we're friends."

"Are you Sarah's mother?"

My simple question threw her. She gaped at me as if I'd landed on her lawn from another planet. "How do you know Sarah? Is it Leroy you want or her?"

"I need to talk to Sarah. Does she live here?"

The woman gave a derisive laugh. "Sometimes."

"Does she live mostly with Leroy?"

She laughed outright at that. "No, no. Sarah has nothing to do with him."

"Where does she live when she isn't here?"

"She stays with a friend in El Paso. But I won't tell you where. I don't know if Sarah wants to see you. Why are you here?"

At that moment, a small blue car pulled into the drive. A young blonde woman jumped out of it and hurried towards us. Sarah?

"Honey! Go back!" The woman stepped off the walkway and stood between her daughter and me.

Seriously?

The young blonde looked startled and turned to run, but I yelled, "Sarah! Can I ask you about Randy Green?"

She stopped so abruptly she almost fell. Meanwhile, her mother began to claw and swipe at me.

"BACK OFF!" I yelled so forcefully it even scared me. I grabbed one of her flailing arms and twisted it hard enough to get her attention. "Stop it right now!" I didn't want to hurt her, but I needed her to understand that if she kept on, I didn't plan to fight lady-like.

The anger seemed to drain out of her, so I freed her arm.

"Let's talk like adults," I suggested.

"My daughter doesn't know anything about that pervert!"

"Mom!" screamed Sarah. "Stay out of this! Let me speak for myself."

"Sarah, will you let me talk to you about Randy?" Then I turned to her mother. "You can stay with her while we speak, but don't touch me again."

"Sarah can speak for herself. I don't want any part of this." She went back inside, rubbing her arm.

"That's just as well," Sarah said.

The door slammed hard. Then we were alone in the yard.

"Sarah, I'm a private investigator working on behalf of Randy Green. Could we go somewhere more comfortable?"

"I don't know if I want to talk to you."

"What can I say to convince you that I need your help? It's for Randy's sake.

"But how do I know that?"

"Has anyone else offered you information about him in the last seven years?"

"No. And I've asked a lot. How do I know if you'll tell me the truth?"

"What reason do I have to lie? Wait. Think about this. You could hear me out first, and then decide if what I'm telling you is true."

"Okay. Let's go in the backyard."

I followed Sarah to a table on a covered patio. The backyard was nicer than the front. What lawn existed had been mowed, and marigolds and petunias bloomed in terra cotta pots near the back door.

"With your permission, I'd like to record this conversation." I had already gotten out the recorder.

"Why?"

"Because what you say is going to help Randy."

She looked confused, but she agreed to the recording.

I asked her to state the usual information for the record, and then asked, "Do you know what happened to Randy after you left Carterton?"

"No. No one would ever tell me anything."

"Randy served seven years in a state prison for raping you."

"You lie!" She bolted out of the chair, but then her face crumbled, and she began to cry. "That can't be."

"It's true, Sarah."

"Why?"

"He didn't rape you, did he?"

"Nobody raped me," she sobbed. "I've never been raped. I never said that. Who said I was raped? Randy was my friend. He would never hurt me." She continued to cry, more out of control than when she started.

I waited while she calmed down, wiped her eyes, and blew her nose. I easily imagined what a cute child Sarah had been. Her hair was still blonde and curly, and an essence of little girl remained with her.

"You signed a statement which told what happened. It was a sworn statement saying Randy raped you. Do you remember signing it?"

"I signed something, but it wasn't about Randy. It was about the nasty man, or I thought it was." She still swiped at her eyes.

"Why don't you start at the beginning and tell me whatever you remember?"

"It's been seven years, and I was just a little girl." She took a deep breath and let it out in a sigh. "I've thought of Randy a lot. My father and I moved into a house across the street from the Greens when my parents divorced."

"Your father had sole custody of you?"

"Yes. He was gone a lot, and he'd leave me alone during the day, but sometimes he left me with a maid. I wasn't supposed to leave our yard. I went over to Randy's one day when he was raking and offered to help. He said, 'sit and talk to me while I work.' I craved attention, and he showed a sincere interest in me. We began talking about different things, some important, some not. He told me I could come over any time I felt lonely."

She paused and then said, "I had a crush on him. One day when I was helping him work on his truck, we started telling each other secrets. I told him I thought he was the handsomest man in the world. He laughed and said he only seemed that way because I loved him. Then he told me I was like a little sister to him, and that he loved me too. I was thrilled."

She paused again and when she continued, her voice came in a pained whisper. "A man began coming to our house at night."

"Please tell me about him," I said when she hesitated to say more.

"He came to my room and sat on my bed and spoke to me. I thought he talked dirty, but it was more the way he spoke than what he said. I was only nine and didn't understand much. He put his hands on me and scared me with his heavy breathing and groaning. He said if I told anyone, he would kill my puppy. I forgot to say that Randy had gotten permission from my dad to give me a puppy. That puppy meant everything to me. I was no longer so alone at my house."

I felt a twinge of homesickness for my own puppy. "Did the man hurt you?"

"Not really, but it was frightening because I didn't understand. He never put his penis into me, but he did put it all over me. Sometimes he only wanted me to touch him. I didn't want to, but I had my puppy to consider." Sarah wiped her eyes again.

"Randy noticed something wrong with me, and he asked me to tell him what it was. I cried, and Randy held me, and the story tumbled out. He told me it was not okay for a man to touch me in that way. I thought it was wrong or else why would he have to threaten my puppy? Anyhow, it felt wrong to me even before he made threats."

Sarah took another deep breath. "Now that I'm older, I realize how wrong it was, and that my father knew about it but didn't stop it." She began to cry silently, big tears rolling down her cheeks.

"Sarah, do you know the identity of the man?"

"No. I never saw him clearly because he only came at night in the dark. I had the impression he was small and ugly. Maybe that was only because he touched me, and I didn't want him to."

"What else do you remember about him?"

"He spoke with a stutter, not a bad one, but I noticed it. Also, he chewed gum all the time. I could smell Juicy Fruit when he breathed on me. I never took it when he offered me a stick of it. The smell of it still makes me sick."

"Have you ever asked your father about him?"

"Yes, of course. He denies knowing about it and denies knowing anything about Randy except to say he was a queer who put sick ideas into my head. My father and I are never together. I hardly ever see him. No matter what he says, I know he knew about it and let it happen. I think that creepy man paid my father to let him do that to me."

"Why do you think that?"

"My father always needed money because he gambled."

"I see. Are you sure you never heard a name?"

"Yes, I'm sure. How did Randy survive prison?"

"He survived a day at a time by putting his attention on other things."

"He's way too gentle and sweet to go to prison."

"I agree, but under that gentleness is a rock of a man."

"How is he now? Is he okay?"

"Yes, he is. He seems happy." I didn't mention that he was missing.

"I'd like to think my father would admit to what he did, but I don't have any hope of that. He's become a hard man. Guilt did that, I think."

"How did your mother lose custody of you, Sarah?"

"She's an alcoholic, but I think I'd have been better off growing up with her. At least she loved me. She would never let a strange man touch me."

"What did Randy do after you told him about the abuse?"

"He tried to talk to my father, but Dad was mean to Randy and wouldn't listen. Randy wanted to run away with me, but he didn't have any money and anyway, where would we go?

"My father accused Randy of abusing me and even tried to tell me it was Randy who came at night. I was nine, not stupid. Randy would've never done that, and if he had, I would've known it was him."

"What happened next?"

"Randy tried to find out who it was."

"How did the man get to your house? Did he walk? Was he a neighbor?"

"My father brought him. At the time, I thought it was because he didn't know how to drive, but now I realize it was probably because if people had seen his vehicle at our house, they would've recognized it. If he'd brought his car, Randy could've found out who he was."

She paused in her story to wipe more tears and clear her throat. "This is harder than I thought it would be."

"I know it is. Just take your time."

"One night, I kept underpants on under my gown because I thought that would keep him away. He pulled them down and ejaculated on me, but I didn't know back then it was called that. After he did it, he jerked the panties back up on me and left." She shuddered at the memory. "I fell back to sleep because I'd been sleeping when he came in. My dad's yelling woke me up, and the next thing I knew the sheriff's car came."

"Did the sheriff talk to you?"

"No, and I fell back to sleep. I woke up in the sheriff's office, and he and my dad tried to tell me that Randy had done something bad to me. I knew he hadn't, and I tried to tell the sheriff about the bad man. I never saw Randy again."

"Was a rape exam done on you?"

"I don't know. I wouldn't have known what that was."

"Were you taken to a hospital or a doctor's office?"

"Yes, but I think I was drugged."

"Were you interviewed that night?"

"No. I was hysterical, and somebody gave me a shot."

"Did the sheriff interview you again?"

"Yes, and I told him about the nasty man again, and he acted like he believed me and had me sign something so that he could put him in jail. After that, I was sent to my mother.

"During that time, I asked about Randy. Every time I talked with my dad I asked him about Randy. He always said he was fine. I wanted to talk to Randy, and I pressed my mother about it. She told me I should try to forget the bad things he'd done to me. I knew then that my father had lied to her, and I gave up. It's hard to be nine years old and fight something like that. I kept Randy in my heart and prayed he was really okay." She paused, and her lips trembled. "He wasn't okay, and I think I knew that."

I put my hand on top of hers. "You were only nine. None of this is your fault, and Randy knows that. He's clear on what happened and why."

Sarah sat up straight. "I might have something that will help you. Wait right here while I get it."

She went into the house and came back with a small cardboard box. "I don't know if this will do any good, because they've been in here all this time. I kept the panties I was wearing that night." She handed me the box.

I was stunned and asked how a young girl would know to do that.

"I knew what he did to me was wrong, and I didn't know exactly how it was tied to the wet stuff, but it was on my panties. I kept them as proof that the bad man was doing what I said. Nobody seemed interested in them, but I kept them anyway. I can't say why, but here they are."

I was speechless.

"Do you think it will help you?" Sarah asked.

"Yes, Sarah, this will help."

"Do you think I could talk to Randy sometime?"

"Of course; Randy would love to speak with you. If you'll give me your cell phone number, I'll ask him to call you."

She wrote it on a piece of paper. "Is he still handsome?"

"I think so, but see what you think. I brought you a photo."

She took it from me as if she feared seeing Randy again. "Oh. My. God!" she gasped. "He's so hot!"

When I left Sarah, I promised to arrange a call from Randy.

I stopped at a restaurant to eat something because my last decent meal had been breakfast the day before. I was almost too excited to eat but knew I needed to. After ordering, I stepped outside to call Barney, but my phone rang when I took it out of my pocket.

"We haven't found him yet," Barney said, "but we can't panic."

"Oh yes, we can."

"Well don't."

I told him about Sarah's amazing cardboard box. He was as hopeful as I was that the evidence it held would lead us to the guilty man. Barney agreed that I should go on to Midland to leave the box at the crime lab before returning to Terlingua.

As I got back in my car after eating, the rehab place in Midland called to say that Jacob Rawlings would see me now. Could I come today? Yes! Maybe he was ready to spill what he knew. All I needed was a name.

I was excited and called Barney to tell him the developments. Even though Randy had still not been located, he thought I should see Rawlings before he changed his mind. He suggested I "step on it," which made me laugh.

"Yeah, I forgot who I was talking to for a minute there," he said.

"My mother would be hysterical if she knew how fast I'm driving her car. On second thought, I could get hysterical thinking about her driving mine. Have you heard anything from Craig?"

"Not yet."

"He'll probably be back today or in the morning. He'll need water and food. And Billy is with him."

"I think that old marine is going social on us."

"It does seem like he's come out of his shell," I said.

"It's hard to picture him tramping around in the backcountry with Billy moaning and wringing his hands."

"Billy can be tough when he has to be."

"If he's not now, Craig will bring him back that way," Barney said.

"Poor Billy."

"Ricos, aren't you excited? Rawlings will give you the name of the man behind this, and it'll be over. You're nearly at the finish line."

I wanted that to be the case for Randy's sake and for Billy's, and even for mine. It was tempting to share Barney's excitement, but I knew it wasn't going to be that cut and dried because nothing ever is.

***

An hour later, Zeke called with information. I stopped in a pull-out so that I could put my full attention on what he had to say.

"The hairs belong to Paul Wilder, an ex-con. He's a petty criminal who has been in trouble many times."

Gee, what a surprise.

"He's just served five years in a state prison for bankcard fraud and is on parole." Zeke gave me his last known address in Midland, which meant I was hauling butt towards Limping Man's home base.

"Listen here," Zeke added, "don't assume that 'petty criminal' means he's not dangerous. It's the repeat offenders who often go from bad to worse. He's already done time for breaking and entering, assault, and fraud."

"He's a charmer all right."

"I'm sure you won't go after him alone, but if at any time you feel you've gotten in over your head, call me. I'm in Austin, but I can mobilize a team in Midland in minutes—or anywhere else in Texas. Remember that."

"I will, Zeke. Thank you."

"Listen. When I was your age, I dove headlong into things and consequences be damned. I thought I was indestructible and was always the last guy to call for help and the first to put myself on the line. You're not like that, I hope."

"No, sir."

He laughed. "There's no point in lying to me."

"Okay, well, I'm a little like that."

"I also know lecturing you won't help."

"I promise I'll call you when I need to."

"That handkerchief you left at the lab contained DNA belonging to Damien Jerome Hall and Randall McKinney Green. Hall was in the system because he worked in law enforcement. Is he someone you know?"

"No. He's a deputy who abused Randy when he was in jail awaiting trial."

"I see. He was dismissed from his last job in Dallas County."

"I bet I can figure out why."

Zeke laughed and then gave me Hall's last known address and phone number. Again, he warned me not to go without backup, and again I promised not to. Parents are so suspicious of every tiny thing.

"Was your friend raped or was it some other form of sexual assault?"

"He forced Randy into oral sex and many more times than once."

"If you want to bring Hall to justice, do your homework. Learn the rest of his history because you know he's probably done it before and since. Find witnesses and other victims. Take it a step at a time."

"Okay, Zeke, thank you."

"If your investigation brings you to Austin, I hope you'll come for a visit."

"I will."

"I'd love to spend more time with you."

After we talked a little more about spending time together, I begged him to rush through one more piece of evidence I'd leave at the crime lab later. When I explained the significance of Sarah's underpants, he agreed. He would probably have done it anyway; such is the power of a daughter.

CHAPTER 22

Midland Recovery, a private drug and alcohol rehabilitation facility, is located on beautiful grounds that are meticulously tended. The grass is so thick and green it looks fake. There are shade trees, rosebushes, and beds of blooming flowers. It's the kind of overly serene place where they stash alcoholics and drug addicts to get them well or out of the way.

Under the trees stood benches in groups, where patients could visit with friends, family, or each other; or they could sit in silent contemplation while going totally nuts.

A friendly attendant took me to the former public defender's private room.

"Good afternoon, Mr. Rawlings," he greeted him as we entered. "I've brought Ms. Ricos to see you, as you requested." He introduced the two of us and left.

"Please sit down," said Rawlings. I knew from records that he was in his mid-forties, but he looked haggard and old. "You said before that you wanted to talk to me about the Randall Green trial. I wasn't ready the first time you called, and I'm still not, but I must face this. I hope you won't judge me too harshly. I did a terrible thing to Mr. Green."

I took out the recorder. "May I record our conversation?"

"No. I don't want that, but I will speak honestly with you. Randy Green never raped Sarah Jones. I believe he lacks the capacity for that kind of violence and cruelty."

I shoved the recorder back in my pocket but turned it on. It would be unusable in a court, but I wanted Randy to hear what he said.

Rawlings stared at me. "Who are you again?"

"I'm Randy's friend, trying to clear his name. I'm a deputy sheriff in Brewster county, but I'm not here in that capacity."

"How is Randy?"

"He's doing fine considering what he's been through."

"After that trial, I became addicted to drugs and alcohol. I couldn't live with what I'd done or failed to do. I was supposed to defend him, yet I didn't. The court assigned me to his case but told me not to exonerate him.

My innocent client would be found guilty and facts be damned. You see, there was no forensic evidence to link Randy Green to any crime."

"Who was behind it and why? Why Randy?"

"Randy was a scapegoat who was in the wrong place at the wrong time, in an evil town run by a crooked sheriff and corrupt judge." Rawlings rubbed his temples as if his head hurt. "Neighbors saw him running from the Jones house that night, so the sheriff easily convinced everyone there had been a rape, and that Randy had done it." He picked at his sweater.

"You asked who was behind it," he continued. "Isn't it obvious? It was Judge Carter. He protected whoever was abusing the girl. The judge was determined to keep the guilty man out of the public eye, and Randy was coldly sacrificed as a result.

"I should never have gone along with it. So much money changed hands in that trial. I was paid two hundred thousand dollars for my part. My life was threatened as well, but I could've moved away or notified the FBI. Money called, and I was weak. It's ironic that I've spent more than that on drugs, alcohol, and therapy through the years that ensued.

"Now I realize I'll never get well if I don't own up to what I did. I'll lose my license to practice law and will probably go to prison. I'm ready for that because I can't keep living in the hell where I've been. I'd rather go to prison a sober man than stay a slave to alcohol and drugs." He leaned back against the chair, as if exhausted by his confession.

"Since Sarah hadn't been raped," I said, "why was anyone picked up at all?"

"Judge Carter knew Randy would stay on top of it until he figured out who the abuser was. He decided to remove that possibility by having him charged with rape and sending him away."

"Sarah had no idea until recently that Randy had been sent to prison. She told me she thought she had signed a statement about the abuse, not about Randy. She never mentioned Randy in her true statement."

"You've spoken with her?"

"Yes."

Jacob Rawlings stood and moved to the window. He sighed as he looked out at the lush grounds. "That innocent child was used to incarcerate the only adult she could trust."

I got up and stood next to him, so the recorder wouldn't miss a word he said. He turned to face me with eyes full of tears. "I assume I'll be served with papers."

"Yes."

"I'm prepared for that."

"Do you have a copy of the trial transcript?"

"Yes. It will take some time to get my hands on it, but I can make sure you get it." He stared at the outdoors a few seconds and then continued. "I'd like to be able to talk to Randy. I need to tell him how sorry I am. Could you arrange that? I won't be able to get fully well until I try to make amends to him."

"If Randy wants to come, I can arrange it."

"I hope he will."

"The judge is dead; who is everyone afraid of now?"

Jacob still stood at the window, but I had started to sit in the closest chair. I have no idea why. I've tried to figure it out since that day, but I still can't explain it.

"The pervert himself calls the shots now," Jacob said, and then the window pane exploded, and a bullet slammed into the back of the attorney's skull, silencing him. Glass sprayed over me, and some of it ended up in me. A second bullet zinged past my ear and barely missed my head, but it did miss because I had been lowering myself into a chair.

A nurse heard the commotion and came to see what happened. She saw that Jacob was gone but called an ambulance for me even though I insisted I didn't need one. I was traumatized by what I'd witnessed, and my ear pained me, but I fared better than poor Jacob Rawlings, who would never feel pain again.

***

The ambulance took me to the emergency room of a hospital in Odessa. I continued to say I didn't need or want medical attention, but nobody listened. One of the EMTs said I'd lost a piece of my right ear, and the injury needed stitches. I also had a few bloody gashes on my right arm, where the shattering window pane had hit me.

My mind replayed the slow-motion way Jacob had slumped

forward with blood, glass, and brains splattering everywhere. The horror of that took away whatever pain I might have felt.

A doctor administered a shot for pain that deadened my ear, so he could close the wound. He and a nurse jabbered as they worked on me, oblivious to my real concern. I had Jacob Rawlings' brains on me!

The nurse said she'd be back in a few minutes to finish bandaging my arm. Before she left, she gave me more pills for pain.

When the nurse came back she said, "Your ear will hurt for a while, but it'll heal fine. After it does, you may want to see a reconstructive surgeon, but I don't think the scar will be noticeable because of your hair."

I lifted my hand to touch the bandage.

"I'm going to put some bandages on this arm. Dr. Timon will be by in a while to check on you and may release you if you feel okay to go."

"I need to go."

"There's a policeman waiting to talk to you about what happened, but I told him to wait until I get your wounds covered. Do you feel up to speaking with him?"

"I saw it," I sobbed. "I had pieces of his brain in my mouth, and it's all over my clothes. And the blood—there's blood on me!"

She put her hand on my shoulder and spoke calmly. "We've cleaned you up. We removed your clothes and placed them in a bag, but I doubt if you want them."

Why didn't I remember that?

"It's in my hair," I moaned.

"Your hair has been washed. I promise you, there's nothing in your hair."

"I can't remember that. Are you sure?"

"Yes, I'm sure. You're having a perfectly normal reaction to seeing a violent act. It'll be a hard thing to forget, and we have somebody here who can counsel you if you'd like that."

"I already have a psychiatrist," I sobbed. "Why does everyone throw psychiatrists at me?"

"Maybe it's because you witness violent acts more often than most people." Her soft, soothing voiced calmed me, and she had a point. I realized I was dressed in a hospital gown. It wasn't fashionable, but it wasn't gore-covered, either.

"What about the policeman?" she asked when she finished the bandaging. "Should I send him in?"

"I guess so. Maybe he can tell me what happened."

"I bet he can."

She went to get the man waiting for me. He was an Ector County sheriff's deputy, not a policeman.

"Deputy Ricos? I'm Deputy Jim Johnson. How are you feeling?"

"How do you know who I am?"

"You were brought here by ambulance and the emergency staff found your ID and notified us."

"Does my sheriff know?"

"Yes, I believe he's been notified."

"Did Jacob Rawlings die?"

"Yes, he did."

"Did you find a tape recorder?"

"Yes, and I brought it with me. I cleaned it up for you." He handed me an evidence bag with the recorder inside.

"Thank you. Do you know who shot Mr. Rawlings?"

"No. We hoped you could tell us."

"I don't know." I leaned back into the pillow.

"There was a man here to see you." He checked his notes. "He's Judge Washburn from Freeman County. He went to make a call."

"How does he know I'm here?"

"Everyone knows you're here because of the news. Is this murder related to a case you're working on, Deputy?"

"I think so. I'm investigating for a friend, not through the Sheriff's Office. I needed the testimony of Jacob Rawlings, and now he's been murdered."

"Can you tell me what you're working on?"

I told him a brief version but left out many of the important things, not because they were secret but because I couldn't think clearly. I did give him Paul Wilder's name and full description, though.

Deputy Johnson left to get coffee but didn't return. I assumed he'd been called to the crime scene. I felt relief that I didn't have to go.

Barney called. "Ricos, what the hell? The sheriff is beside himself with worry."

"The sheriff knows where I am?"

"Yes. The E.R. called him. They had your I.D. The back of the card says to call Sheriff Duncan with regards to this deputy."

"I didn't think of that."

"He wants to know what in the damn hell is going on. You know what it means when he starts cursing."

"I know, but I don't have to explain myself to him. He asked me not to investigate under his name."

"How are you, anyway? The hospital told Sheriff Ben you'd been cut up and shot through the ear."

"I'm okay. They will release me soon. I'm waiting on the paperwork."

"As of now, you're waiting on Sheriff Ben," said Barney. "He's nearly there."

Crap!

"And I have more bad news. Your mother is coming."

Double crap!

Joe came in and made everything else disappear. He held my hand and stroked my face and whispered things that made me feverish.

My mom arrived before the sheriff did, but then she was driving the Mustang, and probably in the same way I drive it. Instead of marching in and demanding to see my chart, she marched in and did a double take when she saw a man holding my hand and whispering to me.

She gave me a sideways glance, stepped up to him, and held out her hand. "I'm Stephanie Ricos, Margarita's mother."

Joe stepped away from the bed an inch or two and took her hand. "I'm so glad to meet you. I'm Joe Washburn."

Joe had come from work and wore a brown tweed jacket with khaki-colored pants and a yellow shirt. He looked sharp enough to draw blood. His hair hung in a braid outside his clothes, and a tiny silver hoop graced one ear, but he still looked professional and not like a biker. It was hard to tell what my mother thought.

After Mom had scrutinized Joe long enough for his hair to go gray, she turned her attention to me. "You look terrible, sweetheart. What does the doctor say?"

"I'm fine. I'm waiting on him to release me. I'm sorry you had to come all that way for nothing."

"Nonsense! I'm your mother, and I want to be sure you're getting proper treatment. Does your arm hurt?"

"It stings, but not as much as it did. My ear is on fire, though."

"I want to speak with your doc. He shouldn't give you such heavy-duty pain medication because—" She glanced from me to Joe.

"It's okay, Mom, he knows I'm an alcoholic."

That told her what she needed to know about my relationship to Joe. She smiled at him and left in search of Dr. Timon.

Joe went back to holding my hand and whispering. A circuit court judge gave me the best treatment I ever got in a hospital.

"I'm sorry about her," I said to Joe. "She just found out I met a man, and that's all I told her, so she's curious. My mom's a doctor, but I guess that's obvious."

"Does she have a practice in Terlingua?"

"She heads up a non-profit clinic, Doctores Fronterizos. They provide medical care on both sides of the river. It's based in Terlingua."

My cell phone rang and when I answered, Sheriff Ben barked, "Are you still at the hospital?"

"Yes, sir."

"Stay put."

He hung up before I could say anything.

I dozed due to pain meds and trauma. When I awakened, my boss was sitting in a chair by my bed. When I'd fallen asleep, the man in that chair had long black hair. I woke up to a much older, white-haired man with short hair, and wearing a sheriff's uniform. It made me feel disoriented.

"Welcome back, Margarita."

"Hello, Sheriff Duncan."

"Are you okay?"

"I'm a little beat up but I'm fine. I'm sorry you had to come."

"Well of course I wanted to come when I heard you'd been injured. I hear you've been running a successful investigation."

"A witness was killed, and I still don't know the name of the man I'm after, so it's not that successful."

"I know you'll get to the bottom of it before long. I sent two more deputies to help look for Randall Green. We're concerned that he hasn't been located."

"I'm worried about him, Sheriff."

He didn't say anything more, so I asked, "Are you angry with me, Sheriff?"

"No. Why would I be angry? You're helping a man who needs it. I have no objection. I'm sure you're conducting yourself in a professional manner as a private investigator."

I didn't comment because Joe and my mother came in together carrying coffee. The sheriff stood and greeted my mom and then introduced himself to Joe as Ben Duncan. When Joe said he was Joe Washburn, the sheriff recognized the name from their earlier conversation.

"Oh, you're the judge," he said, surprised.

"Yes, sir, I'm Judge Washburn. And you're Sheriff Duncan."

It was one of those *well duh* conversations.

My mom's head whipped around to me, and she mouthed, "Judge?"

I nodded. She hadn't had a chance to grill Joe, which was a relief.

The doctor came in and Joe moved to my side and took my hand, which answered Sheriff Ben's unasked question about why he was there.

The doc flip-flopped about letting me go, possibly because my mother was watching him as if she ran the hospital.

"I'll take good care of her," Joe said. "I've already gotten hotel rooms here, and I'll take her there and make her rest. If there's any problem, I can bring her back."

The sheriff's mouth hung open.

"That sounds good," said the doctor—Dr. Timon, not Dr. Mother.

"Her bandages will need to be changed twice a day," said Mom because she just can't help herself.

"I can do that," Joe assured her.

"I'm going to show you how," she said in the voice that causes Craig to salute.

"I'll go now," Sheriff Ben said. "I see that everything is under control here."

"But Sheriff, you just got here," I said.

"Do you need me to stay?"

Joe took charge. "No, sir. I'm going to take good care of Margarita." I thought his comment was directed more at Mom than at the sheriff. Maybe he pictured her going to the hotel with us. That wasn't going to happen unless she drugged both of us.

"Get better," the sheriff said to me. "Keep me posted."

"Yes, sir. I will."

"I'd like to see you when you get back to Brewster County."

"Okay, Sheriff. I'll be back in a few days."

To my mother's credit, she only spent five minutes showing Joe how to properly dress a wound. To his credit, he let her.

CHAPTER 23

Joe took me to a hotel not far from the hospital. He had gotten separate rooms, a detail I appreciated.

"I don't assume things," he said when I commented on it. "The rooms adjoin. I hope that's all right."

I said it was.

"Not assuming things goes double for you," Joe said. "Besides, you need to rest." He gently pushed my hair away from my face as he spoke. "I have work to do. I'll be sitting at the desk in the next room. The door will be open, so call if you need me."

"Thank you, Joe. I want to shower and then nap a while."

I could barely keep my eyes open long enough to bathe myself, but I still had images of being gore-spattered, and I had to be sure I was clean. After the scrubbing, I came back to the bed and collapsed into it.

When I woke it was dark, but light spilled from Joe's room. He stood by my bed wearing cutoffs and nothing else except earrings. His ears were full of tiny turquoise studs, feathers, and intricate silver hoops. His hair hung over his shoulders and lay against his chest. Holy crap. He looked like pictures you see of Native warriors, only he needed face paint and a head dress, and they didn't wear cutoffs.

Joe perused the medications and bandaging supplies on the night stand and wasn't aware that I'd awakened. I was about to say something, although I had no idea what. *Get in bed* was one thing that came to mind.

Then his cell phone rang in the next room, and he went to answer it. He spoke softly for a few minutes. By the time he returned, I had propped myself up with pillows.

"Oh. You're awake. How do you feel?"

"I feel better. Sleeping helped."

I guess I was staring because he said, "This is who I am, but I'm sparing you the paint."

"I'd like to see the paint."

"I'll show you another day. It's time for your pain medication."

"I don't want it, Joe."

"Are you sure?"

"It makes me loopy."

He suppressed a smile. "It's Mom-Approved."

"I still don't like it."

"If you change your mind, say so. I'll be right back."

He returned wearing an undershirt and sat on the edge of the bed and took my left hand. Since I'm left-handed it was fortunate for me that the wounded arm was my right one.

"I need to tell you something, but you won't like it," Joe said.

My heart blocked my throat. I was terrified that Randy had been killed, but it wasn't that.

"Peter Adams shot himself this morning."

I struggled to speak. "That's awful." Then I felt like crying.

"Yes, it is, but don't you think it's more likely to have been a murder made to look like a suicide? Investigators are working on it now."

"Of course, he's killing the witnesses. Oh, Joe! What about Sarah?"

"I took the liberty of calling the El Paso County Sheriff's Office about her. They put Sarah and her mother in a safe house."

I threw my arms around him and hugged him tightly, even though it hurt. He returned the hug, and then rubbed my back with a tenderness that caused tears to come. I was still mortified by the memory of Jacob Rawlings' exploding head, which reminded me of men I shot in Mexico in self-defense, what seemed like a long time ago. When I see one revolting thing, it brings back the memories of all the terrible things I've seen, and those emotions well up and spill out my eyes.

While I tried to compose myself, Joe brought me a glass of water. I sipped it but went back to lying with my head against his chest. He set the water down and put his arms around me again. For a long time, we didn't speak.

"How did you know Sarah's address?" I asked.

"She gives it on the recording you asked me to listen to."

"You're so wonderful, Joe," I said against his chest.

"I'm glad you think so." He continued to hold me, and I continued to let him. After a while, he lifted my face and kissed me on the nose. "Get some sleep. I have work I have to finish but after that, I'll give you some good Comanche medicine if you'll let me."

My heart sped up, but then I wondered if he meant what I thought he meant or if it was the slut putting her spin on things.

He lifted one eyebrow. "Fair warning: one dose and you'll be hooked. I hope."

***

I have no idea what time it was, but Joe had either left or gone to bed. The day's events bothered me, including Sheriff Ben's concern that Randy hadn't been found. He was right, and I was worried. Craig and Billy had found no clues. They kept going out and coming in with the same news.

The land line phone in Joe's room rang shrilly. I heard him fumbling for it. "Hello," he said, and then, "She's not feeling well. Who's calling?"

I clicked on my bedside light as Joe clicked on his.

"Margarita," Joe called out, "Randy's on the phone."

I went into Joe's room and took the phone from him.

The caller wasn't Randy. It was Paul Wilder, the Limping Man. "Sorry, but I had to get past him," he said. "I heard you had a bad day."

"What do you want?" I was alarmed that he knew where I was, down to the room number, but it confirmed what I'd suspected anyway. I was being followed by a pro.

"Are you going to stop?"

"Are you?"

"This is your last warning." His voice dripped ice. "I have Randy, and you haven't figured out where he is. You're not likely to. I have him in a place where he'll never be found. If you don't stop your investigation, I'll leave him there to die a slow death. He's receiving food and water and is moderately comfortable, but all that can change. It's in your hands."

What was there to say? I hate fighting with someone who holds all the weapons.

"I hope you aren't going to make me kill you," he added. "I have a soft spot for women. I've never killed one, but there's a first time for everything."

Damn it! I didn't want to comply with the asshole, but I'd lost two witnesses and was worried sick about Sarah; Craig and Billy were killing themselves searching for a man who wouldn't be found. I'd lost part of my ear, and one hundred percent of my peace of mind.

I looked across the bed at the only good thing to come out of the Randall Green investigation. He watched me with concern in his eyes.

"All right," I conceded. "You win. You release Randy unharmed, and I'll quit."

"You have that backwards. You quit, and then I release Green."

"Okay, I'm quitting. How can I prove it to you?"

"Go home. I'm watching you."

"When will you release him?"

"When you do as I ask."

"I'll go home tomorrow."

"If I find out you're still investigating, I'll kill you and Randy Green, and maybe the Injun, too."

"You could get life in prison for even threatening a judge," I hissed.

"I don't care," Wilder said. "Can you get that?"

"Yes, I get it."

He hung up with no further comment.

"Now he's threatening *me*?" Joe was incredulous.

"He just wants my attention. I'm sorry I got you into this, Joe."

"I've never felt less sorry about anything." He held out his arms to me. As I lay my head against his chest, I heard a soft sigh. It must have come from that One Sane Woman who tries so hard to live in my head.

* * *

The way I saw it in the bright morning of the following day was that two things had to happen before I could proceed: We had to find Randy and keep him safe, and then we had to put Paul Wilder in jail. When I removed Wilder, the powerful pervert might have to show himself.

Joe begged me to stay, and he laid it out like a closing argument, "I promised your mother I would take care of you. You need to rest. You need those pain pills the doc gave you, and you can't take them and drive around. Paul Wilder doesn't care if you stay with me a few days. He already knows the nature of our relationship. I want to keep you close to me." He grabbed a breath and then continued, "Most of all you need love. I could come home from court and make love to you during recess, and love you all night long and all day, too, when I don't have to be in court."

I couldn't think of a rebuttal.

Before I left Joe, I explained that I wasn't working the Green case as a deputy and explained that I was on leave and might or might not ever work as a deputy again. His interest in me didn't seem adversely affected by what I said. I didn't tell Joe I had broken into Sheriff Hancock's records basement. How could I admit everything at once?

When I finished talking, Joe said, "In that case, you're off for a few more weeks?"

"That's right."

"When this is over, let's go away. Really away, like to Spain. We'll see where those tough white men in your ancestry came from."

"Doesn't Spain make you angry? They sent people to the New World and messed up everything the natives had going."

"It was bound to happen sooner or later." Joe pulled me close and held me there. "Since I got you out of the deal, it puts me in a forgiving mood. Besides, there're some Comanche with Spanish blood. What do you think they were doing with the women they stole?"

CHAPTER 24

When I screeched into Terlingua, I went straight to Randy's house and had a look around for myself. Zero in the way of clues, as I'd feared.

From there I went to Tom's and, by the time I arrived, dark had fallen. His Jeep wasn't there, but I knocked anyway in case. Then I tried the door. Locked. I put on gloves and broke out one of the window panes in the back door and let myself in. A penlight and a Beretta guided me through the house as I made sure no one occupied it. I had a surprise for any evil man who wanted to jump me in the dark.

When I established that nobody lurked, I went back to the kitchen and looked around. There was no sign Tom had been there recently, but perhaps he was a man who cleaned up after himself. Nah; I doubted it.

The bedroom was untidy with the bed unmade and clothes thrown all around. It was impossible to figure out how long it had been like that. Maybe he'd come home to change; maybe he was camping and hadn't been home since they took Randy.

Tom had some interesting porn magazines, but I didn't have time to look at them.

"Where are you keeping Randy, you sad sack of shit?" I asked his empty house.

Things got more interesting in the bathroom. Clothes I recognized as Randy's lay in a heap on the floor. They were stained with an oily substance that smelled like pickled jalapeño juice. What the hell? His shirt was soaked with it, much more than a spill while eating. What were they doing to him? I gathered up the clothes and took them.

I went back to the kitchen for a closer look. Under the sink sat two restaurant-sized jars of jalapeño juice, minus jalapeños. My suspicions and panic revved up a notch.

My last search was in the living room. There was a large flat-screen TV with a cabinet full of movies. Crushed Pepsi cans, empty peanut packages, and magazines were strewn across a coffee table. I glanced through the magazines. They were mostly about sports or sex, but one caught my attention. The cover displayed a steely man, ready for combat: camouflage clothing, extra-big rifle, fighting stance, and heavy black marks under his eyes. The magazine was *Combat & Survival*, and it was addressed to Rod Florence. Ah, now things were getting interesting.

A similar publication, *Survival*, was addressed to Brewster Hollings at a Terlingua P.O. box address. I didn't know him, but I thought Barney did. Both magazines had been marked with checks next to various gear that would be good to have if you were marching off to war.

Speaking of that, there was a weapons catalog from an Internet supplier, also with black checkmarks. Tom McAfee had no business with weapons. If Rod Florence had them, he was in violation of his parole. I couldn't say about Brewster Hollings, but if he was hanging with the other two, then he shouldn't have weapons, either.

My cell phone rang, and I nearly jumped out of my skin. Caller ID showed Joe, so I answered it.

He asked what I was doing.

"You don't want to know," I said.

"Are you doing something wrong?"

"You would think so."

"Why? Because I'm a judge or because I'm a man?"

"It's because you know the law. I'm searching the house of a suspect."

"Without a warrant, I presume."

"I don't have time to get one. Anyway, he's a scumbag."

"Scumbags have rights."

"I'm not looking for something to be used in court. I need to know where he's keeping Randy."

"It's still breaking and entering, so let's talk about something else."

"That would be great, but I'd like to call you from home. This place gives me the creeps."

"What if the scumbag comes back and finds you there?"

"I'll shoot him."

Joe groaned. "Please call me when you get home."

As I left the house I would later swear I had never been in, something fell out of Randy's clothes. It was longish and looked like a stone, but it didn't weigh much. I turned it over and studied it. It was a finger bone. Why would there be a finger bone in Randy's clothes? It couldn't be his, gracias á Dios, because it looked old and weathered. Whoever lost the finger lost it a long time ago. I put in into a small plastic baggie and stuck it in my pocket.

***

Before calling Joe, I called Barney. It was dark but not late.

"What are you doing back?" he demanded to know. "Shouldn't you be in bed?"

"I don't need to be in bed. Barney, who is Brewster Hollings?"

"He's that creepy guy that hangs out with Tom sometimes."

"Can you narrow it down? That describes several locals."

"True, but he's the one always dressed in camouflage everything. He's one of those soldier of fortune types, lives way out in the desert off South County Road. He says he shoots people who come on his property uninvited, so I've never been there. Others say he has tons of food in storage. He's got all the right survival gear, but I doubt he could survive a run-in with the tooth fairy."

I laughed at that.

"Why are you asking about Brewster?"

"I think there might be a third local man involved. Brewster would know how to hold a person in the backcountry for a long time, right?"

"True, but so would those other guys. It's a matter of picking a spot nobody will find. How in the hell have those idiots beat us so far?"

"It's because they've picked a good spot. And you and I haven't worked on this together yet. Tomorrow we will, and tomorrow we're bringing them down."

"Take a deep breath, Batgirl. You're saying we'll figure it out together when we haven't figured it out separately?"

"Yeah, that's what I'm saying. We're good together. Haven't we bragged about that forever? Two heads are better than one, like Holmes and Watson or Starsky and Hutch. Think about it, there's Batman and Robin, Goren and Eames, and Butch Cassidy and the Sundance Kid, to name a few."

"Butch and Sundance robbed banks."

"Stop nit-picking. You get my point."

"I do."

"We haven't worked together in so long maybe you've forgotten how good we are since you have Buster now. 'Barney and Buster' does have a nice ring to it."

"What makes you suspect Brewster Hollings?"

Oh crap. "I—um—I looked around Tom's house, and I found a survivalist magazine with his name on it."

"Buster and I went to Tom's, but all the doors were locked."

"Maybe you didn't check the door in back."

"You know I did, Ricos. Unlike Buster, I wasn't born yesterday."

I laughed. "I've missed you, Barney."

"You have?"

"Yes, I have. You can always make me laugh."

He didn't seem to know how to handle something nice from me.

"About Tom's," he said. "Did you find anything else? I assume he'd been back if the door was open. But it's hard to believe he'd leave it open. That's assuming you found it open."

"Let's assume that."

"You broke in."

"You don't know that, and I'm not admitting anything without my lawyer. When I got there, the pane was broken out of the backdoor."

"That's your story?"

"And I'm sticking to it."

He laughed. "What did you find?"

"Not much, other than the gun magazines and a lot of porn." Then I explained about Randy's clothes and the jalapeño juice stains, and he, too, thought it was ominous. We agreed to meet early in the morning.

After that, I called my favorite judge on a different subject.

CHAPTER 25

Barney strode through the front door of my house at 6:30 in the morning, yelling, "Truth is I've missed you, too, Batgirl."

"That's so sweet. I'm in the kitchen."

He entered and dwarfed the room. "I hope you're making food."

"I am, but you never like what I eat."

"What are you eating?"

"Apple juice, a bagel with non-dairy cream cheese, and a banana."

"Sounds fine. Can I have butter and jam on my bagel?"

"Sure. I'll toast one and you can put whatever you want on it."

"In that case, you'd better toast two."

"Only two?"

He took a banana from a bowl on the table and began to eat it and talk with his mouth full. "Buster's dropping by, so he might want one."

"Have you invited anyone else? I don't have enough bagels for all of Terlingua."

"That's not very neighborly, my partner. Look, I invited Buster because he knew we were going to meet, and I didn't want him to feel left out. He has to stay in the office today, so that's hard enough on him."

"I'm glad you invited him."

"You're hot for him, aren't you?"

"If, by 'hot for him,' you mean that I want the three of us to get along like professionals, then yes."

"Nice way to spin it, Ricos."

"You give me no choice when you spout fake news."

"Sometimes I wonder why I'm nice to you." He busied himself fixing a bagel to his liking. "So. Have you figured this out yet, Dick Tracy?"

"I've been waiting for you to get here."

"You look like hell."

"Thank you. That's what a woman wants to hear first thing in the morning."

"I only mean you're all bandaged up and kinda pitiful-looking."

"Oh, that's better."

"I can't seem to say the right thing. People are so touchy these days."

"Yeah, well."

"Craig and Billy came back last night after I spoke with you, speaking of looking like hell. They went to Billy's apartment to clean up and eat. I told them to meet us here at seven."

"Maybe I should fix a lot more food."

"Good idea. Wait 'til you see them. I'm sure Craig has lost weight. I think this looking and not finding is killing them."

I began making burritos, a lot of them. I also made more coffee because Craig likes it, and Barney was drinking the half-pot I made for him. I can't drink coffee when I'm already bouncing off the walls.

Buster called to say good morning, but that he couldn't come because of an altercation between two drunk men in the Ghost Town.

"It's early for dealing with drunks," I said.

"No kidding, but I think these guys are a couple of diehards left over from last night."

"Call us if you need us, Buster."

"I will. Thanks."

I asked Barney, "Do you think they could have Randy at Brewster's place?"

"I thought about that, but it's unlikely. It's way the hell out there, and that would make it hard for Wilder to come and go the way he does."

"True. But maybe that's why Randy hasn't been found."

"We can take a ride out there if you want, Batgirl. God knows, I don't have any better ideas."

"Let's wait and see what Craig says."

Craig and Billy had dark circles under their eyes and looked haggard. I knew Billy would bounce back fast, but Craig was old and had lived a hard life. He was a lean man on his best days, and I didn't want him to become ill. If I mentioned it to him I'd regret it, so I stayed quiet on the subject and comforted myself with the thought that he is *tough.*

Billy made his usual fuss over me, but I could tell he was sick with worry and beaten down by failure. Both men were.

I couldn't think of one thing to say to lift their spirits, so I did what women have done through the ages when their men come home looking like they've been defeated in battle. I fed them until they begged for mercy.

After breakfast, we sat in the living room and listened to Craig and Billy recount the details of their search. They had kept meticulous notes of the numerous places they'd been. They said they'd seen no sign of Randy, and in most places, no sign of humans.

"Now we know where not to look," said Barney. "So where do we look?"

"Maybe he's not really in the backcountry," Craig said, voicing something I had wondered also.

"Wilder could've said that just to keep us busy," Barney said.

"True, but he doesn't know Terlingua well," I said, "so what would cause him to think of 'backcountry' in the first place? And what are Tom and the other guys doing if not guarding Randy?"

"Good point, Ricos."

"They could also be out shooting innocent animals."

"True."

"What now? Think we should go out to Brewster's to see if they're keeping Randy there?"

Barney scratched his head. "Yeah. It can't hurt to have a look around. If they're not there, maybe we'll find a clue about where they are."

"What do you want us to do?" Billy asked.

"Don't you want to rest while we're gone?"

"No. I want to help you find Randy."

"You guys can come if you want," Barney said. "We could use eyes on the road while we check out his place. Brewster's not a man you want sneaking up from behind."

"Yeah, he's like Craig." I affectionately rumpled the old marine's hair.

He grinned but made no comment.

***

"He doesn't just live out South County Road," Barney complained. "He lives way the hell out South County Road."

No kidding. We had bounced, had our teeth rattled, and had our insides shaken so hard that when the truck finally stopped, we gave a collective sigh.

"You guys keep a lookout," Barney instructed as he hopped down from the vehicle. Honk the horn long and loud if anybody comes here."

"You can count on us," Craig said.

"Do you think Randy's here?" Billy asked.

"We're about to find out," I assured him.

He took a deep breath and got out of the truck. He and Craig stood at either end of it to watch for villains.

Barney and I hiked up and over a clay hill that hid Brewster's house from the road. It's an adobe dwelling next to a short, deep canyon that carries runoff from the mountains when it rains.

As Barney and I got closer, we spotted Tom's Jeep parked in a shed but no sign of Brewster's. We took our pistols out at the same time.

"No matter which one of them is driving that," Barney whispered, "he'll be armed and dangerous."

I nodded my agreement.

We banged on the front door, but no one came, and the place remained as silent as stone. While Barney tried the door, I peeked through the windows.

"No illegal searches," he said.

"That depends."

"On?"

"On whether or not the place is locked. I'm going in even if I have to kick the door down. Randy's life could depend on it."

"Oh, shit."

"Turn back now if you don't want any part of this."

"I'm with you all the way, Batgirl, even to prison."

Surprise. The back door was not locked. I went into the house while Barney checked out a storage shed to the rear of it. I heard him call, "Randy? You in here?"

I crept all through the house with my Beretta held in front of me. I opened every door, looked in all the closets, under the bed, and every other place a person could hide; I found nothing but dust and silence.

The kitchen held a big mess. It looked as though someone made sandwiches in a hurry. Empty packages of lunch meat and cheese still lay on the counter. A small mayonnaise jar with no cover on it held a knife smeared with drying mayo. Gallon jugs, some empty and some full of water, sat by the kitchen door.

When Barney came in, I was checking the bedroom.

"I can't find any sign of him," he said. "But I found enough ammo, food, and other survival stuff to last to the end of this century. It put me in mind of Duffy Chisolm and his tons of things, except Brewster's is clean."

"Don't go there, Barney."

"Okay."

The last thing I needed was to think about a criminal in another case while working this one. Duffy Chisholm harassed his peaceable neighbors, hoarded every type of junk you can imagine, lived in filth, and beat me up in a cowardly attack. And people wonder why I have anger issues.

During that lengthy, frustrating case, I proved that Chisolm had murdered a young woman and then, 21 years later, killed a man he had considered a friend. He's behind bars awaiting trial, and he belongs there. I know he exists, but that doesn't mean I need to think about him.

"I wonder what Brewster's afraid of," I said.

"Women taking over, probably."

I laughed at that.

Camouflage clothing was strewn on the floor, the bed, and crumpled on the dresser. Barney went to see if there was an attic or basement. I was for getting out. My gut said Randy wasn't there.

We looked around but found nothing resembling a clue. While I searched the living room, where someone had slept on the sofa, Barney went to look in the small canyon that abutted the side of the property.

When I finished in the house, I waited behind it for Barney. A cage full of scorpions leaned against the back wall. What kind of person keeps scorpions? Their skittering made me feel crawled-on.

"Maybe he eats them," Barney said behind me, causing me to jump. "You know, to stay tough." Short pause. "Scorpions would have a nice crunch, lightly seasoned and fried."

"I'll tell him you want to have dinner with him, when we locate him."

"On second thought," he said, and didn't need to say more.

After the fruitless searching, we went by my house for cold drinks and to regroup. I brought out the finger bone that had fallen out of Randy's pants. When I mentioned that I had Randy's pants, Billy grabbed them from the floor and held them against his heart. When he did, a reddish-brown piece of crystal fell to the floor. I set both items on the coffee table where everybody could see them.

"Maybe these things are a message to us," Billy said. "Why would they be in his clothes otherwise?"

"That's a good point," said Barney. "But what message?"

"What else?" Billy replied with impatience. "He wants to tell us where he is!"

I passed the bone to Barney. "Don't you think that's a finger bone?"

He took it from me and turned it over in his hand. "I think it is. Is Randy in a graveyard?"

At the same time, Craig said, "That crystal is cinnabar. Margarita, you should know cinnabar."

Barney and I looked at each other. "Cinnabar mines," we said in unison.

Cinnabar is mined for the extraction of mercury, but hasn't been mined in the Terlingua area since the 1940s. However, several mines with open shafts still exist in the area. A mine made sense and narrowed our search. It was true that Randy would never be found if that creep Paul Wilder and his apprentices put him in a mine shaft; if left there, he'd die of hunger, thirst, and exposure.

"I think we should start with Buena Suerte," Barney said.

Buena Suerte is an abandoned mining village in the mountains near Lajitas. It's owned by the man who gifted me the thousand-acre bluff. He lives in Wyoming, and the chances of anyone else going there would be slim. Barney and I had once made a discovery of bodies in two of the still-open shafts, so it made sense that Buena Suerte was his first guess. We did have a finger bone, after all. Also, as Barney said, "Those buildings would provide a shelter where a bunch of chickenshits could hide out of the weather and pretend to be tough guys."

We laid out a plan, such as it was. We'd put my ATV into the back of Barney's personal truck. When we neared Buena Suerte, he and I would go in on that ahead of Craig and Billy, in case we were right about the location and the men were armed. I would fire a shot into the air if Billy and Craig should proceed. At that point, they would come forward in Barney's Sheriff's Office truck.

We high-fived and hugged each other in anticipation of finding Randy. Craig took Barney to pick up his truck and our Kevlar vests.

Billy sat next to me on the sofa, hugged me, and then began to sob. "What if they killed him?"

"Don't start thinking like that."

"If they didn't kill him, then this might set him back even more."

"We don't know that. Let's see what's going on before we panic."

"Bad things happened to him in prison," Billy said when he calmed down. "He only talks about it bit by bit."

"That's probably all he can stand. At least he trusts you if he's talking."

Billy let out a long breath.

"Don't spare him your sense of humor, Billy. I hope you make him laugh."

He chuckled. "We do have a lot of laughs."

Soon after that, Craig returned and, about 15 minutes behind him, Barney. We loaded up and headed out.

CHAPTER 26

It's seventeen highway miles to Lajitas, and then eight miles from the highway to Buena Suerte on a dirt road. We caravanned until we were a half-mile away from the mine and then we unloaded my ATV and put on our Kevlar vests.

"Let's do this thing, partner," growled Barney as he hopped on behind me.

We went to do the thing, and left Craig and Billy behind temporarily.

The abandoned mining village of Buena Suerte sits in rugged terrain, surrounded by cliffs and mountains of various sizes. Normally, I would approach slowly, and not just because of the rough road. The area is scenic and peaceful, with only the sound of the wind and birds. We couldn't stop to admire the wildflowers, the birds, or the views. We didn't have time to think about any of that.

We flew. Barney gripped the ATV with one hand and held his Beretta ready in the other. We came around a bend in a cloud of dust and skidded to a stop at the entrance to Buena Suerte. Our three suspects were waiting with the gate open wide. When they heard the ATV, I bet they thought it was their buddy Paul Wilder approaching. Whatever they expected, we were not it. Three mouths dropped open in surprise.

Brewster wheeled around and high-tailed it towards the closest building, a former post office and general store.

"Hold it right there," Barney shouted in his booming voice.

The idiot kept moving, so Barney bellowed, "I will shoot you! Get back over here, Brewster. Right now!"

Once we had them rounded up, I shot into the air, so Craig and Billy would know to join us. Barney ran his handcuffs through the gate and then clipped Brewster and Rod Florence together. They called us names, but nothing we hadn't been called before, until Rod started on me.

When he called me a "filthy Mexican whore, wetback slut," Barney tied a handkerchief through his mouth.

"Thanks, Barn."

"It was either gag him or kick out his teeth." Barney turned to

Brewster. "I'm out of handkerchiefs. If you start, I won't hesitate to tear up my t-shirt. If you force me to do that, your teeth are going down your throat. Do you understand?"

Brewster nodded and stayed quiet.

Tom watched without comment. We pondered what to do with him since Barney had only one set of cuffs; the sheriff had mine.

Suddenly, the loud sound of a slamming metal door reverberated against the cliffs. Blam, blam, BLAM! The vibration made my teeth hurt.

"What in the hell is that?" Barney looked at me, but I had no idea. He turned to Tom. "Tom?"

"Don't you know the sound of a prison door slamming?" he said with a lot of attitude for a man with my gun pointed at him.

"We made a recording for the ex-con," Brewster said, "so he wouldn't miss being in prison. We set it on a timer."

"I see," my partner said through clenched teeth. "I hope you guys enjoy that sound, because you'll soon be hearing it a lot."

I stepped forward. "Where is Randy?"

"We think he died," Tom said in an emotionless voice.

"Where is he? Take me to him." I indicated with my Beretta that he should move it. Mercifully, the slamming sound stopped.

Craig and Billy walked up at that point. I knew there was no way I'd get Billy to leave, so I took Craig aside and asked him to take my cell phone and drive out until he got a signal. "Call 911 and tell them you need the ambulance and to stop for Dr. Ricos. Then call my mom and tell her they're coming. Tell her some a-holes stashed Randy in a mine shaft at Buena Suerte, and we don't know how badly he's hurt. After that, call the office and ask Buster to come and bring one of those deputies who helped with the search. The other one can watch the office and notify the sheriff. You'll have to tell Buster how to get here."

Craig nodded and went back to the truck with my phone.

When I jogged up, Barney was attempting to calm Billy.

I took my emotional friend by the elbow. "Walk with me, Billy. We're about to follow Tom to Randy. You're not going to scream and act hysterical, or you aren't coming. Randy doesn't need that. He needs your strength and for you to have hope no matter how bad he seems. Are we clear on that?"

Billy nodded. "You already know that Randy's hurt?"

"Yes, I'm pretty sure he is, but the ambulance is coming with Mitch and my mom. Craig has gone to call them."

We followed Tom to an open shaft. It took every bit of reserve I had not to shove him into it. By the side of the hole sat a boom box, piles of rope, empty food containers, and several large jars greasy with pickled jalapeño juice. A basket filled with dirty clothing and a jumble of empty water containers explained how they lowered and lifted supplies.

A sob escaped Billy when he saw Randy, but he didn't show any other outward sign of his distress. I took his hand and gently squeezed it. "Would you disarm the tape recorder? I'd shoot it, but I might need it for evidence. Then hold this pistol on Tom. If he comes at you, shoot him."

I kneeled and looked down into a shaft that was not deep, but it was too deep for escape. Randy lay motionless on top of a sleeping bag. The combined odors of human waste and rotting food made me nauseated. Randy had dug a latrine with a rock and a spoon, from the looks of it, but the smell was still overpowering.

Without saying a word, Barney cut a piece of rope and hog-tied Tom. He whined the whole time about police brutality, which just made Barney angrier and more determined.

Billy and I called Randy's name but got no response.

"Lower me down there," I said to Barney.

He turned to Billy. "Go and get my truck. We need it for stability." Barney had lowered me into a mineshaft before. I wouldn't allow myself to think about going into one again.

Billy left without argument while Barney began adjusting the climbing harness that lay next to the pile of rope. We adjusted it to fit me and were ready when Billy came back with the truck and Craig.

"The doctor is coming," Craig said, "and the deputies." He peered into the shaft and shook his head. "Lordy, lordy, lordy." He turned to Tom. "What is wrong with you that would make you treat another human being this way?" Craig never, and I do mean never, speaks to strangers.

Tom couldn't or wouldn't answer the question.

I rappelled down the side of the shaft with Barney letting out rope as I went. The rope was also tied to the truck as a safety measure. Below me lay a bunch of human bones. They had put Randy into a dark hole in the ground *with a corpse*. It chilled me to realize I lived in the same community with these men. Their time in Terlingua would soon be over, but I didn't know if Randy's had already ended.

I thought the bones belonged to one of the murdered women from another case. We had only recovered two bodies from mine shafts, but two more were still missing. If so, one more family would soon know the whereabouts of their loved one. It was barely more than a passing thought, since I was so worried about Randy.

"I just thought of something," Barney said. His voice sounded tinny from my location in the shaft. "Craig, will you take Margarita's gun and guard the guys out front? I don't want Paul Wilder to come back and surprise us."

"Yes, sir," agreed Craig.

It didn't take long to land at the bottom of the shaft. Being in the nightmare was infinitely worse than looking down at it. Dead scorpions made a crunching sound under my feet. I hate that sound. I stomped on a few that still skittered around, but since I wore boots and wouldn't be there long, I gave that up for much more pressing problems.

I felt Randy for a pulse.

"He's alive!" I yelled.

"Let's bring him up," Barney yelled back.

I tried to rouse Randy and finally got a groan but nothing more. As I adjusted the climbing jacket, and then attempted to get it on him, I spoke nonstop in case he could hear me. I explained that we were going to lift him out and that medical help was coming. I told him Billy waited for him at the top. I said every positive thing I could think of as I looked over his ravaged body. His face was so red and swollen he was barely recognizable. The skin around his eyes had puffed over the sockets until he didn't appear to have eyes, the result of jalapeño acid, I thought. He burned with fever and was barely breathing.

"Sing something, Billy," I yelled when I ran out of happy talk.

"Like what?"

"Anything!"

Billy began to sing *Love Me Tender* in a mellow, soothing voice. He sang every verse, and with an intensity that rivaled Elvis.

Bloody, puffy welts covered all of Randy's exposed areas, a result of scorpions. Multiple stings would've put enough poison in his body to cause his condition. I knew enough to know that his situation was grave. My mom would hurry, I knew, but would she get there soon enough?

***

At last, I had Randy ready to be hoisted up. It was difficult getting him into the jacket since he weighed so much more than I did. Once he was trussed, Barney helped me move him to the wall by inching him with the rope while I guided Randy's dead weight.

Barney and Billy began pulling him up. They had to go slowly, or he'd bash against the side of the shaft. At the last minute, I pulled on my heavy leather gloves, grabbed the rope, and hung on for dear life. I couldn't spend one more second down there.

It felt as though we were in a bad slow-mo movie with an insanely repetitive soundtrack of *Love Me Tender*. At some point during that ordeal, I ceased to like that song.

***

Mom and Mitch ran towards us, loaded down with supplies. Buster followed carrying a portable oxygen set-up.

Our partner set his load down. "I'm going to take over for Craig."

"Great idea, Buster," Barney said.

My mother kneeled on one side of Randy, and Mitch dropped to his knees on the other. They attached the oxygen mask to Randy's face, and then Mom took his pulse.

"I've never seen anybody injured in quite this way," she said.

"Me either," Mitch agreed. "It's gruesome."

"We're going to cut his clothes off, so anybody squeamish should stand back," Mom said as she began to cut. Randy's chest, stomach, and legs were covered with the same marks as his face. I took photographs with my phone for the record.

My mother looked up at me. "What's happened to him?"

"I think scorpions were dropped on him and, after that, pickled jalapeño juice."

Barney jabbed Tom with the toe of his boot. "Is that right?"

"Yeah," Tom said.

"You did that to this man?" Mom asked in disbelief. "Why, Tom?"

"He rapes children."

"He's a human being!" Mom's voice broke and she turned to Mitch. "Radio Life Flight, Mitch, and tell them to rush. Randy is in anaphylactic shock and has a serious infection as well. We're about to lose him."

Mitch took off at a dead run.

A sob escaped Billy, and at the sound of it, my mom turned to look at him. She hadn't realized he was there.

"We're going to save him, Billy." She gave Randy a shot as she spoke. "Come here and hold his hand. Tell him you love him and keep talking to him in case he can hear. It will help him get well." Compassion and quick thinking are two reasons why my mother is a superb doctor.

"Margarita, please help Mitch bring the jugs of water and the towels from the ambulance. We need to cool Randy right now. Ask Mitch to bring whatever he has because I'm not sure what I'm going to need next."

"He's not going anywhere," Barney said, indicating Tom, "so I'll help you."

Tom cursed and threatened us, but nobody cared.

Craig joined us at the ambulance and the four of us brought back everything Mitch had that wasn't a permanent fixture. Then we wet towels and Mitch placed them over Randy while Mom started an IV of fluids and antibiotics. When Randy's fever heated the towels, she and Mitch handed them back to us for rewetting.

"He's breathing easier," Mom said after a while.

After a few more minutes, Randy groaned.

"Are you awake, Randy?" Billy kissed his hand. "Please wake up. Squeeze my hand if you can hear me."

We watched and hoped, but Billy shook his head.

"We're doing everything we can for you, Randy," my mother said as she cleaned the welts. "I know this hurts you, and I'm sorry. As soon as you're clean, I'll apply anesthetic cream. That'll feel better. Don't worry that you can't see. Your eyes are swollen shut, but the swelling is going down." She continued to speak soothingly.

Barney and I stepped over to Tom. "I guess you're uncomfortable," my partner said. "I'll tie you in a different way if you'll tell us everything you can about what's happened here. Do you agree to that?"

"Yes, for God's sake, untie me."

"Do you understand that we're making a recording of this conversation, and what you say may be used against you in a court of law?"

"Yes! I already said yes."

"Let me rephrase that," Barney said, taking his time. "You have the right to remain silent." He recited and recorded the entire Miranda reading while Tom cursed and called him names. "Do you understand these rights?"

"For the love of God, man!"

"I'll accept that as a yes."

"Did Paul Wilder ask you to do this to Randy?" I asked.

"No. He asked us to find a place to put the freak where he wouldn't be found, and we did. He told us to bring food and water and to be sure he had enough clothes and blankets and such."

"How did you meet Wilder?" Barney asked.

"We were over at the café talking about how a child rapist had moved here, and none of us liked it. Wilder overheard us and joined our table."

Damn. I knew no good could ever come out of that over-caffeinated group of gossipy men.

"How did you get the idea to torture him?" Barney asked.

Tom shrugged. "We had a bit of fun at his expense. We didn't think of it as torture."

"What about the door-slamming?"

"We were trying to get a rise out of him. He didn't want to talk, and we wanted him to. Rod had the scorpion idea, and we thought it'd be funny. Brewster has scorpions, so we..."

"Did Randy talk?" I asked.

"He claimed he didn't rape that girl, but convicts lie. He admitted he did a seven year stretch for rape."

"That's true. He did seven years, but he never raped anyone. I proved that a few days ago."

"You're just saying that because you don't like me."

"No. I refused to go out with you because I don't like you. The facts of this case have nothing to do with how I feel about you. Randy never raped Sarah Jones. In fact, nobody ever raped Sarah Jones."

"But Wilder said he was guilty."

"He lied, you pathetic tool," snarled Barney.

"What is his interest in Randy?" I asked.

"We don't know. He works for somebody in Austin who has an interest in him."

"Did he ever mention a name?"

"No."

"Who thought of Buena Suerte?" Barney asked. His fists clenched with anger, but he was trying to be civil because of the recording, and because we're not supposed to stomp the crap out of the citizens we serve.

"Brewster had the idea. How did you figure it out?"

Barney put his hand on my back, and we walked back over to Randy.

"What do you think, Ricos? I'm talking about the bones. I already know what you think of the perps."

"I think they belong to either Gloria Abelard or Estella Rodriguez, most likely Gloria since she's been missing the longest."

"Do you think the bones are from that old case?"

"Yes. I hope so. I hate to think there's another young woman missing that we don't know anything about."

CHAPTER 27

A helicopter flew Randy to the medical center in Lubbock. My mom rode along to continue his care and to make sure that Billy could go, too. I promised Billy I would meet him there that evening.

I wandered through the building where the twisted freaks had stayed, hoping for a clue but also for something to do. Barney kept busy overseeing the reading of rights by Buster as each man was handcuffed, formally arrested, advised of the charges, and put into a vehicle for transport to Alpine. The deputies who had come from Alpine to help would take two perps in the vehicle they came in, and Buster would take the third, Rod Florence. Rod's involvement made me sad, only because he was Cissy's father.

"Don't take any crap from him," Barney advised Buster. "If he starts talking filth, warn him once. If that doesn't work, gag him."

After the good and bad guys had gone, Barney, Craig, and I sat in Barney's truck. He radioed Sheriff Ben, who was standing by. "Unit five to base."

"Go ahead five," said the sheriff.

"All's well, but N.F.T." Barney kept his message short because of people listening. *N.F.T.* is "need forensics team." The team would come, courtesy of the Texas Rangers, but it would take a while.

The sheriff already knew Barney's location. "Ten-four," he said. "P.S." Protect scene.

"Ten-four, Sheriff."

Cell phones are easier, but they don't work everywhere we go, and the radio does. Barney and I have a mini-language of radio-speak that even the sheriff doesn't get. We hope.

***

I took Craig to pick up Marine and then to the bottom of the bluff where he kept an ATV of his own. I tried to thank him, and he did let me hug him, but he waved off my thanks. "You'd have done the same for me," he said.

"That's true, but it wasn't you, was it? How'd it go with Billy?"

Craig, never effusive, said only, "He's a fine recruit."

"Please remember to eat, Craig. If you don't look better by the time I come back, I'll come up there and kick your skinny old butt."

"I look forward to your try," he said with a chuckle. "Keep yourself safe."

I went by Mom's clinic to retrieve Missy. We shared a tearful reunion. Okay, I shed the tears; she was so joyful she bounced off furniture and into walls. When she calmed down, we headed home so I could pack for a trip to Lubbock, Midland, and with luck, Simpson.

***

Billy called to tell me that Randy had awakened. He couldn't speak, and he wouldn't be able to see for a while, but he was responsive. When Billy asked him, "Do you know who I am?" Randy had shakily brought Billy's hand to his mouth and pressed it to his lips. I'd never heard Billy sound so happy.

Billy said my mom was flying back to Alpine with the Life Flight crew, and a friend would bring her home from there. "I'm practically in love with that woman," he said. "She saved Randy's life."

I begged off going to Lubbock. Billy started to complain, but I explained that I still had more to do before Randy's name could be cleared in a court of law, and he relented. I didn't mention how critical it was to nab Paul Wilder, the Limping Man, before he could kill me or anyone else.

"Please tell him this will be over soon," I said. "By the time he comes home, the man who should've done his time will be doing it."

"What about the men who did this to Randy? Will they get out on bail?"

"No, Billy. The sheriff is going to talk to the judge and ask him not to allow it. Rod Florence will go straight back to prison because he was on parole. When this goes to trial, he'll get more time on top of what he still has to serve."

"Okay, I'll tell Randy what you said. They're letting me stay in the room with him."

"That's great. It'll help him get well faster."

"Your mom arranged it," Billy said. "I don't know how she did it, but the hospital director put it in writing. If anyone questions it, all I have to do is show them the letter."

***

I sent a text to Cissy asking her to call me when she could. Next, I texted Mom with my thanks and told her where I was going and why. I also texted, "I love you. U R awesome! My Mom makes me proud."

Ten minutes later, Cissy called me in tears. School was out for the day, but before it was dismissed, she'd been told that her father had been arrested. News leaks out when there's an ambulance run, faster than usual when the helicopter comes. Her mother had filled in the rest when she picked her up after school.

"Is it true what my dad did?" Cissy sobbed.

"What have you heard?"

"Mom says he's in jail for hurting Randy. He's going back to prison. What made him do such a terrible thing?"

"I don't know, Cissy. I'm just sorry it affects you."

"Is Randy going to die?"

"No. He's at the hospital in Lubbock, and he's better already. Billy is with him."

"Can you come get me?"

"Yes, if your mother will agree to it. Ask her if you can stay the night with me."

"Mom says Randy raped a little girl, but I know that's not true."

"You're right, Cissy. I've proved he didn't do it, but he spent seven years in prison anyway. Now I'm trying to clear his name."

She cried so hard her next words were incoherent.

"Cissy, I know it doesn't sound like it, but everything is going to be okay. When you hear people say bad things about Randy, tell them what I said. And promise me you'll remember that you have special gifts. Don't let people put you down because of what your father did."

"Okay," she sobbed, and then went to talk to her mother.

Twenty minutes later, I picked her up. She got in and threw herself against me. A long time passed before she would let go.

That night, after Cissy fell asleep, I called Joe to tell him the good news about Randy. I gave him a brief synopsis and promised the details later.

"I've been thinking about your case," he said. "Can I give you my thoughts on your unknown perp?"

"Please do."

"This has been bothering me because Carter was wealthy in his own right, so a bribe wouldn't appeal to him the way it did to the others. I think it was Carter bribing people to protect someone close to him. If I had to guess, I'd say he was protecting a son. Parents will kill for their children. It would've been hard for him to swallow the fact that his son had abused a small child, but his instinct, I believe, would have been to get the boy help and cover up his crime. Otherwise, a child-molesting son would've brought down the whole family. Imagine the scandal."

"Wow, Joe, you've put a lot of thought into this. It makes sense."

"I'm highly motivated by thoughts of you and me in Spain and thoughts of you and me anywhere. And I'm familiar with criminal behavior. Also, the Carters are from old Freeman County money and enjoyed a status similar to the kind royalty enjoys. Carter's mother was a Freeman, one of the founding families. The more a person has, the more there is to lose."

"Thank you, Joe. I'll do some research when I get there."

"You're coming here?"

"Yes, but I'm not sure when. I'm going to see Paul Wilder's parole officer tomorrow, and I won't know where I'm going next until I speak with him."

"Do I need to say that I want you to stay with me?"

"No, and that's also what I want."

"I have court tomorrow, but call and leave a message, okay?"

"I will."

"Margarita, there's a Native saying I've heard all my life. 'Certain things catch your eye, but pursue only those that capture your heart.' In your case, you've captured both my eye and my heart. Please don't make me wait a long time."

* * *

Early the next morning, I left Cissy with Barney, so he could take her to school. As we said good-bye, I asked her for her sister's full name.

"It's Lesley Marie Florence."

"I also need her date of birth." After she told me, I asked, "Do you know where she is now?"

"No. Are you going to find her?"

"I don't know if I can, Cissy, but I'm going to try. Please don't mention this to anyone else until I find out more."

Her face lit-up. "Are you going to adopt us?"

"Right now, I'm just trying to get you two together for a visit."

"That'd be great!" Then she grabbed me and clung on. "That'd be the most awesome thing anybody ever did for me!" She began crying again. "I love you, Margarita," she sobbed. "I love you more than anybody."

"I love you too, Cissy. Now be brave. Call me if you need to. And don't forget that you can stay with Barney and his family if your mom has to leave."

"I know, I know. You worry enough for two mothers."

* * *

I stopped to see Sheriff Ben since he'd asked me to, and I wanted to find out the latest about the prisoners. He said the judge had agreed to our no-bail request until things could be sorted out. Among other things, he wanted to see the forensics reports. Getting them would take a while since the team hadn't arrived yet.

The sheriff was busy, so I didn't have to stick around long.

CHAPTER 28

Paul Wilder's parole officer was a man named Jerome Handley. I stopped to call him rather than arrive at his office without warning.

"Wilder is no longer on parole," he informed me.

"How can that be? He got out of prison three months ago."

"You'll have to talk to the governor. He pardoned him of his remaining time."

"Why would he do that?"

"I have no idea."

"But surely you know what kinds of things would make a governor forgive a man's parole."

"Wilder would have to be proven innocent, which is not the case, or the governor has some use for him, or else they're related. Or the governor did it as a political favor to someone else."

"I see. There's nothing in your file to explain it?"

"I have a signed letter and paperwork from Governor Cardenas, and that's all. He doesn't have to explain himself to a parole officer."

"Does Wilder still live in Midland? That's the last-known address in his jacket."

"Wilder's ex-wife Flo lives there. I think he now lives in Austin. You could check that with her."

I thanked Handley for his help and hung up. Then I had no choice but to call the governor. I was passed from a receptionist to a secretary to several different aides and still didn't reach him. Their job was to protect him from people who would waste his time. I got that, but it was aggravating. After being transferred all over the Capitol, I was informed that the man was gone for the rest of the day. When I mentioned making an appointment, an aide passed me back to the secretary. She said the first opportunity he had would be in one month. Would that work? No. I thanked her and hung up. I'd have to figure out another way.

As they say, it's all about who you know. I called Joe.

Jeanie, true to form, ran a defensive play. "He's in court."

"Do you know when he'll be free?"

"When he dismisses court, I suppose."

"Will you tell him I'm heading his way?"

"He won't be able to see you today, Ms. Ricos. He probably won't get out of court until 4:30 or 5:00."

"I understand that. Will you just give him the message, please?"

"All right, but you shouldn't count on seeing him."

"I won't, Jeanie. Thank you." I was not just counting on it; my heart pounded hard at the thought of it.

After that, I called Wilder's last known phone number in Midland. It had been disconnected, so I felt compelled to drive by the house.

An attractive redhead came to the door in a wrinkled Waffle House uniform. She stared at me and said, "Go away."

"Does Paul Wilder live here?"

"He hasn't lived here in over three years."

"Are you Flo Wilder?"

"What do you want with me?"

"I need to speak with you about your ex. Please."

"Listen, if he got you pregnant, I don't want to hear about it. That's not my problem. We're divorced."

"It's nothing like that. I'm a private investigator working on a case."

"I just got off work." She touched her nametag. "What's he done now?"

"I'm not here for him. I have a few questions for you."

"Oh. I assumed you were here for Paul."

"May I come in?"

"Come on." She stood back and held the door open.

"Thank you."

"I need to smoke, so we're going out back," she said over her shoulder as I followed her through the house into a fenced backyard.

Flo indicated a picnic table with a wave of her arm. "Sit." She lit a cigarette.

"Do you know where Paul is working now?"

"If I had to guess, I'd say he's doing something illegal." She blew smoke out in a whoosh. "But he may be working on a get-rich-quick scheme that's only immoral instead of illegal, or it could be both."

"Do you know why the governor pardoned the remainder of his

parole?"

Flo jumped up. "You've got to be kidding me! Only P.W. could pull off something like that. Shit, he doesn't even know the governor." She threw up her hands in exasperation. "Leave it to him to wiggle out of something everyone else is required by law to do. That's my ex in a nutshell. Shit!"

"His parole officer thinks he's living in Austin."

"That could be true, or he could be anywhere."

"Do you know anyone who'd know what he's doing now or where he's living?"

"No."

"Do the two of you have children?"

"No."

"What about a friend or relative?"

"Paul has an old pal from Carterton who probably knows where he is, but I don't know where he is, either. They could be together doing whatever irresponsible, illegal, immoral thing they've got going on now."

"What's his friend's name?"

"Aaron Carter."

Whoa. "Is he related to the former judge of the same name?"

"Aaron is Judge Carter's son. P.W. and Aaron have been friends since elementary school, even though Aaron is a few years older. He was socially behind, so the age difference never mattered."

"What do you mean when you say he was socially behind?"

"Slow to develop, I mean. Aaron was inept in social ways. I don't know how to explain it. He could never talk to girls without stuttering."

"Stuttering?" It took effort to keep my butt planted on the bench.

"Yes, s-s-stuttering. And he still does. I think he's one hundred percent weirdo, but Paul has always loved him."

"Is he a large man?"

"No, he's small, but he's probably wearing lifts in his shoes. For a homely man, he's vain like that."

"Does he still live in Carterton?"

"I doubt it. If P.W.'s in Austin, then Aaron is probably there. Aaron inherited his father's wealth, so he doesn't have to work. He might be the governor now for all I know. He did have some plastic surgery a while back, according to P.W."

"Governor Cardenas is Latino," I said.

She shrugged. "Okay, I guess Aaron couldn't have made himself into a Latino. I wish I could help you, but I don't know anything about either of them anymore."

"You said he had facial surgery. Was there a problem with his face?"

Flo chuckled. "He was ugly, so that was the problem, I guess. He changed his face and his name and disappeared from Carterton."

"Do you know what name he's using?"

"No, but Paul would know. Of course, the trick is to find Paul. He might be using an alias too, for all I know. He does that."

"I met Paul once," I said, "and I noticed that he limps. One of his legs is shorter than the other, right?"

"That's right, but he has orthopedic shoes to correct that. He shouldn't be walking with a limp unless he's naked. Don't tell me you saw him naked!"

"He was fully dressed."

"Well, that's weird. I wonder what he's up to."

"Are you familiar with a man named Randy Green?"

She thought about it. "No, I don't think I've ever heard that name. Is he a friend of P.W.'s or—wait—he's somebody Paul screwed over?"

"If you've never heard the name, then it doesn't matter." I stood. "I appreciate your help. It would be good if P.W. didn't know I'd been here."

"Well, don't worry about that, little gal. I'm not likely to see him again in this lifetime. I hope."

***

I didn't want to argue with Jeanie or give away my relationship to her boss, so I sat on a chair and waited for Joe in the hallway outside the courtroom. People began coming out after ten minutes, and soon I was the only one in the place. The small room next to the courtroom had to be his chambers, so I knocked on the door.

"Come in!"

When I went in, Joe looked up in surprise. "Oh! I was afraid you'd be Jeanie."

"Are you hiding from her?"

"Well no, but, what a pleasant surprise to see you instead!"

"Thanks."

We smiled at each other.

"Hey, do you wear clothes under that robe?"

He laughed. "I love the way your mind works." Then he stood. "Why don't you come over here and find out?"

I went to him and we kissed a long time. In case you wonder, judges do wear clothes under those robes.

CHAPTER 29

The next morning, I left for Austin to take my chances with the Gov.

"You can't just walk in on the governor of Texas," Joe said when I called him from the road. He still insisted he should make an appointment for me. He knew the governor and yada, yada, yada.

"Yes, Joe. I heard you the other fifty times."

The truth is I didn't want to involve Joe. What if the governor was in deep in all this? What if I screwed up? I didn't want any of my actions to tarnish Joe's reputation. Mine had already taken a few hits, so I proceeded at full throttle, my favorite way.

"Look," Joe said, "I don't want to fight, so I'm going to drop it. Besides, I have something important to tell you. Peter Adams' death was ruled a murder."

That wasn't a surprise, but it still knocked the words out of me.

"It makes me fear for your safety," Joe continued. "Why don't you call in some other law enforcement to help you?"

"Oh sure; he won't notice me and the National Guard sneaking up on him."

"No need to get that tone. I was talking about one or two deputies or the Texas Rangers."

"Men, in other words."

"That's not what I meant at all. You've been recently injured. You're going after a dangerous man, and I don't like to think you're all alone."

"I'm only going to speak with the governor."

"You just said you were sneaking up on Wilder, so don't lie to me, Margarita. It's not fair. How do you think I felt when I heard you'd been injured?"

"I'm sorry I said that, Joe. I'll call my Texas Ranger father once I find out where Wilder is. He already said he'd help me."

"You act as if you're made of indestructible metal, but I've held you in my arms, so I know better. Don't be angry with me because I don't want to lose you."

After that, our conversation slipped into talk best not repeated.

***

The Honorable Lucas Cardenas has secretaries, aides, and other personnel whose job it is to run interference for him. I could understand that he was a busy man and deserved protection from countless unimportant interruptions and people who would waste his time. But I wasn't one of them, dammit!

His receptionist said with an attitude of superiority that Governor Cardenas was busy for the rest of the day. I asked if I could make an appointment for the following day. Next week would be the earliest, she informed me. She was so snotty I wondered what happened to the hospitality the state brags about. It's pervasive in tourist hype, but wasn't evident in the Capitol.

I took a deep breath and insisted I see him today or tomorrow; I had come far, and I was talking about a murder investigation, not lobbying pet causes.

Then the story changed, and she said he wasn't in; someone different claimed he was busy, and then someone else said I should've called ahead.

I made enough waves to get moved along and eventually ended up with the governor's personal assistant, Rex Wilson. He was a young man, just out of college, with a big fake smile and perfect teeth. He dressed impeccably and was efficient in his manner, but I got the impression that people from Brewster County were low in importance. I was from the least populated of Texas counties, where there are not many constituents.

I wished I had let Joe get me in. Nobody would be giving me crap. Effective police work is about having good contacts. Now I had a powerful one and didn't feel comfortable using him because I was sleeping with him. Oh, irony.

"I don't have to see the governor," I told Rex Wilson, "if you can tell me who requested his intervention on behalf of Paul Wilder. That's all I need to know."

He had no clue.

"Would you please ask him for me?"

"I'm sorry I can't help you. You'll have to arrange a meeting with the Governor."

"Tell me how to do that. This can't wait until next week."

"I wish I could help."

"He's supposed to be working for the people of Texas," I said, but it fell on deaf ears, the coldhearted little twerp.

It rubbed me wrong every way, but I would have to call Joe after all. Then I thought of Zeke. Maybe he had a way.

"Come and stay with me," my father said when I called, and I agreed. He asked me to come by his office to get the key to his house.

When I got there, Zeke came around his desk and hugged me tightly. "Please sit and talk to me a minute. I like to look at you."

Truthfully, I like looking at him, too.

"Do you know Governor Cardenas?" I asked.

"I know him professionally. Why?"

"Do you think you could get me in to see him?"

"I'm willing to try. I only know him from protection details."

"What does that mean?"

"The Texas Rangers assist the Governor's Protection Detail when asked to. I've accompanied him on several trips around the state and to Washington, D.C. twice. We aren't friends, but I think I could get you in to see him. Can you tell me why?"

I explained the governor's weird connection to my case. Zeke listened and nodded and seemed to agree that I needed to see him.

Zeke picked up his phone. "Maggie, please connect me to Governor Cardenas. Tell his assistant that Sergeant Ezekiél Pacheco of the Texas Rangers would like to speak to him as soon as possible."

He hung up. "We'll know something in a minute. What would you think of going out on the town tonight? I'll take you to the nicest restaurant in Austin."

"I'd love to go!" When my Zeke father says, "out on the town" he doesn't kid around.

"That's a plan, then."

"We'll have to tone it down a few notches, because I don't have any fancy clothes with me."

Zeke took out his wallet and handed me a credit card. "Buy what you need and let it be my treat."

"No, Zeke, I don't feel right about that."

"Why not? How much money have I been able to spend on my only daughter in the last twenty-eight years? Take the card and buy something and shoes to go with it. Buy anything you need."

"Thank you, Zeke, but you don't want to give me a credit card and tell me to buy shoes."

"How about limiting your purchases to two pairs? Can you do that?"

"I think I can."

Zeke grinned, and then his phone rang. "Sergeant Pacheco," he said. "Good afternoon, Governor." He winked at me. They went through the how-are-you-I'm-fines. Zeke laughed at something the governor said, and then, "Listen, I'm calling on behalf of my daughter. She's a deputy working on a case of wrongful—" He stopped because I was shaking my head.

Zeke took the hint. "I'll let her tell you about her case. Could she come see you this afternoon?" Pause. "Yeah, fine. That's great. Thank you, sir. She'll be there."

That is how the Big Boys in the great state of Texas get things done.

CHAPTER 30

My second trip to the State Capitol was different—different the way dry desert air and swamp humidity are different. I still had to get past security and leave my Beretta with them, but after that, Texas Friendly reigned.

"So nice to see you again, Ms. Ricos," the receptionist lied to my face. "Mr. Wilson will be with you in a moment."

I didn't get to sit down before Rex Wilson, the governor's unhelpful assistant, walked in with a big smile plastered on his face. "Please come with me, Ms. Ricos."

I followed him into the governor's office and he introduced us.

"Ms. Ricos," our governor said, and smiled and held out his hand. "I'm pleased to meet you. I think highly of your father." He had the bearing of a wealthy, powerful man, but his smile reflected honest friendliness and his eyes were kind, not shifty.

"Thank you for seeing me, sir."

"Please have a seat."

I sat in a plush visitor chair. It was a far cry from the plain chair in front of Barney's desk, but I tried to keep my mind in Austin.

"I don't think I've met a deputy from Brewster County before. You sure do live in a gorgeous part of our state."

"Yes, sir, I know I do. My father misspoke when he told you that I'm a deputy. What I mean is that I'm not here in the capacity of deputy. I'm working as a private investigator."

"How can I help you?"

"I need to know who asked you to change the status of Paul Wilder's parole."

It seemed he expected anything but that. "Why does that information interest you?"

"Wilder broke into my hotel room in Simpson and threatened me. He's also a suspect in a murder in Midland a few days ago and another in El Paso after that."

"No. That's impossible."

"Why?"

"He's been here in Austin."

"No, he hasn't."

"Wilder works for Senator Lyle Freeman. It'd be difficult for him to be away right now because the senate is in session. If someone threatened you, I'm sure it wasn't Paul."

"I have DNA evidence that says it was him."

"That can't be. I don't see how he could've been anywhere but here. What did you use for DNA analysis?"

"Some hairs I pulled from his scalp."

"Are you sure it was him? Did you recognize him?"

"He cut the lights to my room and attacked me in the dark. In the scuffle I got some of his hair. But say it's a mistake. I'd still like to know who got his parole requirements removed."

"It was Senator Freeman, of course. Paul Wilder is an old friend of his. He wanted to hire him and keep him under his wing. His parole was getting in the way of that. The senator asked me to step in and I did. He assured me he would keep him out of trouble. I certainly wouldn't have done it if I'd felt he'd be a danger in any way." He paused to regard me with serious eyes. "Did he injure you?" His eyes had moved to my bandaged arm. I wore a jacket because of the frigid temperature in the place, but the sleeves had ridden up.

"I was a bystander at one of the murders and got hit by flying glass."

"Ms. Ricos, if you were injured because of Wilder's actions, I feel personally responsible. I can't tell you how sorry I am. I do feel there has been a mistake, but if you find out differently will you let me know? I'll be waiting to hear."

DNA does not lie. The hairs would have to have gotten mixed up with someone else's, and what were the chances of that?

"Maybe there has been a mistake," I said with a smile, "but I'd still like to speak with Wilder. Where can I find him? I assume Senator Freeman's office is somewhere in this building."

"Yes. It's on the second floor. They'll know where Wilder is if he isn't there. Oh, I should tell you that he changed his name. He goes by a different name since he began working for the senator. Clean slate, you know. Senator Freeman will have to tell you what it is because I don't remember."

"Is the senator using an alias too?"

"Not that I'm aware of. He's been Lyle Freeman as long as I've known him."

"How long have you known him?"

"Three years, since he was first elected to the state senate."

Governor Cardenas stood and offered his hand.

"I appreciate your help," I said.

"So, you're Zeke Pacheco's daughter."

"Yes, sir, I am."

"You look like him."

"I'm proud of that."

He smiled and said, "Adiós."

When I started down the hall towards the stairs, a young man flew out the door of the governor's office. He ran to catch up. "Ms. Ricos?"

"Yes." I stopped walking and turned towards him.

"May I speak with you?"

"Sure."

He came close and spoke in a hush. "I couldn't help but overhear your conversation with Governor Cardenas. Could we talk in private?"

The stranger had smooth, coffee-colored skin. He seemed a mix of African-American and Latino, with black eyes and equally dark hair that curled even though it was cut close to his head. He was about six feet tall with an average build, and he was good-looking, reason enough to go to code red on my Imminent Danger Meter.

"Who are you?"

"I'm Ricardo Ortiz, but call me Ric. I work in Senator Freeman's office." That got my attention. He was whispering and heading me towards the front doors. "Please give me a few minutes of your time." He glanced around again. "I can't speak freely here, and you shouldn't be here."

His words made me cold. "Okay. Where should we go?"

"Let's get outside, and then we'll talk. It's not safe here."

Jeez, he was making me nervous.

My new friend watched wide-eyed as I retrieved my weapon from Security. I stuck it into the waistband of my pants. When we got outside, he asked if I had a vehicle.

"Yes, but it's parked several blocks away in a parking garage. It's impossible to park on the capitol grounds without a signed note from God."

"We'll take my car," he said.

"Wait a minute. No, we won't. Couldn't we just walk around and talk? We could walk away from here."

"I understand your hesitation. Let's walk towards wherever your car is parked."

No way in this lifetime would I go in a parking garage with a tall, good-looking man connected in any way to this case, whether I was armed or not. No way. Not happening.

We crossed a side street by the Capitol and Ric continued talking. "I believe your life is in danger, Ms. Ricos. I heard you tell the governor you're looking for Paul Wilder, and I strongly advise against that. He's a dangerous man. Governor Cardenas is wrong. He hasn't been in Austin."

"I'm listening."

"Senator Freeman told me that Simpson—that's the name he uses—was running important errands, and the rest of us have had to cover for him. Of course, if the governor asked Senator Freeman about it he'd say he's around here somewhere, in Austin I mean."

"What is your position with the senator?"

"I'm an aide. I've just graduated from the University of Texas."

He wore a Capitol photo I.D. attached to the lapel of his suit. It gave his name as Ricardo Ortiz and the I.D. matched his face. My meter backed down to code orange.

"Let's duck in here," he said, indicating a small bar.

I hesitated because small bars are dangerous territory; large bars are dangerous territory; all bars are dangerous as hell. I ducked in with him anyway, and we sat at a booth towards the back of the room.

"What's your plan?" He faced the front door and watched it as though he were a wanted man.

"My plan?"

"Your plan regarding Simpson. You have one, right?"

"First of all, how do you know that Wilder is Simpson?"

"Because I've seen things I wasn't supposed to see and heard things

I wasn't meant to hear."

"I see. And what is the full name he's using?"

"Christian Simpson."

"Oh, please."

"Yeah, I know," Ric said. "He and Freeman yap on about Christian values and family values—but look, that isn't important. What's important is that they want you dead. It has to look like an accident or you'd already be buried."

"You've heard them say that?"

"Well, yes, but not in those words."

"What did they say?"

"Wilder said, 'I'll take out that nosy little investigator while I'm there' and Freeman said, 'Wait. It has to look like an accident. That investigator is also a sheriff's deputy. There can be no questions, understand? We'll be looking at a full-scale investigation if anyone thinks she's been murdered.'"

"I see."

"Freeman is powerful. He's not a formidable politician or a decent one, but he has a formidable amount of money at his disposal."

"Do you know where he's from?"

"Some small town, I think. I don't know the name of it."

"Does he speak with a stutter?"

"Yes. He's touchy about it, too. He's worked to eliminate it but hasn't succeeded one hundred percent. Do you know him?"

"No. Please tell me more about him."

"He bought his way into politics, I think. He's not smart, but he thinks he is. I personally don't like the guy, but there're a lot of these politicians I don't like."

"What causes you not to like him?"

"For one thing, I overheard Freeman talking about 'the blacks and Mexicans and queers,' and not in a good way. It was offensive. I'm the son of a black father and a Mexican mother. I guess he hired me to fill a quota or to show his goodwill towards his constituents of color. It's hard to imagine brothers or home boys as his constituents, but whatever. He hired me, and I've tried to do a good job. He's hard to stomach though."

"What were you doing in the governor's office?"

"I was trying to get a job there. He has a posting for a clerk, and I'd like to leave Freeman before I overhear something they have to kill me for, you know?"

"Have you heard them talk about Carterton or Peter Adams or Jacob Rawlings?"

"No. I don't think so."

"What about El Paso or Simpson the town?"

"No, but I know Wilder was in El Paso a few days ago because I accidentally saw his expense report. He's also been in Midland and Simpson. Say, would you like something to drink? I was thinking about getting a beer."

I thought I needed something also, but a mental image of Sarah's old young mother changed my mind. "I'll have club soda with lime, since I'm working."

Ric got the drinks and returned. "I heard you say you witnessed a murder, and that's how you got hurt. Do you think Simpson did it?"

"Yes, that's what I think."

"Can a deputy who's not from this county arrest a man here?"

"No, and I'm not acting in the capacity of deputy."

"I guess that explains why you're not wearing a uniform."

"I got involved in this to help a friend."

My phone rang. The caller was Zeke. "Excuse me, Ric. I need to take this call." I stepped away from the booth. "Hey, Zeke."

"Did everything go all right with Governor Cardenas?"

"Yes, it did. Thank you, Zeke."

"Listen honey, I don't want to do this, but I have to change our plans. I won't be home until late because I'm working in place of the man who was scheduled for a detail."

"That's okay, Zeke. I understand. Maybe we can hang out tomorrow before I go home."

"I would love that. We'll make a plan over coffee in the morning."

"That sounds great."

I went back to the booth.

"Tonight, there's a reception for the senators," Ric said. "If you'd like to go and observe Freeman, I could take you as my date. Aides and their dates are invited."

"Surely you already have a date."

"I don't actually, and I would be honored to take you."

"But Wilder will recognize me."

"You could wear a wig. My mother has one. She had to have chemo a few years ago and before she did, she had a wig made from her hair. It's beautiful and long. Nobody would ever know it's not your real hair."

"But surely she wouldn't want to lend it to a stranger. And besides, I don't have the proper clothes."

"Come on, you can buy a dress anywhere in Austin. It should be something fancy, and it should cover your arms. Everybody dresses up for these things. And Mom will lend you the wig. That won't be a problem. Then we can change a few other details about your looks."

"Do you think Wilder—I mean Simpson—will be there?"

"I know he will. Senator Freeman will want everyone to see that his right-hand man is present and accounted for."

"I need a copy of the expense report you mentioned. That would be proof Paul Wilder was in El Paso at the time of the murder and in Simpson and Midland when I know he was. Otherwise, Freeman will lie for him."

"Come to the reception with me and afterward, we'll go to the office. I'll find that stuff again, okay? Just say yes."

"It's life or death important that nobody recognizes me."

"Stop worrying. My mom will help. She'll be ecstatic I'm going to this thing with someone real."

"I'm real, all right. But Ric, I have to tell you that I'm in a relationship."

"That figures."

The expression on his face made me laugh. We talked a while longer, and I agreed to go.

CHAPTER 31

"You should be here resting," Joe insisted when I called to update him. "I'd like to demand that you get back here right now, but I don't want those to be the last words I ever get to speak to you."

I laughed. "You barely know me, and yet you do."

"Well, you haven't kept certain attributes a secret."

"As long as we're clear."

He laughed.

I asked him if he had access to Child Protective Service's records. The answer was a cautious, "Yes."

I gave him the information on Cissy's sister with some background on why the two girls mattered to me.

"I can find out where she is, but I can't interfere without issuing a court order with good cause. Do you suspect she's being abused, or was she wrongfully placed?"

I explained what I wanted to do.

"I can call her social worker and ask her to contact the foster parents. If they agree to a meeting with you and Cissy, then you can proceed. Will that help you?"

"That's perfect! Thank you, Joe."

For a while we talked about other things. Then I had to get ready for the party.

* * *

My date failed to mention that the reception was being held at the Governor's Mansion in downtown Austin, not far from the Capitol. I don't know what I expected, but not that. Also, my father had failed to mention that he was part of the security detail covering the event. I was surprised to see Zeke standing near the governor. He wore a tuxedo and looked like royalty.

Both men were smart, and I was afraid one or the other would recognize me, but neither seemed to. Ric introduced me to Governor Cardenas as Victoria Morales. I think the long, luxurious hair threw him, as well as the glasses and the tiny mole Ric's mom had painted on my face near my lip.

The governor was preoccupied with greeting people, meeting spouses of senators and aides, and he barely saw me. As for Zeke, I glanced at him, but he maintained a stone face, covertly checking the surroundings for possible threats. Ric and I moved on to the main room and joined the party.

I wore a medium-length, form-fitting, red cocktail dress with long sleeves that covered the cuts on my arm. I looked sexy, and it gave me a feeling of power. A pain pill had dulled my physical complaints, so I felt ready to kick some butt. However, I was not dressed for it.

After Ric and I grazed the buffet tables and danced a few times, he led me onto a balcony overlooking a lush garden with several fountains.

"Are you ready to meet my boss?"

"My father is here, Ric."

"He is?"

"Yes, he's a Texas Ranger on security duty."

"I've never been on a date with a girl's father on the scene."

I heard Ric talk, but it didn't connect. "I want to speak to him," I said, "but I don't know if that will give me away or get him in trouble."

"Which man is your father?"

"He's standing close to the governor and dressed like everybody else, but he has a transmitter in his ear for communicating with the other members of the security staff."

"It might not be a good idea to speak to him right now," Ric said.

I took a deep breath. "Never mind, maybe I can speak to him later. I'm ready to meet your boss."

"I want Senator Freeman to eat his heart out that I have such a gorgeous date."

"Thank you, but let's be low-key about this, okay?"

"Okay. We'll make it fast."

Ric took my hand and led me towards a group of people I could have gone the rest of my life without meeting. The man I least wanted to meet had his back to us at first. I'd been hunting him for days but coming face-to-face with him was less thrilling than I imagined and more chilling.

Freeman was short, and I thought he must be extra-short if he wore lifts in his shoes. "He's a weirdo, but P.W. loves him," the ex-Mrs. Wilder had said of Aaron Carter, now Senator Lyle Freeman.

Ric interrupted him. "Senator Freeman?"

The pervert turned, taking in the two of us. "My, my," he breathed at me, and I longed to put the heel of my shoe through his chest. "W-who do you have here, R-Ric?" He looked me up and down, pretending that a grown woman turned him on. It's a wonder I didn't start screaming for my daddy. Here was the man who should have gone to prison, the reason Hell had swallowed Randy whole.

I needed to vomit.

"I'd like to introduce you to my friend, Victoria Morales. Victoria, this is Senator Freeman, my boss."

I willed myself to take the hand he extended. My legs tried to buckle.

"You're l-lovely."

"Thank you," I said without throwing up, screaming for my daddy, or falling down.

Freeman held a glass in his hand that would have his DNA and fingerprints. If I could take it, Zeke would have tests run for me at his lab. He could get it done fast, and then I'd have proof. But I had nowhere to stash a glass. No way would it fit in my dollar-bill-sized evening purse.

Ric swept me away to dance again, and I told him about the dilemma of the glass that held two things I needed.

"Wait," he said, "when he goes out to smoke we can get a butt."

"You're brilliant."

"I'm just trying to impress you."

When Ric pointed out Paul Wilder/Christian Simpson, I was shocked by how normal he looked, how different from when I'd last seen him. He was dressed in a fashionable tuxedo and was busy dazzling everyone with his easy smiles and good humor. He was not as large as he'd seemed in the dark, and he wasn't limping.

"He wears a built-up shoe," Ric explained when I said I thought it wasn't him.

"He's two people in one," I said. "Paul Wilder is a goon who does things by brute force and murder. Christian Simpson is his opposite."

Ric nodded. "I think you're right."

"I feel afraid," I whispered. "What if he recognizes me?"

"You don't have to meet him if you don't want to. He's heading this way, though."

Without being asked, Ric steered me away from him. "He's really checking you out," he whispered, "but it's not what you think. It's not your face he's staring at. It's um—it's your rear end."

"Great. Let's get out of here."

"Don't you want some of the senator's DNA first?"

"Oh, yeah, thanks for reminding me."

Just as the old-folks-tunes band finally went into some serious dancing music, Zeke cut in without a word. He smiled innocently at Ric and raised one eyebrow. It was a smooth move and happened in seconds.

Zeke whirled me away from Ric, pulled me close, and whispered, "Forgive me if you're not my daughter."

I laughed. "How did you know?"

"It's my awesome power of observation, and you didn't scream when I grabbed you."

"Aren't you supposed to be working?"

"Even security drones get a break now and then."

"How did you guess it was me?"

"I heard your voice when you met the governor, and I looked over and saw a woman exactly the right size. That, plus your voice, made me suspicious. Then I watched and observed some of my own mannerisms. It's unnerving. You look lovely, by the way."

"Thanks, so do you. Zeke, do you still head the UCIT team?"

"Yes. Why?"

"Why are you protecting the governor?"

"I'm here because the man scheduled to work is with his wife. They're having a baby. Long story short, I'm here because of a scheduling crisis. I rarely have this duty now. But when the governor needs us, the Texas Rangers accommodate him."

"I see."

"Are you serious about the man you're with?"

"No, Zeke. I just met him today."

"And you already got invited to this high-powered function?"

"He's trying to help me."

"Why are you undercover?"

"Paul Wilder is here, along with the perp I've been chasing."

"I want you to leave. Right now! I'll cover your exit."

"I'm not leaving yet."

"Point them out to me, and I'll take it from here."

That would have been the prudent thing to do.

***

Zeke went back to work. I think he was both disgusted with me and proud of me for not wanting to turn my case over yet.

After a few more dances with Ric, Lyle Freeman finally made his way to the balcony. We gave him a head start and then moved in that direction. First, we stood by the door talking quietly about nothing. Even though I was trying not to, I kept glancing around to see where Freeman was. He puffed on a small cigar and took his time, chatting with an old, obese white man who Ric said was probably a senator or lobbyist.

We walked out onto the balcony holding hands. When Freeman glanced at us, Ric said, "This fresh air feels good." I wanted to laugh because it was stifling and stank like a city, but I smiled at him instead. It was a heroic effort, considering I was close to the villain and barely maintaining my cool.

"Nice evening, isn't it?" Lyle Freeman addressed us.

I nodded mutely.

"Yes, it is," Ric said.

The fat man waddled back inside. Freeman took a final drag on the small cigar and then ground it into the soil of a flower pot, even though there was a container for butts on the balcony. Ric and I exchanged disapproving glances.

Freeman took out a stick of gum and the unmistakable smell of Juicy Fruit filled the still air. Nausea overtook me. He discarded the wrapper into the same flower pot he used for the butt, and then he walked away. Ric and I moved to it, trying to appear casual. He reached down to pick up the prize.

I grabbed his arm. "Don't touch it!" I took a tissue from my tiny purse and picked it up with that, wrapping it into the folds to protect it as much as possible.

"Let's go, Ric," I said. "We have an office to raid."

He grinned and nodded, and we got out of there.

***

At the security desk, Ric showed the unsmiling man his Capitol I.D. card and said he was there to retrieve something for Senator Freeman. Ric presented me as his wife, which seemed exactly the ruse it was. The man asked to see my identification, so I produced my driver's license. Fortunately, he only glanced at it and went back to watching a tiny T.V.

I faxed copies of Wilder's expense reports to Zeke's office, and then called him to explain what I had sent. I thought I would have to leave a message, but Zeke answered.

Typical father, when I told him where I was and what I was doing, he freaked out. "Get out of there right this minute! You can't get caught there!"

"Okay, okay, we're leaving." *Jeez.*

I searched Freeman's desk, hoping for any condemning thing, and then checked his wastebaskets. One provided a graveyard for chewed gum and Juicy Fruit wrappers. I couldn't resist taking some of the wads of gum. We probably had all the DNA I needed, but the gum couldn't hurt. I lifted the wads with a clean sheet of typing paper and folded it into a tiny square I slipped into my purse. I saw nothing else of interest, but we didn't have long to look.

Ric turned out the lights, and Paul Wilder came in and flipped them back on. "What are you doing in here?" he demanded.

"I—I left something," stammered Ric. "I just came to get it."

Wilder focused his attention on me. "She doesn't have security clearance to be here. What did you leave that's so important it couldn't wait until tomorrow?" Before Rick had a chance to respond, Wilder's gaze returned to me. I thought I saw a glimmer of recognition, and it made me feel naked and afraid.

"Let's go," Ric said, and he grabbed me by my injured right arm. I gasped at the sudden pain and Wilder's face changed expressions. *He knows,* I thought. Ric shoved me out the door ahead of him.

I ran hard towards the stairs, and then I heard the muffled sound of a gunshot fired through a silencer. Ric wasn't with me! I turned in a panic as Limping Man came out the door. In the half-second I had, I saw Ric's prone body on the floor behind him.

"You're coming with me." Wilder pointed a gun at my chest.

"Where are we going?" I asked. Yeah, it sounded stupid, but I was panicking from deep in my gut, making it hard to think.

My nemesis grabbed my injured arm. Pain shot through me like a hot knife. In a blind reaction, I kicked him in the ankle as hard as I could. Then I stomped on his foot, driving the sharp heel of the pump into his shoe as hard as my weight allowed. Oh, the cursing that followed. But I still hadn't hurt him enough to make him drop the weapon.

Wilder leaned forward to rub his injured ankle, and I attacked with everything I had. I karate-chopped the back of his neck, but that didn't work for me the way it would have for Bruce Lee. It only irked him more. Then I leaped onto him, and for a few seconds I rode piggy-back style, clawing at his face with one hand while I strangle-held him with the other. He snorted, cursed, and bucked. If he'd been a bull, he would've been pawing the ground and slinging snot.

He yelled every curse I ever heard, called me everything, even things that didn't make sense to call a woman. He managed to throw me off his back, and I fell to the hard floor. It knocked the wind out of me, and for a second, I thought every bone in my body had broken. My head smacked so hard I saw stars.

I heard, "Drop your weapon!" but after that, I passed out.

When I came to, Zeke was holding me against his chest. "Are you all right?"

"Where's Ric?"

"He's been rushed to the hospital, sweetheart. Wilder shot him in the back."

"How did you know to come?"

"I'll explain everything later."

"My purse—it has the senator's DNA."

"I've got your purse. They're ready to put you into the ambulance now."

"I don't need a hospital."

"You hit the floor so hard your head make a cracking sound."

"But I'm fine. My head is hard."

Zeke laughed at that. "I'll say. You still need to be checked out to be sure you don't have a concussion. I'll meet you at the hospital, but I have to put you down for now."

"Please don't let me go, Dad."

My father's eyes glistened with tears. "Margarita, I've waited twenty-eight years to hear you call me Dad."

Then he hugged me to him so tightly it hurt and felt wonderful.

CHAPTER 32

An E.R. doctor named Fleming said I was only bruised, which I knew, but nobody listens to me. Zeke stood next to me holding my hand.

"Thank you for saving me, Zeke."

"I didn't do anything any other father wouldn't have done. Ric is the one you should thank."

"How is he?"

"He's in surgery, but his prognosis is good."

"How did you know to come for us?"

"Wilder left the party after you did. After a lifetime of chasing criminals, I'm a suspicious man. I was running hard towards the Capitol when Ric called. He had picked up your phone, which you'd dropped, and he knew you'd just spoken with me. All he had to do was hit re-dial."

"Ric called you?" I marveled at that. How had he had the presence of mind to do it? How had he even been conscious?

"He sounded like a dying man, and he was, I guess. I was terrified for him and for you."

"I want to see him."

"You can't until he gets out of surgery."

"But it's my fault."

"No, it's not. Stop thinking like that. You didn't shoot him, did you?"

"But I dragged him there. Did you kill Wilder?"

"No, but he may wish I had. I shot him in the leg, which is bad enough. But he's looking at life in prison, and that's only if he cooperates by giving up information on the senator. If he chooses not to, he'll get the needle, most likely."

"Zeke, do you think the Texas Rangers would take this case now?"

"Yes. Rigged trials with corrupt judges are what we do. This was justice system corruption on a grand scale and has 'Texas Rangers' stamped all over it." My father hesitated.

"What's wrong, Zeke?"

"In truth, Freeman is already under investigation for corruption."

"By the Texas Rangers?"

"Yes. I couldn't tell you before, but now that you've broken open the case, you deserve to know."

"I'm surprised nobody stopped me."

"Oh, they would have, but you were turning up valuable info right and left. You brought Wilder out of the woodwork, and that explained some things."

"There's an evil sheriff in Freeman County who has kept this wicked scheme under wraps for seven years."

"Yes. He's part of the investigation."

"He should be taken into custody as soon as possible, but he'll be armed and deadly. In addition to what he did to Randy, he has instigated other hate crimes. People there are afraid of him."

"He's on my list."

"What about Senator Freeman?"

"He's stewing in the Austin city jail for now."

"You already arrested him?"

"At my request, a fellow Ranger grabbed him before he left the party. I hope you're not too disappointed."

"Disappointed? I'll do a jump-up-and-down happy dance once they let me up. All I want is for Randy to be freed of his sex offender status and for the man who should've done time to do it."

"That's going to happen, I promise you."

"There's important evidence in the storage basement under the sheriff's office." I gave him the roadmap for finding it and the details about the evidence.

"How do you know all this?"

"Let's just say I know and let it go at that, okay?"

"It sounds suspicious."

"I was acting as myself and not as Deputy Ricos."

"Oh, I see. That makes me feel better."

"There's no harm done. Nobody knows but you and me, and you can get a search warrant and pretend you found the evidence. The sheriff will be in jail, so he won't have a clue how you found it. But you need to move fast, or he might freak out and find it himself."

"I may look young, but this is not my first case."

"Sorry. I get carried away. It's exciting to think about the great big fist of justice crashing down on that creep's head. Sheriff Hancock, prepare to meet my daddy."

Zeke laughed. After a moment he asked, "Do you want to come along?"

"No."

"It's not like you to turn down an ass-kicking."

"I have a hot date. I'll come to Hancock's trial, though. I wouldn't miss it."

"Tell me about this date."

"You wouldn't know him."

"Your mother says you're dating Joe Washburn."

"Why are you talking to my mother?"

"We have a mutual interest in our child. She called me to see if I knew him."

"She is now dead to me."

He laughed. "Your mother has your best interests at heart."

"Save it, Zeke."

"I know Joe from when he lived in Austin. He's a fine man."

"Right, I believe that. I know him, too."

He laughed and started to ask something, but I interrupted him. "I'm trying to move on, Dad."

"That's good. I'm proud of you, Margarita."

"There's one thing I forgot to mention. Remember that handkerchief I asked you to have run for DNA?"

"Sure, I remember. We had a hit."

"Yes. It was Damien Jerome Hall. He's the one who abused Randy when he was in jail awaiting trial."

"You want me to pick him up?" Zeke asked.

"Yes, please. I was going to do it, but now I think it'd be better if you did. If he did one teeny thing I didn't like—for instance, if he made a face or said one word that didn't suit me, I'd stomp the crap out of him. He wouldn't be fit for trial for a year."

"Right." Zeke coughed. "It's better if someone less personally involved goes."

"If you go, I want you to tell him that I gave up my burning desire to kick his head in out of respect for the law. He might think, because I'm a woman, that he could beat me in a brawl. If that's so, he hasn't met a strong woman with a burning desire to shove his face into a brick wall."

Zeke chuckled and didn't argue.

"Joe's good for me," I said a few minutes later.

"Yes. I imagine he would be."

***

I went home with my father, but Joe came for me and we went to a hotel. I feared he would carry on about the dangers of my work, but he surprised me by carrying on about Spain instead. He spoke of rest and relaxation and being together. I couldn't think straight because my conscience was nagging me.

"Joe, there's something I have to tell you."

"What is that?"

"I don't know where to start."

"Start somewhere and I'll figure it out. I'm used to piecing together the truth."

"My problems started before I asked for time off—way before. I met a man who was everything I wanted and, at the same time, everything I detest. I know that sounds crazy, but it's the truth."

"Margarita, I know about your connection to the Martez Cartel."

"I wasn't connected to them, Joe, but I did fall in love with Emilio Martez, the youngest son of Emmanuel Martez, who was the head of the organization. I knew his son as Diego Romero, and I was planning to marry him."

"I know that, and I'm sorry."

"But how do you know anything about it?"

"When you called and threatened me with a subpoena, I looked you up online. I didn't know if you were someone real or only a person trying to make trouble. I found scores of newspaper articles about you or that referenced you. Some of them were about your big drug bust in Terlingua and your subsequent troubles."

"And you still wanted to go out with me?"

"I had no plan of it until I met you."

"What made you ask me?"

"When I introduced myself as Judge Washburn and you said, 'really, I'm here to see the judge' with that great big smile on your beautiful face, my heart went bumpity-bump-bump."

"You're weird."

"And you're not?"

I laughed and then got serious. "If you know about the Martez Cartel and my connection to it, and you're still here, I guess there's nothing more I need to say."

"Margarita, I want you to hear this, please. The way I feel about you, it's too late to care about any of that. If you were running the cartel, I'd have to figure out a way to live with it."

"That's the sweetest thing anyone ever said to me."

"Don't make fun of me."

"I wasn't making fun, Joe."

"Do you know there's an FBI file on you?"

"I didn't know for sure, but I assumed it. Is it bad?"

"It isn't bad per se, but you refused to cooperate with them."

"That's true, but they wanted me to lure a man I loved onto U.S. soil so that they could capture him, or more likely, kill him. I cooperated with their investigation in every other possible way. He's dead, so they got what they wanted without my help."

Joe stayed quiet.

"Does it upset you to know I didn't help them capture him?"

"No, I wouldn't have helped them, either."

"It was wrong for them to ask."

"I agree."

"Do you always look up the FBI files on the women you date?"

"This was the first time. Are you angry?"

"Should I be?"

"No. I saw references to the FBI and DEA in some of the articles I read, so I was curious to see what they had to say. Neither of those agencies has any understanding of how to get other law enforcement agencies to cooperate with them, so what they think didn't surprise me. Anyway, I don't care what they say."

"That's good."

He stood and stretched. "Now, you need to get undressed and into bed."

"But I don't want to rest."

"Who said anything about rest? It's time for another dose of Comanche medicine."

* * *

The next day, I convinced Joe to take me to see Ric. My heroic friend looked pale and awful but grinned when he saw me. I tried to apologize about getting him involved, but he waved it away. I had to put my ear close to his lips to hear him say, "That was the best time I ever had at the Capitol."

"That's pathetic."

"I know, but it was so exciting!"

"Thank you for everything." I kissed him on the cheek. "You saved my life, Ric. If you hadn't called my dad, I wouldn't be here now."

"Did we get the bad guys?"

"Yes, we did."

"Then it was worth it."

"You should get a commendation."

"Maybe I should go into law enforcement."

"When you feel better, call me, and I'll talk you out of it."

"Are you going to quit?"

"No."

"Then, how can you talk me out of it?"

CHAPTER 33

Joe took me back to his place and wanted me to stay a few days, but I needed to go home. I missed my puppy, and I missed my house with my personal view of my mountain. It was hard to leave Joe, but I went home anyway.

Watching the rugged, red-brown stone hulk that is Cimarron always made me feel better. It never moves and has no mouth, yet it speaks to me. Its boulder-strewn run-offs are like wide scars down its sides, and its jagged peaks ache to touch the sky. My mountain knows a lot about life, so anything I tell it is taken in stride.

Missy lay beside me, exhausted from happy dancing over my return and from sniffing out yard faeries.

Sunset was playing tricks with its colors, making Cimarron look burgundy, when Randy came over to hear the whole story. Billy was working, and we planned it that way. This needed to be between us first.

Missy lifted her head and her tail beat the porch, but then she sighed and rested her head on her paws, the little drama queen.

I stood to hug my friend. He was barely able to stand alone, but he held me a long time. He smelled like the anti-bacterial wash he still had to use on his wounds and something I had come to think of as the sexiness that oozed from his pores.

After a while, he cupped my face in his hands. "I have no words for thanking you, Margarita. I'm indebted to you forever." His lips were still swollen and red and tears ran down his face, but his eyes sparkled.

It was beyond me how he was still sane after everything he'd been through. "I already told you that your debt is paid, Randy."

He collapsed into a chair. "Yeah, what does that mean?"

"When I started doing something for you, I began to feel better. I regained my focus and got out of my miserable self."

He nodded in understanding.

"Also, Randy, you're a poster boy for graciousness and forgiveness. I wanted to be like you instead of feeling angry and bitter all the time. When I got on a new track, Joe Washburn came into my life."

"Is he the Native American man Billy told me about?"

"Yes. He's someone, well, he's exactly who he seems to be."

"That's wonderful."

"I would never have met him if I hadn't set out to help you. I went to demand answers at the courthouse and met him there."

"He works there?"

"He was appointed to Judge Carter's position after he died."

"He's a judge?"

Randy's hair had grown enough to stick out comically, except nothing about him was funny. A ball cap hid his scorpion-devastated head, and loose-fitting cotton pants hid his legs. Even with sores, scabs, and scars, he exuded sex appeal. How did he do that? Even injured and pitiful, the man was deadly.

"Those things are great," Randy said, "and I'm happy you met someone wonderful, but don't downplay how amazing you are. I'm not going to let you do that. You did a brave and selfless thing. Admit it, Margarita. Say, 'I'm an amazing woman!' Say it like you mean it."

"I am an amazing woman! Thank you for noticing."

"It'd be hard not to." Randy grinned at me. Then he became serious. "I need to tell you that Billy and I are moving. We want a fresh start where nobody knows anything about me. Billy is fed up with the questions and snide comments. He gets the brunt of it because I rarely go out." He took a deep breath and looked towards my mountain. "We'll miss this scenery, but most of all, we'll miss you. You can come and visit us anytime. One day, we'll be back to visit you."

"I'm sorry, Randy. Maybe if you gave it time people would move on to the next big thing that is none of their business."

"We don't want to wait. Billy and I have something special, and we deserve a chance to make it."

"Nobody ever deserved it more. Do you know where you're going?"

"Not yet, but you'll be the first to know."

"Randy, you'll still have to appear before a judge to be officially absolved of the crime you never committed and to get the sex offender status removed."

"Yes. I know."

"The governor wants to be there. He has a statement to make on behalf of the State of Texas."

"Zeke told me. You made friends everywhere, didn't you?"

"The good news is that the hearing will be before Judge Washburn, and he's doing everything he can to speed it up."

Randy's eyes gleamed.

"And they'll want you to testify at the trials of Aaron Carter, Paul Wilder, and Damien Hall. You know that too?"

"Yes."

"I'll come with you if you like."

He let out a long breath. "I would really like that."

"Randy, there will be a trial in Brewster County, too. The men who kidnapped you will be in court soon, if our district judge and the sheriff have their way."

"While they held me captive, I hated them so much. I cursed them and wished everything terrible on them. Now I want to forget them and move on."

"How do you do that, Randy?"

"It's for me, not for them. If I hold on to what they did, it will only hurt me more. I always try to keep my attention on what I want, not on what I don't want. Thanks to you, I can live my life free of the black cloud of being a sex offender." Randy looked towards the mountain again. "I can see the blue sky, Margarita, and it's so beautiful it almost burns my eyes."

His comment caused my eyes to well with tears.

For a few minutes, neither of us spoke. Dark was overtaking the desert, and when you watch that moment-to-moment magic as it occurs, words are superfluous.

Randy was the first to break the silence. "Zeke said you found Sarah, and I'm dying to know about her."

"Sarah told me the truth from her perspective. She'd like to speak with you as soon as you feel like talking to her." I handed him my card with her phone number and address on the back. "She loves you and never stopped thinking of you."

That news caused Randy to weep.

I spent more than an hour telling him everything about my

investigation. Zeke had made me a copy of the recordings I made with each of the witnesses, including the ones I made illegally that were for Randy's benefit only.

I saved Sarah's until last. When her voice said, "This is Sarah Jones, and I'm giving Margarita Ricos permission to record this conversation so that I can help my friend Randy," the look on his face made every effort worth it. How often do any of us have the chance to put a look like that on someone's face?

* * *

The next morning, I was sitting on my porch reading. Okay, I was holding a book. My mountain was so resplendent in the morning sunshine even the birds were all worked up about it.

Barney pulled into my drive and turned off the motor. He waved, jumped down, brought his uniformed self onto the porch, and plopped into the chair next to me.

"Good morning, Barney."

"You don't look too bad, all things considered."

"You've got to stop with all the compliments. My head's gonna swell up."

"Yeah, I love to sweet-talk the women."

I laughed. "You don't look too bad either, you big lug. How's it going?"

"You've been gone so long, I guess I'll need to retrain you."

"It'll go easier on you if you don't try."

"You know, I meant to tell you that the old bones in the mine shaft do belong to Gloria Abelard, as you thought."

"Maybe the other missing woman is at Buena Suerte, too."

"Yeah, that's what I've been thinking."

"But you're not thinking about looking for her?"

"Well, not until you feel like going."

"Why don't you take Buster to have a look? He's an able-bodied young man."

"Anyone except you would look down into a dark shaft and wet his pants."

"So, you're admitting that I'm a brave and awesome partner to have?"

"Yeah, I guess so."

"Thank you for the enthusiasm."

"When do you come back to work?"

"I don't know if I want to."

"You know you want to!"

"I won't be back for a while. I'm going to Spain."

Barney shook his head and pawed at his ears. "I thought I heard you say you were going to Spain."

"I did say that."

"Spain, as in the country?"

"Sí señor, españa."

"Whatever possesses you to go there?"

"A friend invited me to go."

"A friend I know?"

"No, you don't know him."

"Huh. Did you meet him during your recent investigating?"

"Yes; now stop it. We're not playing Twenty Questions."

"Are you ever coming back to work?"

"Yes, unless I decide to stay in Spain."

* * *

A few days later, I had an appointment with Sheriff Ben. He was worried that I'd decided not to return to work, but I set his mind at ease. I wanted to come back, but since I still had vacation time left, I was going to Spain.

He grinned at me. "That's the kind of vacation I had in mind for you, not running around investigating grand-scale corruption in the justice system."

For a while, we spoke of the Randall Green investigation. He congratulated me on the success of it and said he'd already made a public announcement of Randy's innocence. All area newspapers and the radio had carried the story. He had called the schools and other places that were notified of Randy's sex offender status to rescind the alert. Sadly, facts have little effect in our county, but I kept my thoughts to myself since the sheriff had done everything he could to right a wrong that wasn't his fault.

***

It was past midnight when I got to Simpson.

Joe opened his door wearing only red boxer briefs. His hair was loose and messy and hung over his shoulders onto his chest. He'd been asleep. Or else he was modeling men's underwear.

"I need another dose, Joe."

He grinned and pulled me to him.

***

A few days later, I arranged to take Cissy to see her sister and meet Tim and Sally Barstow, the couple caring for Lesley. While Cissy was inside the house getting her things, her mother came out to the car.

"I want you to take her permanently," she said. "Don't bring her back to me."

I was speechless.

"I can't handle her, and she'd be better off with you. Those people are adopting Lesley, and Cissy will never forgive me for that."

"But Cissy is—"

"If you don't want her, then figure out somethin' because I'm taking off. I won't be here when you come back. Can I count on you or not?"

"Yes, you can count on me, but this isn't as simple as that. You have to formally relinquish your rights as a parent. If you abandon her, the state will decide her fate, not me and not you."

"What should I do?"

"You should wait until Cissy and I return from her visit. Maybe the Barstows will want to adopt her, too." That was my fervent hope. "If you can't wait to leave, at least let me know where you are. You have my contact information, right?"

"Yes."

"Will you promise to let me know where you are?"

"Yes."

Cissy was coming out the door. "Thank you, Margarita," her mother said. There were tears in her eyes.

"Are you sure?"

She nodded. "I know you'll do right by her, and I never have."

Later, when I saw Cissy reunited with Lesley, it me made me sorry I didn't have a sister.

CHAPTER 34

I went to see Joe and found him in his chambers. I breezed in, kissed him, and then collapsed in a chair across from him.

"I can't go to Spain with you, Joe. I'm sorry, but I can't go. It's too soon and too far, and I'm afraid I'll do something to mess this up."

He got up, came to me, kneeled, and took my hands. "How would you mess it up?"

"I don't know but, believe me, I will. I feel a big, hard fall off the wagon coming. It's been coming for a while. Do you want to take a drunk across the ocean?"

"No, but I will take a woman who is struggling to be the best she can be. We all have demons, Margarita." He pushed a curl of hair back from my face. "Have you been drinking?"

"No. I just want to."

"Is this about the man you loved?"

"No, yes. I—I don't know how to explain it."

"Why don't you try?"

"My heart is not all mine yet. I want to give it to you, but I still feel connected to a dead man—two dead men, if I'm honest about it. Going to Spain for two weeks feels like a commitment, and it's too soon for me. I hope you can understand without getting your feelings hurt. It's about me and not you. You're wonderful."

He put his head in my lap and I caressed it. Neither of us spoke for a long time.

"Last time, I jumped in too soon and too hard." As I spoke, I brought his ponytail out of the back of his robe and held it against my face. "Could we spend two weeks getting to know each other better? Spain is not going anywhere."

He lifted his head and smiled. "Okay. Yes. We can do that."

"I'd like to spend a month with my face in your hair."

"We can do that, too," he said softly.

CHAPTER 35

Cissy spent three weeks with Tim and Sally Barstow instead of a weekend. They were crazy about her and wanted to adopt her so that the two sisters could grow up together. Cissy's mom was fine with that, and Cissy was overjoyed. I was relieved to be off the hook. I wasn't ready to raise two young girls since I was still raising myself.

Joe said he would get the name of the judge who was scheduled to hear the motion and put in a good word with him. It seemed that this was going to work out in the best way for everyone.

Joe went with me to check on Cissy. When we pulled up, she flew out the door into my arms. "I'm gonna stay here! They want me to stay! I'm gonna live here!"

"Oh, Cissy, I'm so happy!"

"But it makes me sad that I won't get to see you much."

"You and Lesley can come visit me. And Cissy, I'm only a phone call away, so don't forget that."

"Can I email you?"

"Every day if you want." I hugged her close. "I'll always have you in my heart."

"You're in mine too," she said with tears in her eyes.

For a moment we just took each other in.

"They make me do homework and eat vegetables."

"I hope you're cooperating."

"They're as annoying as you." Then, "Sally did my hair. Do you like it?"

"Oh, yes, it's beautiful!"

Cissy was clean and had gained weight. Her jeans and blouse looked new, and there was a purple ribbon in her shiny blonde hair. It matched the colors in the blouse. She looked loved and cared for, all I ever wanted for her.

"Lesley and me, we're gonna be together forever!"

Her arms were still around me, but her wide eyes moved up to Joe, who stood behind me.

"Cissy, this is my friend, Joe Washburn."

She stared with her mouth open.

"Hello, Cissy," he said with a smile and offered his hand.

She cleared her throat. "Hello."

"I'm happy to meet you."

"Do you know that Margarita is my best friend in the whole world?"

"I know she loves you."

Cissy nodded, and her blue eyes shone.

I put my arm around her shoulders and we headed towards the house to speak with the rest of the family.

Cissy glanced back over her shoulder at Joe. Then she looked up at me. "I guess you finally have a boyfriend."

"Yes, Cissy."

"Ooh-la-la."

Other Deputy Ricos Tales

One Bloody Shirt at a Time
The Beautiful Bones
Darker Than Back
Border Ghosts
Hard Falls
Raw Deal

Other Titles from Beth Garcia

The Reluctant Cowboy
The Trail of Rattler

Read more about Beth and her work at www.elizabethagarciaauthor.com
Her Facebook page: www.facebook.com/ElizabethAGarciaAuthor/
Reach her by email at beth@elizabethagarciaauthor.com
Follow her on social media with **#garciabooks**

Made in the USA
San Bernardino, CA
01 May 2018